'*The Trawlerman* is an excellent, totally absorbing crime novel which can only augment the reputations of William Shaw' *Shotsmag*

'A powerful, scary suspense mystery which had me swiping over pages at speed while savouring every word. This is a brilliant novel' Lesley Thomson

'Shaw never lectures; his crucial imperative remains ironclad storytelling and razor-sharp characterisation, both in evidence here' *Financial Times*

'It's another clever, thoughtful mystery from one of the best authors of Brit crime fiction's new wave' *Sun*

'[A] terrifically atmospheric thriller mixing a twisting plot with a considered meditation on the lasting effects of close contact with violence' *Daily Mail*

'Atmospheric descriptions of the coast and landscape, a cast of believable characters and a twisty plot combine to create an engaging read' *Choice Magazine*

'Pacey, intense and riddled with gripping twists' *Surrey Life*

William Shaw has been shortlisted for the CWA Historical Dagger, longlisted for the Theakston's Old Peculier Crime Novel of the Year Award and nominated for a Barry Award. A regular at festivals, he organises panel talks and CWA events across the south east. He worked as a journalist for over twenty years and lives in Brighton. William Shaw's *The Trawlerman* is the fourth in his series set in Dungeness and featuring DI Alex Cupidi, who originally appeared as one of the characters in his 2016 novel *The Birdwatcher*.

THE TRAWLERMAN

William Shaw

riverrun

First published in Great Britain in 2021 by riverrun
This paperback edition published in 2022 by

riverrun

an imprint of

Quercus Editions Limited
Carmelite House
50 Victoria Embankment
London EC4Y 0DZ

An Hachette UK company

A CIP catalogue record for this book is available
from the British Library.

Paperback 978 1 52940 183 7
Ebook 978 1 52940 184 4

10 9 8 7 6 5 4 3 2 1

Typeset by CC Book Production
Printed and bound in Great Britain by Clays Ltd, Elcograf S.p.A.

Papers used by riverrun are from well-managed forests and other responsible sources.

For Tom

Also for Luke Noakes for taking me out on his trawler Valentine,
*with apologies for depicting the trawlermen of Folkestone
as other than the fine community that they are.*

ONE

Something really, really bad was about to happen.

What it was, Alexandra Cupidi wasn't sure. She was sitting on a cafe bench with a coffee that could have been worse, surrounded in every direction by happy people. The sun was out. Summer bugs dipped in and out of the wild flowers that squeezed their way through the shingle beach. Multicoloured nylon kites flew in a blue July sky.

It was there in her chest; a cold, dark, malevolent slug.

Something really, really bad was about to happen.

However hard she looked around, she could see nothing that would explain what it was that made her so anxious.

The Light Railway Cafe was the terminus for the Romney, Hythe and Dymchurch Railway, close to the house on the promontory in which she lived with her daughter.

It was July, the time of year when the misanthropes, artists, nature-lovers and eccentrics who lived on Dungeness were already

1

tiring of the crowds of tourists who flocked here, disgorging from the comically small train to queue to climb the stone stairs of the old black lighthouse, and to wander around photographing the houses and the locals like they were exhibits, wondering what else you were supposed to do here in this strange, flat place.

Bungalows and shacks dotted the scrubby landscape as if scattered there like dice. The Light Railway Cafe was like most buildings here; a hotchpotch of rough rectangles joined at any angle the builder had fancied, held together with paint.

Something was wrong.

It made her skin itch. If only she knew what it was.

The next train was on its way, clattering down the curve of narrow track that ran along the shingle. This one, Alex noticed, was different. It was decorated with flowers; garlands hung from the windows, fluttering as it moved. She squinted through the afternoon sun at it.

Steam from the funnel drifted slowly south towards them, ahead of the train.

There was something comical about the small train. The light railway had been built as a tourist attraction, its terminus this ramshackle cafe. When the war broke out a few years later, the army commandeered the railway to shift the materials needed to build sea defences all along the shore, and the few tourists it attracted then vanished. This small train still ran, driven and tended by disproportionately large men, and dwarfed by this landscape. The huge bulk of the nuclear power station to the west only made it look more like a children's toy, casually abandoned.

Abrupt laughter travelled ahead of the train, carried by a gust of wind. The passengers in the flower-decked carriages were having a party.

'Wedding party,' said someone. They were right. As the tiny train slowed at the Dungeness station, the engine driver blew the whistle – *poop-poop!* – and Alex saw the glimpse of white inside the flower-decked carriage. A weekday wedding. The bride emerged first, red hair buffeting in the wind, and then everybody piled out behind her, screaming and shouting, carrying bottles of sparkling wine by the neck. They were drunk, thought Alex, joyfully so.

And then a second white wedding dress stepped out of the carriage: a younger woman with short bleached hair; a wedding of two brides.

The wedding party poured out of the station and made their way to the cafe where Alex was sitting.

'Congratulations,' the tourists called out to them.

The red-haired woman, older than she had looked from a distance – late thirties perhaps – smiled a little shyly. 'Thanks.' Women in heels tottered on the shingle. Men moved among them, shirts half untucked, eyes losing focus from drink.

Alex recognised one. Curly was local; he had grown up close by in one of the wooden houses. His family had been fishermen here, and he still kept his twin-hulled boat here.

Curly smiled goofily at Alex when he spotted her there.

'Who's the happy couple?' she asked.

'That's Tina,' he said, pointing to the red-haired bride, 'and that's Stella. We're stopping here for lunch.'

She had never seen Curly in a suit. It looked wrong. He had the sunburned leathery skin of someone who spent his days here on the beach; his hair was thin, a mixture of pale grey and sandy yellow. 'Can I get you a drink?' He pointed towards the small hut named 'Ales on the Rails'.

The day yawned in front of her. 'Why not?'

She had nothing at all to do today. It was driving her crazy.

They had arranged two of the tables in a single row, the brides at one end, and they had ordered fish and chips, and sandwiches. Alex joined them, squeezing onto the end of the picnic table bench seats.

'You ever married?' Curly asked.

'Just the once. Zoë's dad. You?'

'Nobody wanted me,' he said.

'Can't say I'm surprised.'

'Lovely girl, Tina,' said Curly. 'Known her since she was a baby. Worked with her dad on the trawlers. She deserves a little happiness.'

Squeezed on the end of the table, Alex looked up towards the two women. They were holding hands across the rickety table, smiling. It didn't look like a little happiness to her; it looked like a lot of it. She felt that familiar pull in her guts; that something was wrong here. Nothing would make this feeling go away.

'Not working today?'

'Off sick,' said Alex.

'Oh. Nothing bad, I hope?'

Alex didn't answer. She picked up the wine Curly had brought her and took a generous swig. The guests chattered.

4

Everything was bright with summer sunshine. She took in every detail, as if looking for something out of place, something that could spoil this perfect day.

She looked at children playing tag in the car park. She looked at a kite shaped like a comma, dipping down over the flat ground, then soaring up again. She looked at lovers, holding hands as they walked by the tiny art gallery by the lighthouse.

And then she saw a woman, a long way off, striding with a sense of purpose.

As the guests chatted, she approached. She was walking towards them at speed.

'Excuse me,' Alex said to Curly. She untangled herself from the packed picnic table and stood. The woman was in her fifties or sixties, dressed in a plain grey mac, gloves still on, as if defying the summer.

Alex's skin prickled. From a distance, Alex could see the sheen of unwiped tears that ran down her face; occasionally she gulped for breath.

By now Alex had left the group she had been with and was approaching the woman walking along the concrete track. Alex called out, 'Is everything OK?'

The woman ignored her; strode up towards her, and then straight on past. Alex turned to look where she was heading and saw that she was unbuttoning her grey coat.

Nervous now, Alex ran back towards the group to get ahead of the crying woman, and as she did she saw, tucked into the belt of the woman's dress beneath the open coat, a long, grey steel blade.

Ants were suddenly crawling all over Alex's skin. 'I'm a police officer,' Alex said, voice as low as she could. 'I can help.'

The woman paid no attention yet, grasped the handle with her right hand and pulled it out, holding it horizontally out in front of her.

'Stop,' said Alex, louder this time.

The woman blinked, twisted to her right to point the weapon straight at Alex's midriff.

'Shut up,' the woman screamed.

The chatter and laughter stopped abruptly.

Alex stood, arms raised up, drawing her midriff back from the machete in front of her. The edge had been sharpened recently and glittered in the brightness. The woman shook.

'Put it down. Let's talk about this.'

One of the revellers saw the blade and screamed; the scream stopped as quickly as it started.

'Put it down,' pleaded Alex.

Everything was suddenly quiet. The wind seemed to drop. Gulls hung, stationary in solid air.

And to her surprise, the woman did as she had been told, dropping the weapon onto the ground where it clattered on the tarmac.

The woman in grey raised a finger of the hand that had dropped the weapon and pointed it at the red-haired bride.

'Murderer!' the woman screamed. 'Bloody murderer.'

And the red-haired woman, open-mouthed, eyes huge, paled; her skin almost as white as the dress she was wearing.

6

TWO

The wedding party broke up; most of the guests caught the next train back to Hythe, shaken by what had happened. Taxis arrived to collect others, who muttered apologies before they departed. Curly stayed behind with the two brides, who sat close on the bench, arms around each other, whispering together, shocked by what had happened.

The first police car to arrive was driven by a Civil Nuclear Constabulary officer. He was based at the nearby power station. He offered Alex handcuffs and started collecting names and addresses while the woman in the grey coat sat in his car waiting for someone from Kent Police to come and collect her.

'You're the police officer who lives round here, aren't you?' The young CNC officer was new. Alex didn't recognise him.

Curly had brought Alex a fresh glass of wine because he said she looked like she needed one. 'Yes.'

'Weird place to live, isn't it? Right next to that lot.' He nodded at the power station.

'Weird place to work, when there's nothing for you to do,' she answered.

The boy looked hurt; but it was true. The CNC were a heavily armed unit, guarding a nuclear facility that no one wanted to attack anyway. 'You not at work today, then?'

'I have been told to take a little time off for the good of my mental health,' she said.

'Sick leave?'

'Yes.' She held up the glass.

'Unlucky for you; lucky for everyone else here, by the sound of it. Did you know the woman with the machete?'

'Never seen her before in my life,' said Alex.

'Only, some of these people . . .' He looked around. 'They're telling me you stood up and approached her well before she pulled out the weapon.' He looked at his little dark-blue note-book. 'And you had some words with her. Why did you approach her?'

'I'll be honest,' said Alex, 'I have been asking myself exactly the same thing.'

'She was acting suspiciously?'

She had been dressed for the wrong weather, that's all. 'Not really. I just . . .' She tried to think what had made her do it. 'I just knew something really bad was going to happen,' she said.

'That's a copper's instinct, then. Seeing something out of place. Knowing that something was wrong.'

Alex shivered.

'Pretty bloody impressive,' said the copper. 'I'd buy you a drink too, only some of us are still on duty.'

★

Back at the table, Curly lit a cigarette and said, 'Poor cow.'

'You know her?' asked Alex.

'Mandy. Tina's mother-in-law. Ex-mother-in-law, I should say. She's not right.'

'Ex-mother-in-law? You mean . . . ?'

Alex looked at the woman, stationary in the police car, staring straight ahead, no regret on her face for what she'd just tried to do.

He lowered his voice so the brides could not hear. 'Mandy Hogben. Tina used to be married to her son Frank Hogben. They married young, you know? Tina was eighteen years old. Frank's dead. Died in a fishing accident. Nothing to do with her, but Mandy never believed that.'

'What kind of accident?'

'Fell overboard on a trawler out of Folkestone.'

'Why does she blame Tina, then?'

'Like I said, not right in the head. Not her fault. Just tough on Tina.'

At the other end of the table Tina was crying; her new wife was trying to make fun of her, wiping her tears with her veil.

'Not a great thing to happen on your wedding day.'

'You said it,' said Curly.

'So he just fell overboard?'

'No life jacket. No harness. No chance at all.'

'Why didn't anybody save him?'

'Nobody saw it happen. The other guy on the boat was asleep down below. Came back on deck, engine running, nobody on deck.'

Alex thought for a while. 'So how can they be so sure he fell overboard, then?'

'I thought you were off work.'

9

Alex had two more weeks of counselling ahead of her. She would soon be returning to work on what they called 'light duties'. The phrase filled her with dread. 'So?' she demanded.

'If you're on board a trawler one minute, and the next you're gone, that's about the only explanation there is.'

She studied his face for a second. The sun never reached the bottom of Curly's wrinkles, she noticed; little deltas of white skin beneath the reddy brown.

'I used to go out on that boat sometimes,' said Curly. 'It was called *The Hopeful*.'

'Some name. Did they go back and look for him?'

'You have any idea what it's like to lose a man at sea? Worst thing in the world that can happen. They called out the coastguard and everything. But there wasn't much point. They were in the Channel. It was March. Unless you've got an immersion suit on, you've got ten, maybe twenty minutes in the water and then you're gone.'

'Find his body?'

'No life jacket on. They never did.'

Alex looked round. The face of the woman in the car was like iron.

'When was all this?'

'Seven years ago.'

'So his body never turned up in all that time?'

The sound of waves on shingle a long way off. 'That's right.'

Seven years dead; it takes seven years to make a declaration of presumed death. 'That's why they're getting married. They never found the body, so Tina couldn't marry again until now.'

Curly didn't answer.

'How long have they been lovers then?'

Curly turned his head and looked at her for a while. 'You've got a bad mind, Alexandra Cupidi,' he said eventually.

At that moment, as if she knew what they were talking about, the dead man's mother turned her head to the left and stared at them, unflinching. In those eyes Alex recognised that dangerous kind of emptiness. She was beyond caring what anyone thought.

The younger bride, Stella, stood, picked up a bottle of wine and approached Alex with a glass. 'I wanted to say thanks,' she said. Her eyes were an extraordinary bright shade of blue. 'You were cool. She could have hurt you.'

'Not a great thing to happen on your wedding day.'

She handed Alex the glass and poured wine into it without asking if she wanted any. 'Well, it's a day we're never going to forget, at least.'

'Sorry about your guests.'

'We wanted to get rid of them anyway. We're on our honeymoon now.'

'Here?' Alex looked around. This wasn't the sort of place people usually came on their honeymoons.

'We're staying over there.' She pointed to a low, pale-blue bungalow, the far side of the new lighthouse. 'A whole week. Mostly in bed,' she added with a mischievous smile.

Over her shoulder, Tina sat alone at the end of the table, wedding dress already grubby at the hem. Stella had shrugged off the attack; Tina still looked shaken, her face pale and her eyes red. 'I can't wait,' said Stella.

When Alex looked towards the pale-blue bungalow with white-framed windows, she saw also the flashing blue lights of an approaching police car.

THREE

It was an unmarked vehicle, a green Skoda, blue lights flashing through the grille. It was coming to take Mandy Hogben into custody. Even at this distance, coming down the straight track, disappearing between houses and patches of scrub, Alex could see that there were two people inside. As it rounded the corner near the old lighthouse, slowing for a gaggle of tourists who loitered on the single-track road, Alex recognised one: the driver.

'Here they come,' said the CNC officer, sounding relieved to be about to have the woman off his hands.

The Skoda pulled up next to the CNC car, and a small, neat young woman got out. 'That her?' she said, looking at Mandy Hogben sitting alone radiating hatred.

No hello or anything. Which was odd, because Detective Constable Jill Ferriter was Alex's colleague and her best friend. That corporeal sense of unease was back; a dream-like feeling that something was still very wrong. It wasn't the woman in grey.

Something was still setting off bells in Alex's head. She scanned the horizon looking for anything else that felt out of place that would explain this conviction.

'This is Detective Sergeant Cupidi,' the CNC officer was saying, suddenly eager to talk to this younger, so much prettier policewoman. 'She's the one who apprehended the alleged assailant. Perhaps you two know each other already?'

'How come they're sending you out to something like this, Jill?'

'We were just down the road, doing . . . something.' Jill's voice was unsteady, her face pale.

'Doing what?'

'Some bad business,' said Jill quietly.

At that point, Jill's passenger, a uniformed officer, opened the passenger door, leaned out, and was sick onto the compacted shingle next to the car.

'Is that Colin Gilchrist?' asked Alex. She looked from one to the other. 'What's wrong?'

'Like I said, dead bad business.' Jill looked shaken herself.

'What bad business?'

Jill walked to the back of the Skoda. 'Listen, Alex. You're supposed to be taking time off from all this. We're only here for that one. Don't ask.'

'What's been going on? You look genuinely like shit.'

'Drop it. Just not now, love, OK? Please.'

Jill opened the boot and pulled out a tactical vest for herself and another for Gilchrist, but when she realised Alex was standing next to her, Jill slammed the boot shut, though not before Alex had seen what else was in it.

Inside the boot was a clear plastic bag stuffed full of used white forensic coveralls and blue overshoes. Blood had soaked into the blue fabric of the shoes, turning it a deep brown. There were patches of blood on the coveralls too. Alex had been to too many crime scenes. That's why she was on sick leave. For their forensic clothing to be that stained, there would have had to have been a great deal of blood.

Jill was already opening the CNC car door and leading Mandy over towards her Skoda. The woman got in the car without any protest at all. Afterwards Jill called over to the CNC officer. 'You got the witness details?'

He nodded; held the weapon in a gloved hand. 'You'll be needing this too,' he said, holding up the machete. 'Evidence. Can I stick it in your boot?'

Jill looked at the weapon and baulked. 'Oh. We can't take it.'

The man looked confused. 'You'll want it though.'

Jill looked as much panicked by his statement as by the sight of the weapon.

Alex stepped forward between them. 'They can't take it with them,' she explained. 'She's right. They can't have the weapon inside the vehicle with the suspect for obvious reasons, and they can't put it in the boot either because there's a danger of cross-contamination of evidence.'

The man blinked, confused, holding the weapon between finger and thumb.

'They have . . . some stuff in their boot already, from another case. They've just come from another serious crime scene.'

She looked at Colin, who gave the smallest of nods.

'You'll have to arrange for someone else to collect it.'

15

Jill looked gratefully at Alex, then got into the car next to Colin, who hadn't said a word the entire time they had been there. 'Come by later,' called Alex as she started the engine. 'I need the company. I'm going mad out here with nothing to do.' Which was more than half true, she realised.

Jill said nothing. She put the car into gear and all three drove away. Where the car had been, lay the small splatter of Colin's sick.

If she hadn't been off work, Alex reflected, it would have been her witnessing whatever they had seen, and whatever they had seen had not been good.

She watched the two brides leave, hand in hand, walking unsteadily across the uneven shingle towards the low pale-blue cabin, picking their way uneasily between the gorse and the sea kale.

They had left her with the bottle of wine. After maybe twenty metres, Tina stumbled and fell. Stella bent and took her arm, hauled her up. After another few yards, Tina stopped, hitched up her dress and Stella bent her legs to allow her to jump up onto her back, and carried her all the way to the bungalow.

Curly said, 'Fancy a couple more at the Pilot?'

He was drunk. So was she, she realised. The day was scarily empty. She could stay and drink like she would have done when she was a younger officer on the force in London. She hesitated and said, 'No thanks, Curly.'

She turned and made her way down the track towards her house, hair blowing in her face as she walked.

*

It was stupid, drinking at lunchtime. She was supposed to be straightening out her head, not messing with it. The afternoon had become a blur.

By the evening she was sat on the sofa with the TV on, sound down, and was struggling through one of the books her mother had left behind on her visits. Her mother went through two or three novels a week. Alex was trying to fill the empty days off work, but reading books took her forever and she found it impossible to believe in any of the stories.

Alex gave up, looked up at the silent television and saw a young woman holding a microphone outside the gates of a large house. There was police tape across the gates. The caption underneath read *New Romney*, a town a little further up the coast.

'Oh,' she said out loud, and remembered the bloody coveralls in Jill's car.

She scrabbled around, looking for the remote control as the reporter talked to camera with the sombre face of someone delivering terrible news. Behind her right shoulder, crime scene officers dressed all in white, just as Jill would have been, emerged from the front door. Where was the remote? It had been here next to her on the sofa a minute ago.

She felt a prick of irritation. Normally she would have already known every available grisly detail. All she could guess was that something very awful must have happened in that house, a little way down the coast from her.

By the time she had found the remote, tucked between cushions, the news had moved on to an item about an old people's home.

FOUR

Zoë came in late, non-verbal, walking dirty footprints onto the kitchen tiles.

'Nice day?' Alex asked her daughter.

Zoë didn't answer; instead she started opening and closing cupboard doors, then moved on to the fridge in which she found half an avocado. She scooped it out of its skin, methodically mashed it with a fork for two whole minutes, then squeezed a little lemon juice in it and mashed it some more.

'See any lesser spotted wood pigeons?'

'No such bird.'

'A great booby?'

'Mum.'

'A little bustard?'

'Unfunny, Mum.'

'Where were you all day, then?'

'Where do you think? I was volunteering at the Wildlife Trust. I told you that this morning.'

'Did you?' Her strange misfit daughter who loved wildlife more than people. Alex looked at the small bowl of green mush her daughter had made. 'I could cook something.'

'No worries,' said Zoë, picking up the bowl and walking towards the staircase.

'Is that all you're having?' she called up after her. Zoë didn't answer; just closed the door to her bedroom behind her.

She had not been a good mother; she knew that. It was a warm evening still; she stepped outside into it. The air was rich with bugs, swallows swooping after them. Her house had been built inside a low shingle rampart that had once been part of a Napoleonic-era gun battery; to the north, smoke was rising. Beyond the hummock of stones, someone was starting a bonfire somewhere on the shingle.

At ten she called Jill on her mobile. 'Are you home?'

'Just. The longest bloody day.'

'Why?'

Jill didn't answer.

'You were at New Romney, weren't you? That's where you came from. That house where the people were killed.'

'I don't think I should be talking to you about any of this,' said Jill.

'Why not?'

'Because the whole point is you're supposed to be forgetting about all this shit.'

'What happened?'

'You're insane, you know that?'

'That's why I'm off work.'

19

'You really don't want to know. Just it was . . . super bad. Super fucking bad.'

'Maybe it's you that needs therapy, not me.'

'The stuff you see, Alex. Nobody should have to see it. Poor old Colin. That was the third time he chucked up.'

Somewhere someone was playing a guitar; it was hard to tell if the music came from nearby or far away. Sound travelled easily across this flat land. They could hear the noise of the drinkers gathered outside the Britannia.

'And as for you, even when you're supposed to be off work, you're arresting people,' said Jill. 'What was all that about?'

'I don't know. I looked up and there was this woman. I knew she was going to do something. I just knew something bad was going to happen, and then she pulled out a knife. The weirdest bloody thing.'

'Like a premonition?'

'Yeah. Like a premonition. And then when I saw you, I knew something else had gone on. Another premonition. Except I don't believe in premonitions,' said Alex.

'How can you actually say that? You just had one.'

'I believe in the rational world.'

'I believe in vibrations that only sensitive people can feel,' Jill said. 'Like yogis and enlightened people.'

'I've never been accused of being sensitive.'

Jill said nothing for a while. Finally she spoke. 'How can you actually believe in a rational world anyway? What we saw today . . .'

Above Alex, stars struggled to shine, competing with the orange glare of the nuclear power station.

'. . . nothing rational about it,' Jill said.

That night another terrible thing happened. As she lay on her bed, the ceiling fell on her. She woke with weight of debris pressed so hard on her chest that she could not breathe.

The attic must have been full of earth; she could feel its thick wetness crushing her, paralysing her. The smell of it was all around her, dank and rotting, full of unseen creatures. She needed to get up and find her daughter and make sure she was OK, but she was trapped, unable to move any limb.

And then a cool hand rested on her forehead. 'Ssh,' said a quiet voice. 'It's OK now. I'm here.'

By the time she woke, Zoë was already gone. It was late; she had the feeling that she had slept badly but she couldn't remember the dreams she had had.

There was a message written on the envelope of an electricity bill:

Don't forget counsellor @ 11. Z. x

It was a hot Friday morning. Her counsellor had told her that exercise was good, so she was using her bike whenever she could. On the bike on the way to his office, Alex passed the two brides walking hand in hand along the road towards her and gave them a wave, but they were too deep in conversation to notice her. Normally from here she would cycle up the narrower lanes that ran inland among the marshes; today though she rode up the coast road, air cooling the sweat off her.

The other thing that was good about cycling was that it was hard to think too much when you were on a bike. You had to concentrate on the journey, especially on this coast road where lorries were impatient to pass you even on the blindest corners.

— *How do I feel today? I'm bored and frustrated. I want to be back at work.*
— *Do you think you're ready?*
— *Honestly? No.*
— *Why not?*
— *This is going to sound strange.*
— *Try me.*
— *It's weird.*
— *Go on.*
— *You see . . . I keep feeling I can predict the future.*
— *What do you mean?*
— *I had a premonition. Premonitions, really. And they turned out to be true.*
— *Like a superpower?*
— *Sometimes I have a terrible feeling that something is going to happen, and then it does. Does that sound nuts?*
— *In my line of work, I'm not really supposed to use the word 'nuts'.*
— *But to me it feels nuts because it calls into question everything I thought I was. I am a rational person. I don't believe in God or higher powers. I'm someone who believes things happen in a causal sequence. My job as a police officer in a crime unit is to understand that sequence. That's what we do. I understand the order in which things have happened. I don't judge it. I just need to figure it out. What causes what to happen. But now I seem to have this terrible feeling that bad things are about to happen and then they do. That's like . . . things have happened in the*

22

wrong order. Or even that I caused them to happen because I knew they were going to. If somebody told me what I've just said, I would assume they were having psychotic episodes.

— But you don't think you are?

— Would you know if you were having a psychotic episode? Isn't that the whole point? Yesterday I was absolutely sure something really bloody terrible was going to happen. And . . .

— It did?

— Yes.

— And do you still feel like that? Do you think something bad is about to happen now?

FIVE

It was not hard to find the murder house, cycling home. It was just north of the village; a police car was parked across the driveway, blocking the entrance. The house was surrounded by high, well-trimmed hedges at the front and to the north, as much for privacy, she guessed, as to keep out the constant winds that winter brought to this flat land. To the south there was a small copse of scrubby willows and ash trees. She slowed on the single-track road and stopped just behind the car.

Dropping the bike onto the grass, she walked up towards the driveway, the pedal cleats on her shoes clicking on the tarmac. A small, tarnished copper sign on the open gate announced the house was named 'The Nest'. Looking down the drive, she could see that the space to the left of the house was crammed with vehicles. The forensic teams would be inside the house, carefully picking over everything.

'Can I help you?' The young constable sitting inside the car had seen her peering past.

'Pretty grim in there, I expect?'

'Are you a friend or a neighbour?' he asked.

'No . . . just passing,' she said.

'Right,' said the man, looking at her with the contempt coppers feel for rubberneckers. 'On your bike, love.'

'On my bike?' she said. 'Seriously?'

Instead of staying to argue, she turned away because a gangly young man had emerged behind the large cypress hedge, phone against one ear. It was Colin Gilchrist. Not wanting to be recognised lurking at a murder scene, she picked up the bike and pushed it on up the road.

She had walked about thirty metres the far side of the gate when a Qashqai coming from the other direction pulled up alongside her on the lane.

'Flat tyre?' A red-faced man leaned out of the window. 'Want me to help?'

Woman on her own, dressed in Lycra. 'No. I'm fine,' she said.

'Take off the front tyre. We can bung it in the boot. I'll give you a ride if you like.'

'You don't know where I'm headed.'

'Nor you me,' he said.

'You pick up a lot of women this way?'

He looked offended. 'I was trying to help. It's not safe around here. Haven't you heard?' He put his hands back on the steering wheel, ready to drive away.

'Heard what?'

'About the killings? Didn't you see the police back there? He was a member of my golf club,' he said.

'Who was?'

25

'Ayman. The man who was slaughtered with his wife. In that house just there.' He pointed back towards the high hedges. 'Sweetest people. Some bloody lunatic.'

'How do you know?'

'Friend in the police.'

'Golf club?'

The man frowned. 'Yes, actually. So like I said. It's not safe for you around here, OK?' Offended, he drove away. Alex stood for a minute, then pushed the bike off and swung her other leg over onto the pedal.

When she reached Five Vents Lane, she couldn't help feeling that the darkness in that house was chasing after her; that this would not be the end of it.

At Burmarsh church, she stopped and drank from her water bottle. Inside the cool of the Norman arch, a pointy-toothed imp scowled down at her. The noticeboard said the church was four metres below sea level. She could imagine the weight of water this land was holding back. A certainty of bad things about to get worse.

Suddenly weary, she lay down on the grass and sorrel. Had she slept badly last night? She tried to remember the night, but it was a blur.

'Hey.'

She was almost home when she heard the voice and braked.

Jill was sat at one of the wooden tables outside the Snack Shack, a converted freight container that became a pop-up restaurant during summer months.

'What are you doing here, Jill?'

Tourists in swimming trunks lounged in deckchairs, eating fish perched on their bellies. 'Came to see you, obviously. Hadn't eaten all day, and now I've just scarfed a plate of chips. Colin Gilchrist says he saw you. At the house.'

Alex nodded. 'Did he? I was passing.'

'Hell you were, Alex.'

'I was curious. That's all.'

'You're supposed to be protecting yourself from all this shit so you can get better, and here you are noseying around like you're still on duty.'

Alex propped her bike against the table and sat down. 'I was going to my counsellor, that's all. It was on the way back.'

'I was worried you weren't going to go. How was it?'

'Yeah. Well. Early days.'

'Course, that house is only on the way if you take a detour.'

'I'm still a police officer. I'm interested, that's all.'

Jill grunted. 'Want to finish my chips? I can't eat them all. I'm stuffed.'

'Poor lamb,' said Alex, leaning over to take one. 'Let me help.'

Jill stood to buy another bottle of water. A dad, eating a fisherman's roll with his kids, looked up as she passed, followed each step of her walk across the shingle, oblivious to his wife next to him.

'How's Zoë?' Jill asked when she was back.

'I barely see her. She's clearing grass to let the orchids grow, apparently.'

'She's got a job?'

'Of course not. She's just volunteering.'

Curly appeared, trudging up across the beach towards them

27

in a pair of wellingtons that had been worn so thin in places you could see the canvas that held them together. From his right arm a large fish dangled; he had one finger slipped through the gill for purchase.

'Good day?'

'Bass,' he grinned. 'Big bugger. Caught three. This one's for Tina and her . . . you know, wife.' As if he found the phrase slightly awkward to say. 'See if they want it for their supper.'

'Thought you were only allowed to take one.'

'Yeah. Obviously.' He grinned shyly. 'I wouldn't go telling a copper if I kept the others for myself. I chucked them back.'

'Believe that, you'll believe anything,' muttered Jill.

'Hope you bloody did, Curly.'

'Is Tina OK – after what happened?' Jill asked.

'Bit shaken up. She's mentally ill, that Hogben woman.'

'In the car,' said Jill looking up at him, 'taking her to the nick, she said Tina had murdered her son.'

The grin vanished from Curly's face. 'He was lost at sea. I know for a fact.'

'Yup,' said Jill. 'I went and checked the records when we got back. They said it was an accidental death. Lost overboard.'

The sun dropped lower. The red light flooded the flat land around them. ''Xactly,' said Curly, and without another word he marched off again, silver fish swinging by his side.

Alex watched him heading across the road, towards the shack Stella and Tina had rented for their honeymoon. 'You went back through the records?'

'Course. Mentally ill or not, she was making an accusation of murder.'

'Does it bother you?'

'Course it does. That doesn't mean there's anything in it.'

Alex smiled at her. She was a good copper. 'Tell me about the Younis family then. What happened to them?'

The names of the people murdered at the house called The Nest had been on the television this morning. Ayman and Mary Younis; a retired couple in their early sixties.

'Nope,' said Jill. 'Fuck off.'

They sat a little while longer and watched the sky turn red.

'You know I'll find out anyway.'

'Nope.'

'Suit yourself.'

Eventually Jill said, 'It's driving me nuts. Might as well drive you nuts too.' She sighed. 'I wish I hadn't had the chips now. You'll be wishing the same, time I'm finished. First thing I've eaten since yesterday lunch.' She looked around. 'Let's walk somewhere quieter,' she said. 'Quieter' meant heading south, away from the huts and chalets, towards the industrial bulk of the nuclear power station.

They walked side by side until they reached the tall boundary fence.

There had been a Waitrose supermarket delivery due at the Younises' house at eleven in the morning on the Thursday, Jill said. When the delivery woman arrived at the house, she noticed that all the curtains were closed, upstairs and downstairs, but she didn't think anything of it, because though she had been working in this area for six months, she had never delivered to this house before.

She took out her box of groceries and rang the doorbell, but nobody answered. Unsure if the doorbell worked or not, she opened the porch door and went to knock on the door inside.

The inside door to the Younises' house had a clear glass panel. The lights were on, but she didn't look inside at first. She knocked a couple of times, called out, but nobody came, so she leaned forward and put her face against the glass.

At first she could not make out what she was looking at.

Sitting at the bottom of the stairs was a woman, legs splayed out on the floor, back against the newel. The driver thought at first she had fallen and perhaps passed out there. As her eyes accustomed themselves to the low light, she realised that the woman was not dressed at all. She was completely naked. The darkness covering her torso was not clothes, but blood.

Some people panic when they come across scenes like this. Others find a strange calm takes them over, almost as if their mind has been hijacked. The woman couldn't explain why she acted so rationally, but she felt inside her pocket and pulled out her mobile phone, switched on the torch and looked again.

SIX

'Colin Gilchrist was the first responder,' Jill said, looking out over the evening sea. A ferry, navigation lights on, was heading south to France. 'Poor bastard. On his own. When he got there the woman from Waitrose was back in her van, bawling her eyes out.'

'The victim was Mrs Younis?'

'Yep. It was her. Her throat had been cut. I was the first person from Serious Crime. I went in, kitted up.'

'There was more?'

Jill didn't speak again until they reached the far side of the gaggle of fishermen who sat on the beach casting lines out towards the hot-water pipe that took the water from the reactors and pumped it out to sea.

Jill stopped, sat on the shingle facing the Channel. 'And then I went outside to look for signs of an intruder and I found Mr Younis at the back of the house. Naked, like his wife. Single gunshot to the neck, right at the jugular. He bled out on the grass, poor bastard. His nose and lips were missing, but forensics say that was probably foxes or badgers. And then there were two dogs. They had both been stabbed.'

'Where were his clothes?'

'In the kitchen.'

'The killer made them undress first, then murdered them?'

'Looks like it.'

The stars were starting to appear now; Venus and Mars were high and bright. 'See what I mean?' Jill said. 'Horrible.'

'I'm sorry.'

'Don't be. It's what we have to do, isn't it? Go to places like that.'

Alex nodded. 'What sort of dogs?'

'Labradors. Why?'

'I just like to have it all in my head.'

In the disappearing light, Jill looked at Alex. 'You like to have it in your head?'

'Wrong phrase.'

'Your trouble is you have too much in your head already.' Jill sucked in air. 'That's not all.'

'I didn't imagine it was.'

To the east, a fishing boat, port light showing as it headed in to Folkestone. The Channel was busy.

'The man was killed where he was. Mrs Younis was murdered in her bed. The bed was soaked. It was disgusting.'

'Whoever killed her took her downstairs? But they left Mr Younis where he died?'

Jill nodded. 'The thing was, the killer had written a message on the mirror in the bedroom in her blood.'

32

'What?'

'*Kill them all. God will know his own.*' Jill shook her head. 'It's psychotic. Like, serial killer stuff. Colin found it on Wikipedia. It's from the crusades, apparently.'

'Yes.'

'You actually knew that?'

'It was a monk,' said Alex. 'These soldiers were going to attack some town where Catholics lived alongside a sect that the pope had declared to be heretics. A general asked the monk, "How do we know which are Catholics? They all look the same. They live alongside each other perfectly happily." The monk replied, "Kill them all. Let God tell them apart."'

'*God will know his own.*'

'Exactly.'

'Weird, huh?'

'Prints?'

'Nothing significant yet.'

'This time of year, too. Not going to be easy.'

Jill knew what she meant without asking. Most of the year it was dead around here, but it was July: high summer, and the tourists were filling the caravan parks that were dotted throughout the marsh and its shoreline.

'How long was Colin Gilchrist alone there?'

'Twenty minutes.'

'Poor lad.'

'Yep. Poor lad. I went home last night and bought a packet of cigarettes for the first time in a year and smoked so many I felt sick.' She looked at her watch. 'I better go.'

'You could stay over. Zoë hasn't seen you for ages.'

Jill shook her head, looked up the coast towards where the Younises' house was. 'Sorry, lovely. Going to be a long day and a half tomorrow. If I stayed here, I know I'd just get pissed up.'

It *would* be a long day, Alex thought. They turned and headed back towards the Snack Shack, where Jill had left her car.

'What about the murder weapons?'

'Not found either yet. The gun was a nine-millimetre.'

'Two different weapons. That's strange. She was moved, and he wasn't. Two different murderers?'

'Maybe. Someone who had different ideas about men and women. Frankly, we have no bloody idea at all, right now.'

They walked north, past the solid red brick coastguard lookout station that had been converted into a luxury holiday home, past the contrasting tumble of sheds and wooden outbuildings that were clustered around an old first-class carriage, past the little art gallery that one of the owners ran.

Jill drove a mint-coloured Fiat 500 which she had hand-cleaned every Sunday. It was parked by the side of the road. The lights winked as she pressed her key fob.

'Did they have any children?'

They were at the car now. 'You have a dark mind.'

'I do.'

'They have a son, but if you're thinking it could be him, then no. He has profound multiple learning disabilities. He's in a care home up in Tunbridge Wells.'

It was after Jill started the car that Alex had another thought: 'What had they ordered?'

Jill turned her head through the open window to look at her senior officer. 'What?'

'Find out what the supermarket order was.'

Jill's head tilted back a fraction. 'Is this all that, "I like to have it all in my head"?'

'Good luck tomorrow,' Alex said. She saw the light go on in the bungalow that Tina and Stella were renting. Reaching through the window, she put her hand on Jill's resting on the steering wheel. Jill nodded.

— *When we first talked, Alexandra, you said there were three incidents which you think might have been responsible for your trauma. Are you ready to talk about what they are?*

— *I don't have any difficulty talking about them.*

— *It's bright. Let me lower the blinds a little.*

— *I'm fine, honestly.*

— *Go ahead, then.*

— *The first was a stabbing. It was over a year ago now. I was the first to arrive at the crime scene. The victim turned out to be a young police constable I knew a little. Anyway, it was obvious he had lost a lot of blood. He was slumped against this bedroom wall and it was dark . . . The thing was, I couldn't even find where the knife had gone in at first because there was so much of it, everywhere. I knew I had to put pressure on the wound, but I couldn't even find it. I remember checking for a pulse and there wasn't one, at least not one I could feel, but I waited with him until other officers arrived – and then the ambulance. It turned out he was still alive, but only just. I remember that feeling of the warmth of his blood. I was kneeling in it and it was soaking*

35

into everything I was wearing. When I left the room and went outside into the street I remember the looks of horror on people's faces because I was literally covered in blood. I had it on my hands and my face. Even in my hair.

— *That must have been awful. What happened to him?*

— *He didn't make it. They weren't able to revive him.*

— *I'm sorry.*

— *I'm sorry too. I had never liked him. I remember thinking, if I had liked him more, maybe I would have tried harder to save him.*

— *I'm sure it wasn't like that.*

— *Are you?*

— *Go on.*

— *The second was in a cellar in a house in Gravesend. It wasn't really a cellar. The homeowner was mentally ill. It was a really strange place. Over years and years he had dug out these tunnels and chambers under the house. The whole building was unstable. Long story short, I ended up being trapped in one of these chambers with a man who was . . . He was trying to kill me, pretty much. The fight dislodged one of the props that was holding the ceiling on us . . .*

— *Jesus.*

— *Right? When I say ceiling, it was just bare earth.*

— *Jesus Christ.*

— *It came right down on top of us. Most of it fell on him, the other guy . . . We were both trapped in there, in all this crap, in complete darkness. They got him out in the end, but he's paraplegic now. The weight of it broke his back. I was lucky.*

— *Jesus.*

— *Are you OK? You don't look great.*

— *Sorry. I'm not great in enclosed spaces. They give me the hee-bie-jeebies.*

— *Neither was I. I couldn't breathe for dust.*

— *I was just imagining it. Do you need some water or something? I do.*

— *I'm fine.*

— *OK. Let's carry on. And the third?*

— *Another sad story. I sent a friend to prison; a fellow officer. During the course of an investigation I discovered that when this man was a boy he had killed his own father. His father had been abusive. He had beaten his mother over years. One day this boy had just had enough and he killed his father. His father had a gun. The boy had found his father's gun and he shot him with it. At the time there had been an investigation but the murderer was never found. This was in Armagh during the Troubles, so there were a million other things going on. The man's father was caught up in all that business too. People were getting shot all over the place and people weren't exactly owning up to things. Nobody imagined it was his thirteen-year-old son, so he got away with it. Except . . . I figured it out and I ended up having to arrest him. He went to prison. He was a good man who was only trying to protect his mother, but he'd got away with it. Because of me he lost his job and his pension and everything.*

— *And?*

— *That's it. He's out now, but I don't think the same. He used to be a respected man around here.*

— *You blame yourself?*

— *I'm not sure what I could have done differently though.*

37

— *The first two events were violent. I don't see where the violence was in that last one. At least, not in relation to you.*

— *I didn't say it was violent. You just asked me what were the things that I thought had contributed to my trauma.*

— *And that story . . .*

— *It's just like the others in some ways. Because you're a police officer you have to do this stuff. And I think it leaves a mark.*

Alex pushed her bike across the shingle to the pale-blue cottage with the white windows. It was a sweet-looking place, the sort of building a child might draw: a symmetrical roof with a red terracotta chimney at one end. There was a light on in the main room. Alex knocked on the wooden door. Nobody answered. She stepped to the right and put her face against the glass.

SEVEN

A crunch of stones underfoot; Stella appeared around the side of the house. 'Oh. It's you.' She stepped forward and threw her arms around a startled Alex, hugging her tightly.

Another voice came from the far side of the shack. 'Who is it?'

'That beautiful woman copper who lives in the Coastguard Cottages who saved your bloody life from the madwoman. Come on. We owe you a drink. We're round the back.'

Tina was sitting on a small, two-seater sofa that sat on the shingle behind the bungalow. She had a glass in her hand and there was a small bamboo table in front of the sofa with an ashtray and a packet of cigarette papers with a tell-tale tear on the cover. 'Curly said you're all right for a copper.'

'I should have that on a T-shirt.'

'We're having some cava. Want some?' asked Stella.

'Still celebrating?'

'God, yes. It's been a bloody long time coming.'

Stella went inside to the kitchen and returned with a wine glass full of pale, bubbling liquid in one hand and a deckchair in the other. She handed Alex the glass and then set about the task of unfolding the chair.

'Thanks,' said Tina quietly. 'For what you did. You were amazing.'

Stella was still struggling with the chair. 'Hey. That double murder up in Romney? Curly says . . . he says you do that kind of thing. They slit the woman's throat, I heard.'

'Who from?'

'Friend works for Ocado. It was one of them found her . . . So there's some kind of weirdo loose, then?'

'I'm not working on that. I'm on sick leave right now. Otherwise I would have been there instead of having a coffee at the station cafe yesterday.'

'Here's to sick leave then.' Stella raised her glass. 'What's wrong with you?'

'Stella! Don't be rude.'

'Stress,' said Alex.

Tina leaned forward, picked up the ashtray and laid it on top of the packet of cigarette papers, probably hoping that Alex hadn't noticed them. Then she sat back and made room for Alex on the small sofa while Stella arranged herself in the deckchair.

The air was warm and balmy. Around them, hidden in the sea kale and gorse, the crickets had started singing. 'How long have you been together then?'

Tina and Stella exchanged a glance. 'Eight years,' said Tina.

'Oh.'

Stella chuckled. 'She was working in the chip shop. Her old man was one of the fishermen supplying the fish there. Awkward.'

'The one on The Stade?' The Stade was the town's old dock, where buildings huddled onto the quay overlooking the harbour.

'Not the posh one,' Stella said. 'The one that does proper fish and chips.'

'So you were already going out when Tina's husband disappeared?'

The noise of crickets filled the silence. Stella took a large swig from her glass.

'We kept it secret,' said Tina quietly.

'Back then I was out. Everyone in town knew I was a dyke. But nobody knew Tina was.' Stella picked up tobacco from the table and started looking for the papers that Tina had hidden. 'Not even Tina. Came as a bit of a shock to me first time she kissed me.'

'Shock to me, too,' said Tina.

'Her, a married woman.'

'Don't,' said Tina. 'None of it is funny. I didn't know I was gay when I married him. I was too young.'

Stella had started looking under the table. Alex leaned forward, lifted the ashtray, picked up the papers and handed them to Stella.

Tina blushed.

'I'm hardly going to shop you,' said Alex. 'I'm all right for a copper, allegedly.'

Somewhere people were having a party. The low repetitive bass from a hip hop record pulsed in the darkness.

'Stella was really cool. She made her own clothes. I once saw her walking through town in this skirt she'd made from pink and yellow Marigold gloves. I was, like –' She dropped her jaw wide.

41

'Only wore it that time. It was a bit sweaty.' Stella laughed.

'I thought you were so cool. Nobody I'd grown up around was like that.'

'Her ex would have gone ape if he'd ever found out Tina loved me.'

'Would he?' asked Alex.

Another nod.

'Did he ever find out?'

Stella looked at Tina. 'Nope. Never did.' Stella lit her cigarette. A bird cried in the night. It was a sad sound; a short, plangent wailing. An owl maybe. Zoë would know.

'Wouldn't be the first fisherman's wife to play for the other side when her man's at sea,' said Stella.

Even in the porch light, Alex could see Tina's blush deepening, but she smiled.

'It was lovely,' she said, quietly. 'Longer he was at sea, the happier I was. What's bad is I used to pray that he'd never come back. And then one day, he didn't.'

'He fell overboard,' said Stella. 'Did you hear about that? I'd have pushed him myself if I'd been on the boat.'

'Shut up,' said Tina, a little too loudly.

Stella ignored her. 'And a year after he'd gone, we moved in together and ever since then, that psycho Mandy Hogben has been accusing her of killing him.'

'She's not well, Stella.'

'It's not the first time, then?'

'Show her, Tina.'

Tina sighed, then turned her head to Alex, picked up her hand and laid it on her scalp. 'Feel that.'

Alex's finger found a bump of flesh; a line about two centimetres long. 'She did that to me in Asda. I was doing the shop and she was there. She saw me, started screaming and shouting and throwing stuff at me.'

'Tina had concussion after that.'

'A can of something. I bled like a pig all over the aisle. It was horrible.'

Stella sounded angry now. 'At the inquest they said it. He got onto the boat and sailed off in it and never came back. What more does she want? She was bloody there at the inquest but she won't believe it.'

'It's OK, Stell.' Tina's voice was soft.

The pulse of the distant bass continued. The spit of land seemed full of people tonight.

Stella flicked her cigarette butt into the air; it flew in a red arc into the blackness. 'More splosh, anyone?' she said, standing.

'When did you hear that he was dead?' asked Alex.

'They were fishing out of Folkestone. Just a two-man crew. The other man on board called it in to the coastguard the moment he discovered he'd gone over, but he hadn't seen him go, and he wasn't sure when, so the search area was huge. The sea was pretty big too and they knew they'd no chance of finding him alive. I had a copper come to my door to tell me he was lost overboard. I said, "Have you told his mother yet?" They hadn't, of course, because they wanted me to do that. Thanks a million.'

'So it was you who told Mandy Hogben her son was dead?'

Tina nodded.

Alex drank. 'But you had to wait seven years to marry because they never found his body.'

'Controlling bastard, even after death.'

'Stella!' chided Tina.

They drank a little more wine. Satellites and planes moved above them, tiny dots of light. The sky here was enormous, Alex thought. 'You never had kids with Frank?'

'He wanted them. I never did. You got kids?' Tina asked.

'One. Teenage girl. Seventeen. She's out there somewhere. She's gone feral.' She waved in the direction of Big Pit. Her girl spent little time at home these days.

'Short fair hair? Skinny as a pin? Has a backpack?'

'Zoë, isn't it?' said Tina.

'That's her.'

'She's brilliant.'

'You know her?'

'We just met her today. Early this morning I was watching a yellow-legged gull out at the patch, and she was there too.'

'Was she?'

The 'patch' was what some locals called the water just off shore by the power station, where heated water attracted the fish and where the fish attracted seabirds. Zoë had been up early, Alex remembered, before she had woken.

'She's your daughter?' Tina laughed. 'She's absolutely nuts. We love her.'

'Me too,' said Alex.

'Stella's crazy about birds and stuff,' said Tina. 'This was her choice of place to go, not mine.'

'Your Zoë said she'll take us moth-trapping one night.'

'Who goes hunting moths on their honeymoon?' complained Tina.

44

'Me. You've already had one honeymoon. This is my first. I get to choose what we do.' For no particular reason, she stood and howled at the dark sky, like a wolf. 'God, though. They said on the news there's a psychotic killer out there. Pretty scary stuff. Killed two people, they said.'

Alex said, 'Yes. Pretty scary.'

'Don't you worry about your little girl, out here on her own?'

'All the time.'

They were all quiet for a minute. Alex drank a little more of the fizzy wine and realised she was a little bit drunk. Tina broke the silence by asking quietly, 'How did you know she was going to pull out that blade?'

'I didn't. That's what freaks me out. I stood up and walked over towards her, but I don't know why I did.'

'It's like you've got a spidey sense.' Tina giggled.

'What?'

'Like Spider-Man.'

'Tina believes in that stuff. The third eye. Divination and destiny,' said Stella. 'I'm your destiny, aren't I, darling?' And she leaned and kissed Tina on her head, just on the spot where Frank's mother had scarred her, and she left Alex and Tina sitting in the darkness while she fetched another bottle.

On the way back home, she noticed Zoë's bike was propped unlocked against William South's small porch, so she knocked.

William South lived in Arum Cottage, a small red bungalow that faced the nuclear power station.

South opened the door.

'Have you got my girl in there?'

'You want her back?' He opened the door wide.

Zoë was sat at South's dining table, hands in front of her. There was blood on them.

EIGHT

'Jesus, love. What have you done?'

'Been digging,' her daughter answered.

'My grave?'

'I'm not burying you, Mum,' said Zoë. 'I'm leaving you for the crows.' South sat down opposite her and picked up cotton wool. 'An air burial.'

'Thanks.'

'Blisters,' said Bill quietly. 'Looks worse than it is.'

'I said I was volunteering today up at the Romney Marsh reserve, remember? We were clearing out the drainage ditches. I was going for it. And then I was clearing grass with the scythe for the orchids. They have Spiranthes spiralis there. It's a threatened species.'

'Autumn lady's tresses,' said Bill, as if this were an explanation Alex would understand.

Since dropping out of sixth form college, Zoë had filled her time either protesting or volunteering. Whenever Alex had tried to get her to complete a CV, Zoë just replied that she didn't need

47

money and nobody actually wanted young people any more. Alex had given up arguing.

'How could they let you get in that state?'

'She's fine,' said Bill. 'She enjoyed herself.' He went back to sticking plasters on her fingers.

Zoë looked at her wounds with pride. 'Eight hours with a scythe and shovel. Some of your lot were there too.'

'My lot?'

'Police. Asking if we'd seen anyone suspicious.'

South put a tin mug of tea down in front of her without asking.

'You were community copper round here when Frank Hogben went missing, weren't you, Bill?'

He picked up the scissors and cut another inch from the roll of plaster. 'I was. Why you asking?'

Zoë clenched and unclenched her fingers, feeling the plasters on the skin, watching them both closely while trying to pretend she wasn't listening.

Alex narrowed her eyes. 'I've got a question for you. You think there was something off about the death of Frank Hogben?'

South placed the small pair of scissors he'd been using onto the roll of plaster and eventually said, 'Aren't you supposed to be off duty right now?'

'That's what they keep telling me.'

South sniffed. 'Maybe you should take their advice.'

Alex frowned. South was being even more obtuse than usual. 'If you don't tell me, I'll only ask Jill.'

'Before her time,' said South, standing. 'She won't know anything about it.' He crossed the room and put the plaster in a small white wooden cupboard with a red cross on the door.

'Off duty or not, I arrested Frank Hogben's mother yesterday. She had a knife. She was accusing her former daughter-in-law of killing her son.'

'She's not well.'

'You know all this?'

'Yes. Mandy Hogben has been ill for years.'

Alex looked at him. He was avoiding her eye. 'Do you think that's even possible? What Mandy Hogben was saying?'

'Tina and Stella?' interrupted Zoë. 'The two women who got married yesterday?'

'Yes.'

'I like them. Stella has a vintage clothes shop in Folkestone. She says she'll give me a discount.'

'Since when were you interested in clothes?' asked her mother.

'Course I am.' Zoë held up her hands like they were some kind of prize.

'Did you know Frank Hogben too?' asked Alex.

'And his father, Max. Everybody knew them. Max was one of the men who use fists first, then, if you're lucky, talk later. Everyone was afraid of him, including Frank. I saw him walloping his son with my own eyes down on The Stade over some petty family squabble.'

'He still alive?'

'Max Hogben killed himself driving without a seatbelt, stupid arse. He had this car, a Ford Escort RS 1600-i. Supercharged thing. There were only a couple of thousand in this country. They were racing cars, really. His was "sunburst red", they called it. You could see it coming miles away. It was his pride and joy. Another car just overshot the lights at Cheriton Road and went into the side of him. It was just a simple accident. The other car was only going, like, twenty miles an hour, they reckoned. The driver got out to apologise and Max Hogben was dead. Nothing suspicious about it. He'd hit his head on the B-pillar, internal cranial haemorrhage and that was it. Bad luck and not wearing a seatbelt.'

'You were there?'

'Ten minutes after it happened. Never liked Max, or the way he treated his boy.'

He went quiet for a minute, then said, 'Funny thing. Frank Hogben kept the car. The chassis was fine, it wasn't much of a bang, so he did it up, got it back on the road and used to drive it around, just like his father had.'

'The car his father was killed in?'

'Yep. Same seat and everything. Driving it up and down, one arm hanging out of the window. That's pretty strange, don't you think?'

'Pretty strange.'

Zoë interrupted the moment by asking, abruptly, 'Do you believe in ghosts?'

'What?'

'You heard. Do you believe in ghosts?'

'No, I do not,' said Alex. 'I believe in what I can see with my own eyes.'

'I know *you* don't,' her daughter said. 'You don't believe in anything if it's a bit too weird for you. I was asking Bill.'

Bill shook his head. 'Same as your mother. Never seen one. No reason to believe in them.'

'What brought this on?' asked her mother.

'You know Kenny Abel?' she asked South.

'Course,' he said.

Alex recognised the name. Kenny Abel was one of the men who worked for the Kent Wildlife Trust; he ran the group of volunteers Zoë had been working with.

'Anyway. Wednesday night after work he was in the pub. When he came out, he reckoned he saw the spirits of the murdered people flying up into the air. He didn't know what it was at the time. Only when he saw it on the news on Thursday . . .'

'Kenny Abel said that?'

'Today. Yeah.'

South said, 'The clue might be that he was coming out of the pub.'

Zoë chewed on the inside of her cheek for a while, then looked away, out of the window. 'I think it's really sad that as you grow old, you get more cynical. You lose the ability to believe in anything.'

'You're in a funny mood tonight,' said Alex.

'Not really. I mean. What if you could see souls? Only, what if not everyone could see them?'

'He was probably drunk, like Bill said. Things like that don't really happen.'

'You wake in the night and talk to dead people. Who are you to say what's normal or not?'

'Does she?' asked South.

'Zoë!' scolded Alex. 'No I don't.'

'Yes you do,' muttered Zoë.

Alex looked at South. 'Sometimes I have nightmares. It's part of the PTSD.'

51

Bill turned to Zoë. 'It must be scary for you.'

The teenage girl cocked her head to one side. 'It's not every night.'

'You know, if you ever need anything . . .' South said. He stood and looked out of the north window, towards the lighthouses. 'Anything at all.'

Somewhere outside a motorbike roared down the Dungeness Road breaking the stillness. The new concrete lighthouse stood illuminated, a black and white rocket against the black sky. The summer air was moist. Every ten seconds it lit the air with a bright beam; a fixed point in a moving world.

They wheeled their bikes home together, mother and daughter.

It was only a short distance down a single-track road to their more solid house.

'Which pub?' asked Alex.

'What?'

'The pub that man says he saw the ghosts from. Which one was it.'

'Kenny Abel? I don't know. Was near the house where the dead people were, though.' They had reached the back door of the house and Alex had her key in the door. 'He said they flew up from the roof of the house into the sky.'

They flew up from the roof and into the sky, thought Alex that night as she sat awake in bed, listening to owls.

When she woke in the morning there was a cup of cold mint tea by her bed which she didn't remember making.

NINE

Dressed in khaki shorts and a huge T-shirt that hung off her angular shoulders, Zoë was holding a knife in one hand and poking inside the toaster with it.

'Is that unplugged?'

Zoë looked up. 'Yes, Mum. I'm not an idiot.' For a while she carried on digging, until broken pieces of bread started emerging.

'Is that peanut butter on that?' Alex asked.

'Kind of.'

'What do you mean, kind of?'

'Peanut butter and Marmite.'

Zoë had the grace to look embarrassed.

'*Yes, Mum. I'm not an idiot.*'

'I hate using the grill,' Zoë said. 'It takes forever.'

The sun was already high. It was going to be another delicious, slow summer's day and the thought of finding anything to fill it made Alex's heart shrink.

Zoë was now trying to put the burned pieces into the bin,

which was already full. Alex sighed. She crossed the room and pulled the bag out of the container, tied it and took it outside.

As she was making her way back to the kitchen, a young man in a Manic Street Preachers T-shirt, standing by the back door of the house next door with a cigarette in his hand, looked at her nervously and asked, 'I don't mean to intrude, but is everything, you know . . . all right?'

Puzzled, she said, 'Yes. Fine.'

'What did he mean, *Is everything all right?*' she asked Zoë, when she was safely indoors.

'You don't remember.'

Alex blinked. 'Remember what?'

'You were shouting.'

Alex nodded. Pulled out a fresh bag from the drawer. 'Was it bad?'

Her daughter shook her head as nonchalantly as she could. 'Not really. I'm used to it.'

'You made me mint tea.'

'It calms you down.'

'Does it?' she asked. She didn't like mint tea, she thought.

The house next door was rented out to people who wondered why their neighbour was screaming in the night. What kind of people, Alex considered, would leave it until the morning to ask if everything was OK? She wouldn't have. She would have been out banging on the door, but maybe that was what was wrong with her.

Zoë's toast was ruined. Alex offered to make her some more but Zoë shook her head. 'I'm not really hungry anyway.'

Alex looked at her. These last few weeks, Alex had been so

bound up in herself. 'You have to eat something. Especially if you're going digging again today.'

Zoë didn't answer.

'Look. I'll give you a lift there, if you like.'

Her daughter nodded. 'Not that I approve of cars, obviously.'

Twenty minutes later, in the car parked at the Romney Marsh Wildlife Visitor Centre in front of the low, green-roofed building she said, 'I'm sorry. About the shouting.'

'It's OK.'

'Is it scary?'

'Nope,' her daughter said simply. 'Not for me. Probably just for the neighbours.'

Children accepted what you did, thought Alex, because you were their parent.

Instead of getting out, Zoë sat in the car for a moment, rucksack in her lap. 'I just want you to be all right,' she said, then opened the door and got out before her mother could say anything in answer.

Alex watched her stride off towards the building's big front door.

She sat for a minute, checked her face in the mirror, then got out and followed her.

When Alex entered the building, she was already talking to a well-built man in his thirties, with long matted hair. He wore a khaki utility vest over a blue pullover.

'Are you Kenny Abel?'

'Mum,' protested Zoë.

'About her hands . . .' said the man.

'It's not that. She's fine. She chooses to do this stuff, I'd be scared of trying to stop her. But I wanted to ask you something. About what you saw on Wednesday night.'

'Sorry,' muttered Zoë. 'I wouldn't have told her if I thought she was that interested.'

The man raised his head. 'Why are you asking?'

'My daughter said you thought you saw their souls going upwards.'

'Yep,' he said, chin jutting forward a little as he answered. 'I was having a drink in the Romney Hotel after work. Went outside to have a ciggie and to make a call to the wife. I knew what it was when I saw it. Only realised something had gone on next day when I tried to get in to work down Ashford Road and it was all closed off. Then it was on the news.'

'You can see souls?'

'Yes.' The muscles in his face seemed to tense, as if daring her to disbelieve him. 'Not everyone can. I can.'

'See souls?' she repeated.

'Yes.'

'So you've seen souls before?'

Beside him, Zoë was squirming with embarrassment.

'My grandmother's. Only, that was during the daytime in a hospice. She had pancreatic cancer. She was weak as a kitten, barely breathing. The only way you knew she was alive was the beeping of the monitors. I saw her leave her body and go up, clear as anything. Nobody else did. Just me. It was like this pale cloud rising upwards. And, like, ten seconds later the monitors showed her heart stopping.'

He could see the scepticism on her face. 'I know what you're thinking. I was tired and grieving. But I'm not the only one who's seen stuff like that. Same happened to the poet William Blake. He saw his brother rise up from his deathbed and float into the air. Not everyone else saw it then either.'

Alex felt as if she were coming down with something. The world seemed to be becoming untethered from the reality she understood. 'What did it actually look like? What you saw on Wednesday night.'

'It was like a line of silver, shooting upwards. All over in a second.'

'A beam of light maybe?'

'No. See . . . it's not like that. More like the bodies were floating upwards, but fast, like.'

Alex nodded. 'What time was that?'

'About ten.'

'About?'

'Hold on.' He pulled out his phone, opened his messages and flicked up. 'Must have been seven minutes past.'

'How do you know?'

'I told my wife about it. We were on the phone.' He held up the screen to show her his call log.

Alex shivered, peered at it. 'Where were you standing?'

'At the back. There's, like, a smoking area.'

Alex looked at the man still holding up his phone, defying her to disbelieve him. 'Thanks,' she said.

'Go now, Mum,' said Zoë sternly.

She took the route back past the Romney Hotel, stopped in front of it, thinking. It was a long, old, cream-painted building, fifteenth-century, just back from a narrow pavement. The bar was still closed at this time in the morning, but there was a bell for hotel enquiries.

A man in his sixties with long grey sideboards opened the door. 'I just want to check something,' Alex said.

'Beg your pardon?'

'I'm a police officer,' she found herself saying.

'Is this to do with the murders?' the man asked.

She said, 'I just need to see your smokers' area. I'll only be a minute.'

He led her through the lounge bar, unlocked a door and pushed it open. 'Why? What's going on?'

She stood under the electric space heaters among the mess of unemptied ashtrays and looked to the north-west, the direction of the Younises' house. 'Anything in particular?' asked the man.

'That's the house over there, isn't it?'

'Bloody awful thing,' said the man. 'Everyone's on edge, round here. Just had a waitress pull out of all her shifts on account of she doesn't like coming this way now. Not that that's important,' he added quietly, ashamed of the selfishness of what he'd just said.

The murder house's roofline was hidden behind the willows and poplars that fringed a local sports field, but the land between the pub garden and the house was flat. One would be able to see a soul rising up from the rooftop of the murder house; if such a thing were even possible.

She thanked the landlord and left him as bemused by her visit as she was.

★

Turning off the main road, she drove up to the house, where police cars still cluttered the driveway, parked on the grass verge, then looked back over the hedge towards the pub.

Her phone rang. 'I can see you.' Jill's voice, barely heard because the line was breaking up.

'Can you?'

'Your car, anyway. What are you doing lurking here, Alex?'

'I was just dropping Zoë at the Wildlife Centre.'

'Yeah. Right.'

'I was,' Alex said, but the call had dropped.

Ten seconds later, her phone rang again. 'Funny way to drive home. You actually cannot leave it alone, can you?'

'You're still in there, then?'

She could hear Jill's sigh. 'I'm taking a break. Meet you—' But the call had dropped again. A few seconds later a message from her:

Fk my phone. Wait there. Don't talk to NO ONE. Something vv strange.

TEN

Alex's desire to see inside the house, to see the details of the violence, how the bodies had fallen and the blood on the mirror, surprised even her.

It was understandable. Normally Alex would have been inside, or would have access to photos and videos of the scene. She was on the outside now.

Instead, she waited a little way from the murder house until she saw, in her rear-view mirror, Jill emerging from the front gate, half running as she got closer, clutching a pack of cigarettes in one hand.

'Can we go somewhere for a bloody coffee?' Jill blurted, opening the door. 'That place is absolutely doing my head in.'

'Round here? You've got to be joking.'

'Even my phone doesn't work in there. It's spooked.'

The place Alex drove them to was the best she could do. A pub in Littlestone, ten minutes away, that advertised free football on the TV. A tattered England flag sagged on a flagpole over the small paved area at the front where they could sit, but it was open.

Alex fetched two coffees from the bar and joined Jill on the terrace among the Saturday morning drinkers.

'It's not healthy,' said Jill. 'You are not supposed to be thinking about this stuff. It's this stuff that's caused you to . . .'

'Lose it?'

'I wouldn't say you've lost it, not exactly,' said Jill.

'Thanks.'

'Mind if I . . . ?' Jill had already pulled out a cigarette. '*I'm losing it. Not surprised if everyone on this investigation is. When it comes to things like this, maybe they don't make any sense.*' There were dark patches under Jill's eyes.

A teenager sped past on a motorbike, driving well over the limit. They both watched him disappear up the road but said nothing.

'Well. What's so odd?'

'For starters, we have absolutely nothing,' Jill said eventually. 'It's the weirdest thing. The house is clean. Evidence-wise, it's like a black hole. That's what forensics are telling us. No fingerprints that don't match the victims. No footprints, ditto. No tyre tracks. No DNA yet. Yet no sign of it being cleaned either. No wipe marks, no traces of recent cleaning fluid. When does that ever happen?'

'It does happen. Some people just don't seem to leave prints, or bits of skin. It's a phenomenon, but sometimes it happens.'

'Not when two people are dead in some kind of psychotic attack. Tell me. What kind of killer doesn't leave a single trace at a murder scene? It's like someone flew in and out of there.'

Alex said, 'Ghosts, maybe.'

'Very funny. I was thinking, what if it was some kind of

61

ultra-professional killer who pretended to be psycho just to cover up.'

'Around here?'

'Why not?' Jill picked up her coffee and tasted it, made a face. 'And what does that actually mean, *Kill them all. God will know his own*? But to leave no clues at all . . . You'd have to be pretty methodical to do that. See what I mean? It doesn't make sense.'

'No. It doesn't.'

Jill took her time before she spoke again, and when she did so, her voice was cautious. 'One really bloody weird thing's come up, though. That's what I need to talk to you about, Alex. You had that funny question. You asked what they ordered.'

'Yes?'

'Why precisely did you ask that?'

'Tell me what they ordered.'

'I asked first. Come on. I need to know.'

'You tell me. Then I'll tell you why I asked the question.'

Jill made a face, considered this for a minute, then reached down, picked up her bag and pulled out a notebook. 'Here we go. This is exactly what they ordered. Dishwasher tablets. Four bottles of wine. Dog food. Gin.'

'That all?'

Jill looked up. 'Exactly. You'd have thought that you'd order more than that if you're going to go to all the trouble of an online order.'

'Did you check the cupboards?'

Jill smiled. 'I did actually. No shortage of gin – or dog food.'

'How much did it come to?'

'Total value, £41.65.'

'Is that all?'

'Not much for a weekly shop, is it?'

Alex didn't answer. Opposite the pub was the New Romney railway station. She watched someone walk past with a set of golf clubs.

'So?'

'Right. The Younises didn't need the food on the list. They already had gin, at least. What's the minimum amount for a delivery? I'd guess about forty quid?' Alex let that sit for a second. 'That's why I asked.'

'Oh. Wait. I got it.' Jill's eyes went big. 'You think whoever put in the order did it only because whoever killed them wanted the delivery driver to find the dead bodies?'

'Maybe.'

'Oh my God. Oh-my-God-oh-my-God. Why didn't I see that?'

Alex took a sugar cube, dropped it into her cup and stirred it, hoping sugar would give it something, at least.

'And that's why the murderer left Mrs Younis at the bottom of the stairs for them to see when they rang the bell?'

'So who ordered the delivery, Jill?'

'Mrs Younis ordered it online. But it's hardly likely to have been her, is it? It's like an invitation to see a dead body. It's all super-weird.'

Alex looked down at her feet. Butterflies danced around the dandelions that cracked through the paving stones of the patio. 'Yes. It is.'

A young couple joined them in the garden, both drinking lagers, lighting up cigarettes. Alex lowered her voice. 'What about money? Have you looked at their bank accounts?'

'We're looking. Because there's no sign of anything having been taken from the house.'

'Still no suspects? Nothing?'

'No relations we're worried about. No lovers or colleagues. Just one report of Ayman Younis having a heated argument four days before the murder but we've been unable to work out who with. The postman heard shouting coming from the garden behind the house. He thinks he heard the words, "You're going to fucking kill me, you know that?" He's pretty sure that was Mr Younis's voice but he can't be absolutely certain.'

Alex thought about the layout of the house. The front door was on the left, by the driveway. Behind the house, out of sight if you were at the front door, was a large rear garden. 'Could it have been an argument with his wife?'

'No. There was a second voice, he said, talking less loudly, and it was definitely male. We're asking friends if they have any idea of who it might have been.'

'*You're going to fucking kill me?*'

'Yes. McAdam has been calling him the Unknown Male. It's got a ring to it, don't you think? Mind you, pretty much all males are unknown to me.'

'What about time of death?' asked Alex.

Jill frowned. 'Why are you asking me that?'

'Just wondering, that's all.' She thought about Kenny Abel and his souls. If she explained why, she might sound madder than she already did. 'Do you know?'

'Come on, Alex. Why do you want to know?'

Alex shrugged.

'Actually, we might be in luck there.'

'How?' Forensics were increasingly reluctant to name precise times of death these days. Bodies decayed at different rates; temperatures fluctuated from place to place. What had been assumed to be an exact science had proved not to be. It was rare for anyone to hazard even an approximate time of death these days.

'As it turns out, Mary Younis had a pacemaker. It's gone for analysis. The pathologist says if we're lucky, we will be able to discover the exact second it stopped working.'

She drove Jill back, parking fifty metres from the house. A BBC news team was parked just outside the gate now, setting up a camera.

'What are you doing now?' asked Jill.

'Nothing.'

'Perfect. Go home. Put your feet up. Get some rest.'

Alex nodded. 'Yes. Maybe that's what I'll do. Let me know if it was around seven minutes past ten.'

'If what?'

'The time when Mary Younis died.'

'Seven minutes past ten. That's just too weirdly specific.'

'It won't be, then, I promise. It's . . . it's too nuts. Just tell me if it is. OK?'

Instead of turning around to head home, Alex returned to Littlestone. It took a little driving around before she found what she was looking for.

The golf club's main building was a huge Edwardian arts and crafts hulk, red brick, pebble-dash, black beams and white balustrades.

Alex parked on the road close to the front of the clubhouse and walked past it onto the course. Her father had been a police officer in an era in which senior officers had all played golf. He had never played a round in his life; neither had she. But then, nor had he ever been diagnosed with PTSD.

A golf course, she thought, should have rolling hills and trees. This one didn't; like everything around here, it was flat. Today, in the midsummer sun, it was at its flattest.

As she walked towards the first tee, three jolly-looking women strolled past her pulling trolleys, dressed up in loose pastel-coloured trousers and sporty hats. They were in their sixties or older.

Alex retreated to a nearby white-painted bench and observed them as they peered at their watches, waiting for a fourth player.

Eventually one, the shorter of the three called, 'You don't play, do you?'

Alex snapped out of her thoughts. 'Sorry?'

'Fancy a round? We've been stood up.'

'I'm not a member.'

They approached her.

'Oh, don't worry about that. We could sneak you on.' They laughed like naughty schoolgirls.

'I can't actually play, either.'

'Even better. Dawn here needs a handicap.' More laughter.

She looked up at them. 'Can I ask you, did any of you know Ayman Younis?'

The laughing stopped at once. 'What are you? A journalist?'

Alex shook her head. 'Worse. I'm a police officer.'

'Show me,' said the shorter woman distrustfully.

It was true, she was a police officer, but she had no right to be here flashing her warrant card; all the same, she dug into her shoulder bag, pulled out her purse and flipped it open.

'New, I suppose,' said the short woman, peering close. 'I don't recognise your name.'

Alex, still seated, blinked up at her in the bright sunshine. 'Why would you know my name?'

'I was a superintendent. Thirty-one years' service. I know most people from around here. You're not local.'

'No. I came down from the Met.'

The woman made a face, then raised her eyebrows in a small flash of realisation. 'Oh. You're the one who sent poor Bill South to prison.'

Alex knew she had not made herself popular among her colleagues. 'Yes. I was.'

To her surprise the woman said, 'I don't suppose that was very easy, having to do something like that.'

'No. It wasn't.'

The woman stood, scrutinising her. Idly she pulled a wood from her trolley. 'I rather admire you for doing it. It was a big shock to us, of course. Bill South is a good man, but it was the right thing. It must have taken some guts.'

'I don't think most people round here see it that way. William South, mostly.'

A short, high laugh. 'He has hidden depths, that man. I'm sure he respects your decision too. He's up here all the time, you know. He came to do an ecological survey of the course last year. He still comes here bird-spotting sometimes, with that girl. His niece, I think.'

A murmur of agreement from the other woman.

'His niece?'

'I think she must be a relative. She doesn't seem to go to school or anything. I think he looks after her. Trouble at home or something, I expect. He's a very good man.'

Alex bristled, but said nothing. She imagined all these golf women fussing around Bill and her daughter. Zoë led a life she barely understood. 'What about the Younises?'

'Poor Mary wasn't a member. She didn't really do golf, did she?'

'Mary Younis?'

'Yes. You probably know that already.' The woman squinted at her, trying to puzzle her out. If she had been working on the case, she would have known these details.

'And Ayman Younis?' Alex said.

'You'd do better talking to Terry over there.'

An athletic-looking man was putting on the eighteenth hole nearby. He wore a dark-blue polo shirt, white shoes, and baseball cap.

'Go carefully. Terry Neill has been very upset by the whole thing. He usually partnered with Ayman.'

'Neill, you say?'

While the women teed off, Alex watched the man playing alone, tapping the ball towards the hole, missing it, and watching it roll to the other side of the green. She waited until he'd finished and was tugging his trolley towards the clubhouse, then stood. 'Mr Neill,' she called.

The man stopped, peered at her, took off his baseball cap. He had a thick head of salt-and-pepper hair.

She came closer. 'You were a friend of Ayman Younis's.'

From where she stood she saw him raise the white gloved hand that held his cap to his tanned face. He was crying, she realised.

ELEVEN

His eyes were bluer for their red rims.

'I'm sorry. I'm quite the crier.' They sat together on the bench in the warm afternoon sun. 'It's very raw, though. Last thing in the world you'd expect around here. The whole thing is so strange.'

He was in his late forties, she guessed, which made him younger than most of the other golfers she had seen on the course this morning.

'I can't actually imagine him not being here,' Terry Neill said, looking around him at the course, flat and empty. 'I've just been playing a round without him. Saturday mornings, every one for the last couple of years, we're out here. Every time I sliced the ball or knocked it close to the rough, I wait for him to say something, to take the piss, but he's not there. I can't imagine him not being up in the bar now suggesting we have a drink.'

Alex handed him another paper hankie from her bag.

'The thing about men is they don't make friends easily. Me,

at least. It's a physical thing, grief, you know? Statistically, it's known that some spouses die within a few months of each other. Loss alters us in significant ways.'

She looked at him cautiously. 'You're not, by any chance, a counsellor are you?'

He broke into a laugh. 'God forbid. An academic. A biochemist. Former biochemist. Mostly retired now, obviously. Why? Are you looking for one? This doesn't seem like the obvious place to start.'

'No. I seem to have one already. You believe that grief is just a chemical imbalance, then?'

He picked off his gloves. 'That would be a very arrogant thing to say. Grief is huge. But one way to look at it might be neurology. There's a thing called Broken Heart Syndrome, did you know that? Extreme emotions have a physical effect on heart function. You can actually die from a broken heart.'

Alex's mother had not died after her father had passed away. Far from it. She had prospered. Alex, who had loved her father in the way an only daughter could, had resented that.

'You're having counselling?' he asked, wiping the underside of his eyes. 'How are you finding the experience?'

'Good, actually. It's useful to talk. You don't think it's all mumbo-jumbo then?'

'Not in the slightest. I've done a ton of it. Counsellors tend to be a bit sniffy about what we biochemists say, but if it works, it works . . . even if they don't always understand why.'

'What sort of people were the Younises?'

'Good people,' he said. 'Mary was sweet. Quite shy. Very smart in a bookish kind of way. I was closer to Ayman. He

71

was the archetypal Englishman.' He laughed sadly. 'Immigrant grandparents. All he wanted was to be part of all this.' He waved his hand at the land around him. 'Have a nice house. A nice family. Dogs. Golf club. More English than you and me, really. Every time he beat me at golf he apologised, for God's sake.' He smiled thinly, as if grateful for the chance to talk about his friend. 'His father had an electronics engineering business. Ayman sold it about twenty years ago so he could be here with his wife and his son . . .' He paused, took a breath. Alex saw his eyes begin to shine with tears again.

She left it a moment before asking, 'Can I just ask, had Ayman Younis ever been threatened by anyone?'

'Your colleague asked the same. The young woman.'

'The better-looking one?'

'Younger. Not better-looking.'

'Liar.'

He smiled.

Jill had interviewed him. She was already putting what pieces there might be together. 'Was there ever a threat to his life?'

'No. Like I said to her, he was liked. Respected.'

The three ladies had not waited for their fourth partner. They were already on the second green.

'You don't mind talking like this, do you?'

'God, no. To be honest, I was heading to the clubhouse, but it's like a church in there right now after the news. Everyone's talking in whispers. People are afraid to talk about this kind of thing.' He tucked the tissue into a trouser pocket. He stood. 'Do you mind going there with me?'

She stood too, and the two walked slowly to the nearby club-house. 'What were the things Ayman cared about?'

'Mary, obviously. And Callum.'

'Callum?'

'His son. He is devoted to him. *Was* devoted to him. Callum is disabled. Cerebral palsy and other complications. He was born very prematurely. It's no life at all, is it?'

Alex thought for a while. 'Who looked after him?'

'Well, Ayman did. Financially, obviously. He was too much for them to look after on their own. He has spastic quadriplegia and cerebral visual impairment. He's functionally blind. They tried for a while but he needs specialist care around the clock.'

He held the door open, and led her through to a bar, where the curtains were William Morris fabric, the chairs were upholstered in leather, and silver cups sat in rows behind mahogany and glass. 'It was what drove Ayman, I think. He had to earn enough money to keep Callum in the best conditions he could. It's why he befriended me, in some ways. He wanted to talk about it. He always hoped that science would be able to help in some way.'

'Did you ever meet Callum?'

'Just the once. We went up to the nursing home in Tunbridge Wells for his twenty-first. Ayman and Mary held a party for him at Loftingswood Grange not so long ago.' Alex must have looked puzzled, because he added, 'The nursing home. It's why they moved to Kent, so they could be close to him. They kind of organised their life around him. Ayman was one of those people who just wanted everything to be right, do you know what I mean? Excuse me. I've just got to change my shoes,' he said. 'You OK for a minute?'

73

The bar was quiet. The man who had tried to pick her up in his Qashqai outside the Younises' house put his head round the door, spotted her, frowned in puzzlement. Alex smiled and gave him a little wave. He retreated in embarrassment. After that, she sat on a chair and flicked through a copy of a magazine that promised three quick ways to sharpen her short game, feeling a little out of place, until Terry returned. He had replaced his golf shoes for a pair of trainers and had washed his face so that it was not so obvious he had been crying.

There was a small oak table by the door full of leaflets. He paused at it, lifted out his wallet and put a ten-pound note into a yellow collection box marked *Action CP*, then turned towards her, and she noticed that the tears were back.

Alex realised that the initials CP would stand for Cerebral Palsy and realised that Ayman Younis had probably put the box there.

Terry sat down opposite her and gave a small smile, then apologised and wiped his face again with the back of his hand. 'Was there anything else?'

'Was Ayman Younis bitter about what happened to his son? Did he blame anyone for his condition?'

'What does this have to do with the murders?'

At the bar, a man cleaning glasses turned his head towards them. 'Nothing, probably,' said Alex.

'It's a nutcase, isn't it? That's what they're saying.'

'An odd thing for an academic to say.'

'I don't mind calling whoever killed Ayman a nutcase. I keep thinking, what must it have been like to have a madman in your house, to know you were probably going to die? It's awful, isn't it? I wish I had been able to talk to Ayman before he died. Just to . . . I don't know.' He tailed off. 'You will find him, won't you?'

'I should tell you, I'm not part of the investigation team,' she said. 'I was just here.'

'Oh. So why are you talking to me?' he asked, puzzled.

'I'm sorry,' she said. 'I shouldn't have. I should go. I'm just in the area. I was curious. I had no right to be.'

He looked at her for a minute, then said, 'I don't mind. I really don't. When something like this happens, you just want someone to talk to about it, don't you? You have to process it. It's why you're doing counselling. It's the worst thing that's ever happened around here, and look. People are carrying on with their Saturday as if nothing happened. Or avoiding the conversation at the club bar.' He looked around. 'Everyone should be crying, not just me. Weird, isn't it? How people go to such lengths to avoid talking about some stuff. I mean, death and violence happen, but we only want to hear about it in stories.'

'That's true.'

'So I don't mind at all. In fact, I should probably thank you.'

'Really,' she said, standing. 'I should go.'

'I'm here most days if you want to talk some more. In all weathers. Out there or here at the bar.' He stood and shook hands, rather formally. When Alex was at the door she looked back. He had sat down again, alone at the table.

She found Loftingswood Grange easily. It was a red brick Victorian house set in its own grounds, about fifteen miles north of the Younises' house. A discreet sign on the road announced it simply as a 'Private Nursing Home'.

Here, above the marsh, the landscape was softer, more obviously English. A giant cedar sat in the middle of sweet-smelling newly cut lawns.

The countryside was criss-crossed with ancient footpaths. She took one that ran alongside a hedgerow, parallel to an iron fence at the side of the grounds that skirted the house. Tortoiseshells and painted ladies fluttered around the hedgerow. Somewhere close, a grouse cried, then flapped into clumsy flight.

Pausing at a gap in the hedge, she looked down the slope towards a new wing, built onto the side of the house; it was low and flat, with large French windows that stood open onto the lawn so that residents in their wheelchairs could navigate their way out into the garden with ease, or be led there. There were three people sitting outside in their electric chairs. Two seemed to be asleep. The third sat fidgeting. Alex wondered if one of them was Callum, but it was too far away to see clearly.

It looked calm and placid; not the worst place to be. A young man dressed in a blue nurse's uniform held a bottle to one patient's mouth, giving him something to drink.

A crack of a stick ahead of her. Alex looked up. Coming towards her was a young woman, dressed like a serious bird-watcher, in jeans, a T-shirt and a utility waistcoat, carrying an SLR camera around her neck. The camera was dwarfed by its lens. 'Afternoon,' the woman muttered as she approached.

Instead of moving aside, Alex stepped into the middle of the narrow path, blocking her way. 'Get anything?'

The woman stopped. 'What you mean?'

'Out looking for anything in particular?'

The woman smiled. 'No. Just seeing what's around.' A small gap in her teeth lent her face an unexpected charm.

'I hear there are some lesser spotted wood pigeons around,' said Alex.

TWELVE

'Lesser spotted wood pigeons?' said Alex again.

The woman put one hand over her camera, as if protecting it. 'Didn't manage to see any,' said the woman eventually. 'Just my luck. You?' She stepped forward, expecting Alex to move aside, but Alex stood her ground.

'What about a great booby?'

'Sorry?'

'A little bustard?'

The woman seemed to consider this for a second, then said, 'Are you actually taking the piss?'

Alex stepped forward, closer to the woman and said in a low voice, 'That's a very big lens. You know it's illegal to take photographs of people inside their own homes without their permission, don't you?'

The woman frowned. 'I don't know what you're on about.'

'I think you probably do.'

The two women stood, toe to toe on the narrow path. 'Who do you think you are?' asked the photographer.

'Nobody,' said Alex. She took out her phone, held it up and quickly took a photograph of the young woman.

'What the are you doing, doucheface?'

Alex replaced the phone in her bag. 'Public space. It's fine for me to take your picture here. Bit rude possibly, but not actually illegal, because this is a public footpath, clearly marked as such, so there is no expectation of privacy. And if any photographs of Callum Younis turn up in a newspaper, I've got a photograph of you, so people will know who took them.'

'You got some nerve,' said the woman.

'Thanks,' said Alex.

The woman hesitated; her tone was suddenly less hostile. 'You know Callum, then?' she asked.

Alex laughed. 'Got to hand it to you. You're a trier.'

'Aren't we all these days?' In a single swift movement she lifted the camera, adjusted the lens and fired off five or six quick shots.

'Do you know, I suppose we are.'

The woman looked at the screen on the back of her camera and gave a small smile. 'Well. Do you? Do you know him?'

'I should introduce myself. I'm a police officer. At least, that's what I try to be. How about you?'

The woman smiled, showing that cute little gap again. 'Shit,' she said.

'You're OK,' said Alex. 'I'm not on duty. Besides, the offence would be publishing the photographs in a newspaper, not taking them, so there wouldn't be much I could do.' Alex hitched herself up onto the iron railing that ran alongside the path, tucking her feet onto the bottom rungs, leaving room for the photographer, but now the woman seemed less anxious to get past.

'So what are you doing here, then?'

'I can't give you a decent answer either. Not one that makes any sense. What about you? How did you know the Younis boy was here?' She nodded at the house.

'Was at the pub in Rye last night. I had an unexpected windfall. Little bit of money came my way and I went out to celebrate. One of the nurses from the home was in there drinking and after a couple he was on about Callum. Poor lad. Can't do anything for himself except piss and shit, apparently. Bit indiscreet, I know, but the nurse was upset about it all. He's worked with him two years now. You must get pretty close. Thing is, the parents were paying for him to be in there. Now they're both dead, who's going to cough up? The nurse was saying he'd be taken to a state-run home, probably, but God knows what that would be like for a lad like him.'

'That's the story you wanted a picture for?'

'The murders were yesterday's news. What's the follow-up? This was a human angle. So yeah. Not a bad story.'

'I suppose not. Stitches up the nurse, mind you, for leaking confidential details of a patient.'

She shrugged. 'They don't have to know it was him. Besides, it wasn't just me he was telling. It was half the bloody pub. Public space, like you said.' The photographer jumped up onto the fence beside her, making the old ironwork sway. She hooked her legs over one by one, turning to sit facing towards Loftingswood Grange, the opposite direction to Alex. 'Shit life, eh?'

'Could be worse,' said Alex. 'It's a good question, though, isn't it? Who's going to pay for him to be there now?'

'He's one of the lucky ones,' said the photographer. 'He's in there. They must have been paying thousands for that.'

Alex turned, too; both of them now sitting facing the private nursing home and its carefully maintained garden. 'What's that to you?'

The woman looked straight ahead. 'My brother is autistic, categorised as requiring substantial support. Only we can't afford private.'

'Sorry.'

'Don't be. The people who look after him love him just as much as them lot do, only they don't get paid half the money to do it or have half the facilities. And don't think that's me trying to justify what I'm doing here, because I don't actually feel I need justification. It's a story, and people want to know. That's all the justification I need.'

Vapour trails cut the blue sky into parallelograms. Summer hung hot and heavy over them. 'I wasn't judging you.'

'Yeah you were. Kind of.'

Alex smiled. 'The law's there to protect people like Callum and your brother. I'm all about the law.'

'From what I hear, Callum's not going to read anything I ever put in any paper so he doesn't really need a lot of protecting, does he?'

'You've been to the house too?'

The photographer eyed her warily. 'Close as I could get, yes. Was there on Thursday. Crawling with you lot there too. Got one photo in yesterday's *Mirror*.' She reached down and plucked a long stalk of grass, put it into her mouth and chewed.

'That was your windfall?'

81

'Exactly. Quite good money for a change. Nobody else got close.'

'Congratulations.'

The woman turned the camera on Alex again and fired off a couple of shots. 'You want my take on it? I reckon this coast attracts psychos. Something about it. The way the wind blows. I don't know. Not so bad in summer, I suppose, but in winter it can feel like everyone here's just hopped the wall of some kind of institution. All the devils are here . . .'

'You live nearby?'

'Hythe.' A few miles up the coast.

Alex climbed back over the fence and jumped down. 'Do you think I could see your photographs some time?'

'Why would you want to do that?'

'The ones of the house. To see what you saw, that's all.'

'Would you pay me?'

'Not a single penny.'

'Like you said, got to try, haven't you?' Still sitting on the fence, the woman reached into a pocket in her utility vest and pulled out a card. Alex read it. *Georgia Coaker. Freelance photographer.*

'I'll call you,' Alex said, and set off back down the path towards her car.

Georgia Coaker called after her. 'There's actually no such bird as a lesser spotted wood pigeon, is there?'

When she got back to Dungeness it was afternoon, and Bill South was balancing himself on the roof of his house with a hammer in his hand, dressed in faded blue shorts and a loose shirt, sweat showing on its back.

82

Alex parked the car, went inside the shack and emerged with a glass of water, then climbed one-handed up the ladder. 'Nice view,' she said, looking around when she'd reached the top.

She put the glass down carefully on the guttering and, when she had manoeuvred herself onto the slope of the roof, stood, picked it up and approached South with it. 'You must be thirsty,' she said.

'Careful. Not sure how much weight these rafters can take.'

'You're not supposed to say things like that to a woman, Bill.'

He took the glass from her and gulped it down. She could see now that he had cut a rectangular hole in the corrugated zinc roof. 'Putting in ventilation,' he explained. 'Too hot in there now, summers like this.'

'So you just saw a hole in the roof?'

'That's the beauty of a wooden house.'

She looked around at the surrounding landscape from this new elevated angle: the haphazard bungalows, the lines of railway track, the expanse of stones dotted with plants that were strong enough to survive here. 'Maybe you should build another floor up here while you're doing it. The view's great.'

'Works for me like it is,' he said.

'I wanted to ask you something,' she said. She bent to sit down but when she put her hand down, the zinc sheets were sizzling. 'About Frank Hogben,' she said, straightening again.

THIRTEEN

They stood on the roof, a suitable distance apart so as not to put too much strain on the timbers.

'Well?' said Bill.

A gaggle of tourists, possibly Japanese or maybe Korean, who were walking up the narrow track alongside the power station fence, paused and stared. One of them raised a camera to photograph them, up there on South's roof. There must have been something comical about the pair of them, she supposed. Maybe they imagined it was how the locals lived here, on their roofs, and would tell their friends about it back home. Soon another raised his camera, then a third.

'Look. We're an attraction,' said Alex, and waved back. The entire group waved at them now.

'You're encouraging them,' said South disapprovingly.

So she waved harder. The tourists didn't seem to think it was OK to leave while she was still waving at them. They stood there politely waving back until she had finally stopped, then turned and walked on, chattering.

South had the ability to stay silent for long periods of time. He picked up a rasp and started rubbing it against a burr of metal on the roof. The noise was raw and loud, like an animal in pain might make.

'So,' said Alex eventually. 'You were a community copper when that went on, when Frank Hogben was reported missing. You must have heard stuff.'

'Not really.'

'You never thought there was anything in what Mandy Hogben said?'

'That Tina killed him? What makes you think there is?'

'I don't know. There's something about Tina that's off. I can't put my finger on it. She reminds me of a deer caught in the headlights, somehow.'

He got back to work, dulling the sharp zinc edge with the rasp.

'What?' she said, annoyed.

'You're not that different,' he said.

'What do you mean?'

'That look. Sometimes you have it too. Like those rabbits you see on the tracks around here. At night when you catch them with the torches.'

'No I don't,' she protested, offended. 'Don't be ridiculous.'

Irritated, Alex got up and made her way back to the ladder, ready to descend. The tourists were on their way back down the path, waving at them again.

She picked up Zoë from the nature reserve at five, watching her say goodbye to Kenny and the others. 'I thought we could go to the beach and swim. Salt water is good for blisters,' she said. She had put the barbecue in the back.

The tide was out. Unlike Dungeness, Greatstone beach was wide and sandy when the tide was low. They set up camp on the edge of the dunes and wriggled into costumes, then ran across the rippled beach into the water, which was always freezing whatever the season, and plunged in regardless, laughing.

When she had been pregnant with Zoë, Alex had always been determined to be a better mum than her own mother, Helen, who she thought had never been that interested in children. Zoë had done everything to make that task hard. As a young child, she was prone to tantrums and sulks. The only times she had seemed genuinely happy had been in the bath or in swimming pools. There was something mysterious about water.

Alex swam until her arms tired, got out, wrapped herself in a towel and went back to the dunes to light the barbecue and start putting vegetables on skewers, watching Zoë still moving in the water. The charcoal took a long time to heat. She put the first of the skewers on the coals and heard the hiss.

'I thought it was you.'

She looked up to see Terry Neill, the man from the golf club, dressed in a T-shirt and sky-blue swimming shorts. 'I live over there,' he said, pointing towards the houses that backed onto the beach. 'I could see you.'

Zoë was out of the water, teeth chattering. 'Who's this?' she demanded.

'A man I met at the golf club today. Terry, this is Zoë.'

'Golf club?' Zoë had found a pair of dead starfish and brought them with her, flattening the sand and laying them on it, then holding her water-wrinkled hands above the coals to try and warm herself. 'You hate golf.'

'So do I,' said Terry, laughing.

'Do you play it?' Zoë said.

'Yes. I do.'

'That's stupid,' said Zoë.

Terry laughed again. 'It's an addiction. I don't enjoy it at all. What are those?'

'Asterias rubens.' Zoë looked down at the starfish. 'I'm going to take them home and dissect them.'

'Oh,' said Terry. 'A biologist. How splendid. Did you know that the starfish has no blood?'

'Obviously,' said Zoë.

'Don't mind her. Sit down. Do you want some food?'

Terry squatted on his haunches and watched her as she turned the vegetable skewers. The coals hissed as marinade dripped onto them. 'I'm sorry I cried today.'

'It's OK.'

'Why were you crying?' asked Zoë bluntly.

'A friend of mine died . . . very suddenly,' he said. 'I miss him.'

Zoë nodded.

'It's ready,' said Alex, rummaging in her picnic bag. 'I'm afraid I only brought two plates,' she told Terry.

'Maybe we should have some wine with it?' he said.

'Mum always wants wine.'

'I'm driving, Zoë,' protested Alex.

'One won't hurt, then,' Terry said. 'I'm only a couple of minutes away.' He stood and set off towards the houses.

Alex's phone buzzed. It was a message from Jill:

Call me. X.

'I don't always want wine,' said Alex.

'Why did you offer him food? You hardly know him.'

'He's a biophysicist, Zoë. He probably knows all about star-fish.'

Zoë looked doubtful. And then Terry was back with a chilled bottle of Zinfandel and three glasses. 'I didn't know if Zoë wanted some.'

Zoë softened a little, pleased to be counted as an adult, but she said, 'Not much.'

They ate marinaded onions, mushrooms, aubergines, tofu and courgettes, much of it slightly charred, in flatbread, feeling the warm juices run down their chins as the coals faded from red to grey.

'You told me you were seeing a counsellor,' he said. 'Do you mind if I ask why? If it's prying, don't worry.'

'I have been diagnosed with Post-Traumatic Stress Disorder. Work stuff. Nothing serious.'

Zoë watched her as she spoke.

'You've probably seen some pretty grisly stuff,' Terry said. 'I believe it's very common in the police and emergency services.'

'My boss said I should try it.'

'Mum!' Zoë protested.

'What?'

'Stop saying it's not that bad.'

'Loads of people have it worse than me.'

'Mum,' muttered Zoë.

'You shouldn't dismiss it,' said Terry quietly. 'The damage can be real. If you look at an MRI scan of someone who has been through significant trauma, you can often see how their brains have physically changed. The hippocampus can be diminished. You can see the damage.'

With a soft rattle, charcoal settled in the metal barbecue pan.

'I'm not on that scale.'

'How do you know?'

'You think my brain would be like that?'

'I don't know. Imaging shows you physiological differences in traumatised people. You can watch how prefrontal activation of brains is different. The physical changes are visible. What's much less easy to understand are the mental processes that have been rewired through trauma.'

'If that's true, it's hard to see how someone can fix that by just talking.'

'Would you prefer us to go in with knives?'

'See, Mum?' said Zoë, clearly warming to Terry a little.

'I could show you the photographs some time, if you'd like.'

'Is that a kind of intellectual's Netflix and chill?' asked Alex. 'Come up and see my etchings?'

Terry laughed and held up his palms. 'I can think of more exciting dates than that, if you like.'

'Were we talking about dates?' Alex said, a little frostily. 'I didn't realise.'

'Sorry. I didn't mean . . .'

Alex reached out and took his plate. 'We need to get back,' she said.

'Mum. He was still eating.'

'It's OK,' said Terry. 'I should probably go.'

'Why were you like that?' Zoë demanded when he'd left them with his half-drunk bottle of wine.

'Like what?' Alex poured water onto the coals and felt the warmth of the steam on her face.

'He was asking you out.'

'I am aware of that.' Alex made a face. 'Not my type at all. Anyway, I thought it was you who didn't like him.'

'You never go out with anyone.'

'You're a one to talk.'

'I'm seventeen, Mum.'

'When I was your age I was hanging out with boys all the time.'

'And you're my role model?'

Alex sighed; examined her daughter, hair matted with salt. 'Fair point.'

As she tidied up the picnic, Alex heard her phone buzz again in her bag. It would be Jill. 'I don't know. There's something off about him,' she said.

'You think that about everybody right now.'

'I met him today, and then he just happens to turn up when we're at the beach?'

'Because he lives just over there, Mum. You sure there's not something off about you, just like he was saying?'

'He's just one of those men who asks women out all the time.'

'How do you know? You always think the worst of everyone.'

Zoë had always been exasperating; she had an answer for everything. 'I'm a police officer. We see the worst of everyone.'

Finally Alex took the phone out of the bag. Three messages all saying the same thing:

Call me!!!!!

FOURTEEN

'How did you actually know that?' demanded Jill.

Alex had waited until they were back home from the beach and standing in the kitchen, stepping sand onto the clean floor, and then she had called Jill back.

'Know what?' But Jill's phone had been cut off by the time she answered.

She dialled again. It took a minute to connect.

'Phone connection is ultra-shit out here,' said Jill. 'Let me try and find a better signal.'

Alex heard her walking over gravel. 'Where are you?'

'I'm at the house.' She didn't have to explain which house. 'You said to call you if Mrs Younis died at around seven minutes past ten.'

Zoë had removed the swimming towels from the beach bag and put them on the kitchen counter.

'Her pacemaker stopped at just after four minutes past. I mean . . . that's a bit too close for comfort. Is that, like, a fluky guess?'

'The strangest thing,' said Alex. 'I can't say.'

'What do you mean, you can't say? Don't be like that, Alex.'

Alex checked the clock on the cooker. It was half past nine. 'What are you doing still in that house?'

'I'm not even sure myself now. Just came back. I wanted a second look.'

'You wanted to be there at the time the murder happened.'

'Yeah. I don't know if I'll learn anything from it, but it seemed worth a try. Nothing else is making any sense. The whole thing is nuts. Tell me, for God's sake. What made you say seven minutes past ten?'

Alex watched Zoë unwrapping the beach towels carefully. 'I'll be there in fifteen minutes.'

'No way, Alex. You're not coming here. Just tell me why you said that particular time. Because it's pretty much the exact same time she was—'

The call broke up for a second.

'Are you there on your own?'

'Tell me what you know, Alex.'

Buried safely in the middle of the towels was one of the starfish Zoë had found. Zoë picked it up and held it between finger and thumb.

'It might just be a coincidence,' said Alex.

'I thought you didn't believe in coincidence.'

'True. But I don't believe in souls, either.'

'What the hell are you on about?'

'I'll tell you.' But the connection had dropped again. 'Jill? . . . Can you hear me?' The silence changed to a long tone. Redial went straight to voicemail.

She picked up her car keys again and noticed that Zoë had fetched a magnifying glass and was peering at the dead starfish. She watched her daughter put down the magnifier, open the kitchen drawer and pull out the kitchen scissors, putting them next to the dead starfish on a chopping board.

'No, Zoë,' said Alex, taking the scissors off her on her way out of the door. 'Definitely not.'

Alex parked outside the open gates. The house was dark; no lights were on, inside or out. Jill's Fiat was in the driveway, but she was nowhere to be seen.

'Jill?'

As Alex stepped out of the car, the lock screen on her phone told her it was two minutes past ten. She approached the house. 'Where are you?' she called, louder this time.

Two metres from the front door, she was blinded by a security light blasting on. Blinking, she stepped up and knocked. 'Jill?'

The door was locked.

She turned. To her right, the garage was lit up. Jill's car was parked in front of it and beyond the car was the small dense copse that had grown up between the house and the neighbouring field.

A flicker of light in the wood caught her eye.

'Jill? That you?'

She called Jill's number. It rang unanswered.

From the darkness of the copse came the unmistakable crack of a dry stick.

'Hello?'

She walked forwards towards the trees, listening for any other sign of movement.

It could have been a deer or a badger that she had heard, she thought. A reflection of a creature's eye caught in the light.

The security light behind her switched itself off and the copse became impenetrably dark. Switching the torch on on her phone, she pointed it into the branches.

An old wire fence, low enough to step over, held back the lower branches of a laurel. Alex shone her torch up and down; on the ground, something caught the light. She stepped closer, peering at it.

It was flat and round, like the lid of a jar, only darker; a black disc of some kind, several millimetres thick, newly enough discarded to be lying on top of a tussock of herb-robert. There was something sinister about the simple geometry of the shape.

She dialled Jill again. No answer. She checked the time. Four minutes past ten now.

Pushing down on the wire, she lifted one leg over the fence and then the next, steadying herself, then stopped to listen again.

The copse was silent. She had frightened away whatever creature had been in there, she guessed, or it was still somewhere in there, frozen in fear. Taking a step deeper into the thick wood, she pushed her way around the thin trunk of an ash sapling and tried to find the disc she had seen from the driveway. Though she was closer, she couldn't see it. She leaned from side to side, trying to get a fresh angle.

Again, an unnatural shape caught her eye, but it was not the disc. A couple of metres away, in the scrub of undergrowth, was something else that was out of place, she realised. It took a while to understand the shape she was seeing.

A pair of black leather boots. Funny, her first thought had

been, that someone should leave two boots side by side like that in among these trees. Then came the realisation that the boots were not discarded. Two legs, clad in some kind of camouflage material, extended up from them.

A torso.

A person.

She shone her torch up to where the head should have been, but instead there was only blackness.

Confused, chest tight, she took a jerky step backwards.

Lit by her torch, two bright white eyes materialised from the darkness, then below the eyes appeared white teeth and a red mouth.

The mouth roared. There were no words, just an inchoate noise.

Alex stumbled backwards falling hard against the fence.

Light suddenly blazed all around them.

It was a man, dressed from head to foot in camouflage, his face completely blackened.

'I'll fucking kill you,' he screamed, as she pushed herself upwards, trying to find her feet again.

FIFTEEN

The first thing Jill said when her car pulled up back at Alex's house was: 'You are out of your bloody mind.'

'So they say.'

'You were just going to chase after that man?'

'Instinct kicked in,' said Alex. 'I would have done it if you hadn't turned up. He just stood there screaming at me for a second, then he ran way out of the woods and into the field.'

The man in the Manic Street Preachers T-shirt was sitting at the back of his house in the dark, smoking a cigarette. Jill clocked him and lowered her voice.

'Lucky I was there to stop you. What is wrong with you? You were on your own, as far as you knew.'

Jill, it turned out, had been a couple of hundred metres up the lane trying to get a decent signal on her phone when she'd heard Alex shout her name the first time. When she had approached the back of the house, she had triggered the security light.

'Man, approximately six foot tall, dressed in camouflage gear, black army-style boots with black greasepaint on his face,' was the description Jill had called in. 'Probably dangerous.'

'My heart is still beating like the worst drill track you ever heard,' Jill said.

Despite Zoë's professed love of the environment, every light downstairs seemed to have been left on. They went into the kitchen, blinking in the glare of it. 'Wine?'

'How much have you got?'

'That bad?'

'I don't know why you're so calm. You were right next to him.'

It's true. It was before she had seen the man that she had been anxious. In the aftermath she had just been strangely at ease and that had been a welcome feeling.

There was a half-empty bottle of white in the fridge door. She pulled it out, poured two glasses, thought for a moment, then put another bottle into the freezer because, knowing Jill, they'd be needing it soon enough.

Jill took an inch out of her glass and said, 'And? So. Why did you say seven past ten?'

'It's a weird one.'

'Nothing is going to get any weirder than tonight.'

'I wouldn't be so sure. A friend of Zoë's said he saw souls,' she said.

Alex explained how Kenny Abel had claimed to have seen souls rising up from the roof of The Nest at exactly that time on the night of the murder. 'And he said he saw them at seven minutes past ten. He was very precise about it because he was on the phone at the time and he could check his phone records.'

'Jesus. You're not wrong. That's ultra-weird.'

'Did you see anything tonight when you were waiting?'

'Apart from a lunatic in the woods? You seriously expected I was going to see a ghost or something?'

'I don't believe in ghosts.'

'Oh. So just because Alex Cupidi doesn't believe in them means they don't exist? I believe in them, I tell you. That's properly freaked me out.'

'I was wondering whether it was just some trick of the light. Something that anyone would see around there at that time of night. Or that there might just be some simple explanation.'

They looked at each other for a while. 'Souls?' said Jill.

'I know.'

'That gives me the heebies.'

'Me too, as a matter of fact,' said Alex.

'And you don't even believe in them.' Jill had emptied her glass and held it out. 'Can I – you know – stay the night, then?'

They stepped outside the back of the house so Jill could smoke.

'I can't help it,' said Jill. 'One freaky case like this and I'm back on them worse than ever.'

Up on the bank, they sat with their backs to the lights of the house and the power station, looking into the darkness of the nature reserve, a low black horizon dotted with stars and the silhouettes of the delicate geometry of electricity pylons.

'That was crazy tonight. Did you see his mad face? Was that black boot polish, or some Vietnam-era Rambo shit? He must have been hiding in there all the time I was on my own.'

'The Unknown Male,' said Alex.

'Yeah. I wonder if he was.'

'Promise not to tell Zoë. She'd freak out if she knew that happened to me.'

'You're scared of her, aren't you?'

'Aren't you?'

'I think she's the most amazing girl in the world.'

'But I'm still scared of her sometimes.'

Jill laughed, blew out smoke. 'Fags are so horrible, aren't they?' She pulled out her phone and scrolled through her messages.

'Anything?'

'They haven't found him yet. Not likely to in the dark.'

There wasn't much point looking out there at this time of night. They would send officers to scour the area in the morning. Alex went back into the kitchen and pulled the second bottle out of the freezer, then picked up a blanket. Zoë appeared at the bottom of the stairs. 'Is that Jill?'

'Want to come and join us?'

'Is she drunk?'

'Not yet.'

'You're OK.' She turned and went back up to her bedroom. Alex went back out into the darkness.

'Why was he even there? I mean . . . it could be him, couldn't it? He probably had guns.'

'I didn't see one.'

'Someone like that . . . all ninja'd up. You think they could get in and out of a house without leaving prints?'

Alex picked up a stone and lobbed it into the blackness, listening to it land with a quiet *chink*.

'Something else,' said Jill. 'Digging into the Younises' accounts, turns out that in March, Ayman Younis paid out four hundred thousand pounds to invest in a green forestry scheme in Guatemala. It's called Biosfera Reforestation.'

'Jesus. Big money.'

'Very big.'

'Lucre, lechery or lunacy. The three great reasons for murder. You're looking into it?'

'That's quite poetic,' said Jill. Her glass was empty again. 'Course we're looking into it. It was one of them schemes where they plant trees for carbon offsetting. They're supposed to be a good investment because they're backed by local government and the UN and whatever. Put your money in, you can't possibly lose.'

'But you're going to tell me different?'

'Maybe. There are some web pages online but I couldn't find a contact number anywhere. Turns out the Fraud Intelligence mob have a mega file on them.'

'He put his money into some scam?'

'They're sending us some information tomorrow.'

'He had a lot of money then?'

'Yes. Looked like it. Gorgeous house. Everything kind of perfect, you know? She was all into animal charities and the Ramblers. He was Savile Row suits and Church's brogues in the cupboard. New car every couple of years. They liked to keep up appearances, know what I mean? The only person who ever had a bad word for them complained about how they would outbid other people at the Rotary charity auction. Hardly the worst of sins. Ayman liked people to know he was well off.'

Alex thought of what Terry Neill had said: *All he wanted was to be part of all this.*

Jill stood. 'I'm hungry, Alex. I was going to get a takeaway when I got home. All that running around in the dark and I'm starving. What have you got? I could eat anything, right now. Mind if I take a look in your fridge?'

'Go ahead.'

'Want anything?'

Alex lay on her back looking up at a starless night sky. It was true what Jill had said. It would have been crazy for her to chase the Unknown Male into the darkness, when she had no idea if he was armed, or whether he was the murderer, but she would have done it had Jill not been there. It scared her to realise that. Nothing would have stopped her. Not following him deeper into the copse had left her feeling strangely empty.

SIXTEEN

'A bloody starfish cut up into pieces in a Tupperware box,' said Jill when she returned empty-handed. 'That'll give me nightmares.'

'Sorry,' said Alex. 'I should have warned you.'

'Why can't she just look at a YouTube video of it like a normal child?'

After seeing Zoë's cut-up starfish, Jill had lost her appetite. 'Just one more before we go to bed?' she said. 'To settle my nerves.'

Alex still had a full glass.

'How's the counselling going?'

'Good, I think. He just wants me to tell the stories about the things that happened to me that made me this way. I think he thinks if I tell them enough I'll maybe get bored of them.'

'Don't. It's serious.'

'I met a biophysicist yesterday. He said you could see physical damage on the brains of traumatised people. Interesting, no?'

'That's a coincidence. I met a biophysicist too. One of Ayman Younis's friends.'

'Did he ask you out?' She spoke without thinking.

'No. Bit old for me.' For a second Jill looked puzzled by the question. 'I felt sorry for him, though. He was devastated by what had happened.'

'Yes.'

'Bogging hell.' She put two and two together. 'You're talking about Terry Neill as well, aren't you?'

Alex looked away. 'Yes. I kind of bumped into him.'

'You're bloody following us around, aren't you? Christ, Alex! Are you insane? What has got into you? You're on sick leave.'

'I don't know what's got into me.'

Jill seemed to mull this over for a while. 'Why did you ask if he asked me out?'

Alex didn't answer.

Jill grinned. 'Oh, my giddy uncle! He asked you, didn't he?'

'He offered to show me some pictures of brains.'

'I liked him,' said Jill. 'He had nice forearms. Maybe you should go and look at his brain pictures. *Have a look at my delicious cerebellum*.'

'What happened to *Are you insane? What has got into you*?'

Jill lolled back in her chair. 'You've never had a boyfriend since you've been here.'

'No. And I'm happy that way, Jill, so don't start.'

'Are you?'

'You're the one who's always after a boyfriend, not me.'

At twenty-five, Jill was at that age where she worried it might never happen. 'I'm not always after a boyfriend,' she complained. 'Not, like, every second.'

Jill was up early, eating Zoë's granola at the breakfast table, her appetite back in force. As always, she looked fresh and immaculate. 'Is that a clean shirt?' Alex asked.

'I always keep one in a bag in the car. And clean knickers. Just in case.'

'In case of what, exactly?'

'Shut up,' said Jill.

Alex looked in the sink. There was already a bowl in it. 'Zoë up already?'

'Said she was going to get a lift with Bill to the Wildlife Trust. We had a good little chat, her and me.'

'What about?'

'You, obviously.'

'Obviously.' Alex sighed, made herself a coffee and sat down beside her. 'Still no sign of the Unknown Male?'

Jill checked her phone again. 'Nothing so far. Early yet. I'll let you know.' She wiped oat milk from her mouth. 'I had nightmares too,' she said. 'About that bloody starfish.'

'What do you mean, "too"?'

'You. Last night.' She reached out a hand and laid it on Alex's and gave a sympathetic smile. Alex looked back, warily.

— *Let me get this straight. You are concerned that you may be deliberately putting yourself into dangerous situations?*

— *I wanted to chase after the man. He was clearly hiding for a reason. On a rational level I know it would have been a stupid thing to do. But at that moment I felt . . . I won't say great, but I felt . . . connected.*

— *That's an interesting word.*
— *'Interesting' as in 'revealing'?*
— *Let's turn it around. Do you not feel connected the rest of the time? When you're with your daughter? When you're with me, now?*
— *Of course I do.*
— *But you would feel more connected when you are in a situation in which harm might come to you?*
— *You make me sound like some kind of junkie.*
— *It's a question. Why is it important to go to places where you feel harm might come to you?*
— *It's a loaded question. I didn't go there because I wanted a man in commando gear to creep up on me.*
— *But you did want to run after him?*
— *I suppose. Fair point.*
— *OK. Let's leave that. I don't want to push you anywhere you don't want to go. How are the superpowers?*
— *Coming along nicely. Do you believe in ghosts?*
— *Have you seen one?*
— *I'm not sure. Can I get back to you on that?*

There was a traffic stop on the Dymchurch Road. Alex cycled past the waiting cars and recognised the lanky figure of Colin Gilchrist leaning towards one of the drivers' windows.

'About six foot tall, dressed in military fatigues,' he was saying to the driver, a woman who had three children in the car who were craning forward in their seats, trying to hear every word.

'Any luck?'

Colin Gilchrist smiled shyly when he saw her. 'Sorry about last time.' In small, unexaggerated movements, he mimed leaning over and throwing up.

Stepping back from the roadside to let another officer take his place, he said, 'Plenty of people say they've seen him. Hard to miss because he dresses like a squaddie. It appears he's been living rough around here for about six weeks. Even a couple of complaints from farmers about him being on their land, but finding him, not so easy.'

'He's always dressed like that, then?'

'We think it's a man named Robert Glass. Ex-serviceman, Second Battalion, The Rifles. He was living rough around Folkestone for a while. We'd been aware of him. Minor drug offences.'

'Somebody who knew about guns,' observed Alex.

Colin nodded towards the west. 'If it's him, I bet he would have trained at Lydd on the rifle ranges.'

The Lydd ranges were just a few miles away on Dungeness.

'Nice bike,' he called as she pushed off to head home.

She reached the Dungeness estate in twenty minutes, sweating hard, and slowed on the uneven concrete track.

As she passed the bungalow where Tina and Stella were staying she spotted a third figure sitting next to them. She paused and waved, but Zoë didn't seem to notice her.

Jill's Fiat was parked behind the house. Jill had taken one of the pink cushions that she kept on her back seat out of the car and was lying on the shingle slope with her head resting on it.

'Back so soon?' Alex wheeled her bike to the small brick shed behind the house.

Jill sat up and removed her Jackie O sunglasses. 'I'm taking you out for a meal.'

'Why?'

'Do I have to have a reason? You're my mate.'

Alex closed the shed door and walked over to where her friend was lying. 'What exactly was Zoë saying to you this morning?'

'I ain't going to lie, Alex. She said she didn't think you were eating properly and if Zoë, who seems to live on air, is saying that, things would have to be pretty bad.'

'Did she know about this? Did she ask you to talk to me.'

'Yes.'

'Oh God.'

'Because she's worried about you. Go on then. Put something on. I'm not taking you in that cycling gear.'

'I'm tired,' Alex said. 'I don't feel like being around people.'

Jill put her sunglasses on and laid her head back on the pillow. 'I won't tell you what I found out about the Biosfera scam then.' And with that, she knew she had her.

The meal, however, in the nearby town of Rye, did not go well.

SEVENTEEN

'It was a scam,' Jill said as she drove. 'The National Fraud Intelligence Bureau opened a file on Biosfera Reforestation just a couple of weeks ago, it turns out. There appear to be victims right across the country. It's not a particularly original one, but it seems to have been very effective.'

Jill drove fast, braking hard for traffic lights and junctions.

'A once-in-a-lifetime opportunity. Investors were told to keep it on the quiet because the government participation in the scheme hadn't been officially announced yet, but once that happened they would have a guaranteed return because the Guatemalan government were matching investments with local subsidies.'

'Win-win.'

'Exactly. And, as it happens, the Guatemalan government do have reforestation subsidies and there are plenty of companies benefiting from it, but Biosfera Reforestation wasn't one of them. Whoever set it up copied and pasted off government websites and companies that were legitimately involved in subsidy schemes to make it look legit. They made sure that the promised returns weren't astronomical, just enough to make investors think they were being a bit cleverer than the rest . . . that they had found something a little special.'

They reached Rye; an island of ground in a flat land, an old town of half-timbers, red bricks and cobblestones. Jill found a space in the dockside car park and adjusted the rear-view mirror to check her make-up, then turned in her seat, reached out a hand and placed it on Alex's knee in the same unsettlingly sympathetic manner she had this morning. 'There's something else I need to tell you too. And I'm not sure you're going to like it.'

'What?'

She hesitated. 'Why don't we talk about it in the restaurant.'

'You're actually worrying me.'

The restaurant was in an old stone mill just down the road. It was one of those Italian restaurants with red-and-white-striped tablecloths and waiters carrying outsize pepper grinders.

'Well?' said Alex when a man in jeans had seated them at their table. 'What is it you found out?'

But Jill insisted they had to order drinks first, and then the waiter arrived to take their food order. A couple at the next table were talking now. He was complaining about their babysitter who had turned up late. The woman was asking him not to spoil the evening.

'I'll have a caprese salad,' said Jill. 'But no cheese.'

The room was full of noise. Alex was conscious of that pressure in her chest; the same feeling she had had on the day she had taken the machete off Mandy Hogben; that unwelcome conviction that something bad was going to happen. She looked round the room trying to figure out what was making her feel like this.

'You OK?' Jill was looking at her, concerned.

'Zoë's hanging about with Tina and Stella,' said Alex evasively. 'It's strange.'

'No stranger than her hanging around with a fifty-year-old man who's been convicted of murder.'

'Something's wrong with them – with Tina and Stella. I don't know what.'

'Right now you think something's wrong with everything.'

'Yes. I know. I'm sorry. Tell me, who reported Frank Hogben missing?'

Jill looked exasperated. 'I don't know, Alex. It's not what I've come here to talk about.'

'Sorry,' Alex said. 'I'm listening.'

'OK. Listen to this then. This Biosfera scheme actually ran for about eight months, they reckon. There was an office in Guatemala and everything, to make it look legit. The real landowners of the place that was going to be forested turn out to know absolutely nothing about it. The whole thing is an invention.'

The waiter arrived with Alex's wine.

'And then,' continued Jill, 'two months ago, the website disappeared, the phones went dead and everything went quiet. And *poof!* There was no money.'

'Who has it?'

She shrugged. 'No idea. There were names of people on the company website – which no longer exists – but they were fake. The domain registration details were fake.'

'So all that money Ayman Younis put into it is gone?'

'Looking at his bank records, almost half a million we think now,' said Jill.

'And there were others presumably too?' said Alex, looking around the busy restaurant, trying to work out what was making her feel so itchy.

'I'm coming to that,' said Jill. 'A nice man at the intelligence unit said Ayman Younis paid his money into a legitimate-looking UK account in the name of Biosfera Investment. That bank account was paying regular amounts out to banks in Gibraltar and Malta, which are tax havens. In turn they were paying out to banks in much more dubious tax havens and so they can tell where their money came from but they have no idea at all where it went.'

Their order arrived. Alex looked at the seafood spaghetti she had ordered and felt queasy.

'Thing is, they've seized bank records for Biosfera Investments and so they have a list of people who've put money in. They're contacting these people over the next few weeks. Most of the investors still have no idea at all they've been conned.'

Alex was only half listening. The restaurant was full now. There were people waiting in line, and that made her want to finish the meal and leave quickly. The couple next to them had finished their main course and the woman was fidgeting as if nervous about something too. She kept looking over her shoulder as if she, too, were expecting something to happen. Alex blinked at her.

'Did you hear me?'

'Sorry? No. I wandered off somewhere.'

'I said, one of the investors on the list was Terry Neill. He

111

hasn't lost anything like as much as Ayman Younis, but a few grand. Are you OK, Alex? You haven't touched your food or your wine. I'm supposed to be feeding you up.'

Alex realised her arms were crossed over her chest and she was rubbing her upper arms, as if cold. She unfolded herself, picked up a fork. 'So. Terry Neill was caught up in this too?'

'And what's worse, there was another name on the list I recognised too.'

'Who?'

'Like I said, you're not going to like this.'

Alex felt a prickle on the back of her neck. Even the air around her was somehow different. It was just like before at the wedding that Thursday.

And then the next thing, she was standing, knocking her chair backwards, sending it clattering onto the floor.

'Knife!' she shouted, loud as she could. 'Knife.' She pointed.

The hubbub of the restaurant was instantly gone. Instead of looking where she was pointing, at the man who was holding a large silver blade, everyone was looking at her.

Alex blinked. Looked around. There was a look of horror on Jill's face.

Behind the man with the long knife, the waitress stood, holding a cake, her face glowing from the candlelight. The sparkler in the middle of the icing showered golden sparks into the air for another couple of seconds, then fizzled out.

The room was still and quiet for what seemed like an age, until the woman, sitting at the next table with her boyfriend, spoke.

'Surprise,' she said quietly.

EIGHTEEN

— *You asked about my superpowers?*

— *Yes.*

— *I think I've lost them.*

— *Should I be sorry to hear that, or is that a good thing?*

— *I had another premonition last night. Same as the other time. I was out for the evening and I became absolutely convinced that something awful was going to happen.*

— *And did it?*

— *Embarrassingly, no.*

— *But you felt just the same as the time you saw the woman with the knife?*

— *Yes. You're right. Exactly the same. It's hard to describe. You know that thing about the hairs on the back of your neck standing up?*

— *Only this time there was no woman and no knife . . . ?*

— *Well . . . kind of. But not. There was a knife . . . but it was just a knife.*

— *Have you heard of the term 'hyper-vigilance'? It's one of the effects of trauma. When something violent happens to you it affects your sense of time. Typically, you may become unable to put what happened in the past. It's as if it's happening right now and you're still in that moment. Your brain is expecting the traumatic event to happen again and again and again. You're in a state of constant readiness to fight, or to run.*

— *I'm a police officer. Half my job is about predicting whether bad things are going to happen or not.*

— *Well . . . exactly. Like you did with the woman with the knife. Why do you think you were right the first time and not the second?*

— *I would have noticed her anyway, is that what you're saying? I would have noticed her whether or not I thought something terrible was going to happen?*

— *What do you think?*

— *I think I'm probably a pretty good copper to have noticed her when everyone else didn't.*

— *Yes. I think you probably are. I think you're probably a very good copper. That's why you're in this mess.*

— *Thank you. Shame about the superpowers, though. They would have come in useful.*

— *How are you feeling now?*

— *The same.*

— *You feel that something terrible is about to happen?*

— *Something pretty bloody bad, yes. I do. And absolutely nothing I can do is going to stop it.*

There had been another name on Jill's list of investors, just like she had said. It had been Bill South's.

'Again. Maybe not so bad,' Jill had said. 'He only lost around thirteen grand.'

Alex had been shocked. 'Not so bad? You don't understand. That's all the money he has now. He lost everything else. Do you think Bill knows about this yet?'

And Jill had shaken her head. 'I knew this was going to freak you out. It's not your fault, Alex. None of this is anything to do with you.'

But it was. Because of her, he was not a rich man. After thirty years as a police officer, he had lost his job and his entire pension the day he had been dismissed from the force.

'I am an idiot,' Bill said.

'No.'

'It's definitely all gone?'

'I'm afraid so, Bill. Jill says the Guatemalan government say they have never heard of Biosfera Reforestation.'

He sat down on the small weather-beaten bench at the back of his house and put his head into his hands.

'It wasn't just you. Ayman Younis and Terry Neill from the golf club. They both lost more than you did. Terry Neill is a Professor of Biochemistry, for God's sake.'

'Does Terry Neill know yet?'

'I don't know. I don't think so.'

'I'm a bloody idiot,' he said again.

She stood in front of him, an awkward witness to his humiliation, torn between wanting to be respectful and wanting to know more. In the end, she asked, 'Who told you about the scheme?'

'Ayman . . . Terry . . . There were a few people at the golf club who were in on it. It was a conversation in a bar. There will be more names on the list. Tell Jill to check the bank details against the membership list of the golf club. They talked about it all in, like, whispers. I remember Ayman showing me the company website on his phone. I trusted him, you know?'

'And you put everything you had in it?'

'I know. The scheme was going public in September. There was a limit to the size of the fund and everyone knew it would be oversubscribed, so we had to get in early or lose out. It didn't feel like greed because it was doing something good. It sounds so obvious now, doesn't it?'

'Yes.'

'I'm an idiot,' he said for the third time.

She sat beside him on the bench in the afternoon sun and put her arm around him. 'I'm so sorry, Bill.'

It was as if her arm wasn't around him at all. He sat, stiff as a soldier, watching the afternoon shadows lengthen away from them.

After a while he said, 'I wouldn't mind being on my own.'

She took her arm away from him and stood.

'I don't suppose you had any more thoughts about who was on duty the night *The Hopeful* came in . . .'

'Still on about that, are you?'

'Sorry. Not the time. If there's anything I can do. Anything.'

He didn't answer.

Zoë came back that evening from God knows where, skin red from the sun below the sleeves of her T-shirt.

'How many times do I have to tell you to put sunscreen on?'

'Skin cancer usually doesn't show up till you're old. By 2050 a little cancer is going to be the least of our problems.' She poured herself a glass of water. 'What's wrong with Bill?'

'What do you mean?'

'I stopped by to say hello to him on my way home and he was sitting on that bench at the back of his house. He told me to go away. I think he's angry with me about something.'

Alex felt her grief. 'Oh no, love. He's not angry with you. He's had some very bad news.'

'What kind of bad news?'

'He lost some money in an investment that went wrong.'

'That doesn't sound so bad. It's only money.'

'Well . . . maybe it is for him.'

'It's no reason to be rude, though, is it?'

Alex was shocked. 'Was he rude?'

'He was drinking whisky and he told me to just go away.'

Alex went to put her arms around Zoë, but her daughter backed away.

'Whisky?'

'I don't know why people drink it. It tastes absolutely disgusting.'

This time she had been right; a bad thing had been about to happen. And now it had. When Bill South had come out of Maghaberry Prison he had started drinking and it had taken him a while to get sober. He had stayed that way for two years; until now.

NINETEEN

Terry Neill's house was whitewashed; from the road it looked square and unprepossessing, but these were houses that faced out onto the beach beyond.

She rang the bell and Terry appeared at the door in shorts, a white T-shirt and bare feet.

'Oh,' he said. 'You.'

'You weren't at the golf club, so I thought I'd come here and try my luck.'

'How did you know where I . . . ?'

'I'm a police officer, remember?'

He stood back. 'Actually, your colleague was here this morning.'

'Jill? So you heard already then? I'm sorry. I just thought you ought to know . . .' She half turned to go, then said, 'How are you?'

He shrugged and smiled. 'It's more that I feel really stupid and that people like you know how stupid I've been.'

'It was obviously a good con.'

'Yeah, well. That's me. Only the best. Why don't you come in and have a coffee?' He stepped back to let her in.

She hesitated, then stepped inside. If it was unimpressive from the road, inside the house was very different. The 1930s interior had been obliterated and replaced with a male modernist fantasy. The ground floor was a long rectangle with a kitchen at one end and an enormous desk at the other, with a pair of Eames armchairs facing a free-standing wood burner in the middle of the room. White bookshelves lined the wall to the left; on the right hung pictures, a mixture of large modern abstracts, smaller landscapes and a few prints. What saved it from looking like a glossy executive magazine spread were the unwashed dishes in the sink, a scuffed rug, and a pair of socks, discarded on the tiled floor.

'I realise, of course, that I'm the classic fraud victim. I think I'm clever.' He poured coffee beans into the top of a silver machine on his kitchen counter. 'There's plenty of research to show that victims of financial fraud aren't little old ladies who hide their cash under the mattress . . . Is that sexist?'

'Yes.'

'The most common target of financial fraud is in fact a middle-aged man like me who thinks he knows a bit about money. We think we're smart enough to think we can game the system so instead it games us. Do you like it strong?' he asked.

When he'd made the coffee, he opened up the doors beyond his enormous wooden desk to a deck that looked out onto the dunes.

'Who was it who told you about the scheme?'

'You know who it was? And you know why I can't feel bitter

about it? Because it was poor Ayman. He really thought he was doing me a favour.'

He had cut himself shaving, she noticed. A small nick just below his lip.

'I gave your colleagues some other names too. Other people from the club. We all feel kind of stupid.'

The marram grass was almost silver in the high summer light. She looked directly at him. 'Do you think someone might have been angrier than you about what happened?'

'That's exactly what Detective Constable Ferriter asked me.'

'And what did you tell her?'

'All I've learned is that anyone is capable of anything, given the right stimulus. These people are my friends, though. It's hard for me to imagine any of them doing it. Do you and your daughter often come here . . . to this beach?'

'We live at Dungeness. You take your life in your hands, swimming there.'

'And how are you?'

She had come to ask him questions; instead he was asking them of her.

'So-so. My counsellor says he thinks I keep seeking out situations which put me in danger.' She looked directly at him.

He smiled back at her. 'Maybe you are. Back in the sixties, when you could still do these kind of experiments, these two American psychologists took some dogs and divided them up into two groups. The first they gave electric shocks to. The dogs could stop the pain by pressing a lever. The second they also gave electric shocks to, but when these dogs pressed the lever, the shocks kept on coming.'

'Poor dogs.'

'Poor dogs, yes. They did this for a little while, then they put both sets of dogs into boxes which they could escape from just by jumping straight out. When they gave the shocks to the first dogs, out they jumped. But the second dogs just lay there whimpering, even when they were being shocked, doing nothing.'

'The dogs didn't want to leave the situation that caused them pain?'

'Trauma had effectively rewired the dogs' brains so that they became incapable of taking the kind of action they needed to take to stop themselves being hurt.' He stopped.

'Are you saying I'm like the dogs in the second box?'

He lowered his head a little, as if looking over the top of glasses that weren't there.

'That's a scary thought,' she said.

'You're a police officer. You must have dealt with victims of abuse. Have you ever noticed how they return to their abuser? Or find new partners who are just as bad as the old ones? Freud called it the compulsion to repeat. Trauma rewires your brain.'

'You make my emotions sound like parts of a car engine.'

'Sorry,' he said, with a small smile.

'Don't apologise. I like it. It somehow feels less scary if it's just about faulty fuses.'

'Are you scared?'

She thought about this for a while. 'If you'd asked me a week ago I would have said I was pretty much OK, bar the odd bit of unscheduled weeping. I am coming to realise that I'm not OK.' She looked down at the deck. 'I'm not myself any more and I find that scary. My counsellor just told me I was hyper-vigilant.'

'I can try to explain that in terms of fuses too, if it helps.'

'It helps. Go on.'

'Will you have dinner with me if I do?'

'No,' she said.

He barely registered the refusal. 'Shame,' he said. 'Wait there. I need some props.'

A conceited man, she thought. Good-looking, but too sure of himself, like most of the men she regretted sleeping with.

He returned after a while, with a stem of broccoli, a small potato and a banana.

'I said no to dinner,' she said, attempting a joke.

'Sorry. I spent a while looking for the right vegetables. I was looking for almonds which would have been more appropriate in shape and size than a potato. These,' he said, laying them out on the glass-topped table, 'represent various parts of your brain.'

More flippant remarks occurred to her, but she stifled them.

'We think of the brain as a single organ, but it's useful to think of it as many separate organs working together. This –' he held the banana – 'is your thalamus. Among the many things it does is act like a kind of wireless hub, taking in signals from your eyes and ears and distributing them to your frontal lobes . . . here.' He picked up the broccoli. 'That's your conscious brain. So that when you see something that is particularly frightening, the thalamus routes the signal there and, ta-da!' He waved the broccoli. 'You can act rationally in response to the danger.'

'Like, is this a murder weapon or just a cake knife?'

He frowned, not understanding. 'Yes. I suppose.'

'Sorry. Continue.'

'However, it also sends signals here –' he picked up the potato

– 'to the amygdala. If the thalamus is like a wireless hub, this is like a smoke alarm, activating the so-called unconscious brain. Up goes your heart rate, and it triggers the release of stress hormones like adrenaline and cortisol. Fight, freeze or flee? Those reactions are all taking place before your frontal cortex –' he put down the potato and shook the broccoli – 'has even had time to process what's going on. You'll have noticed that in an emergency you start to act before you even know what's going on?'

She nodded.

'Because the thalamus has spoken to the amygdala and triggered a reaction. But then your rational brain kicks in and decides whether that course of action that you're already halfway through makes sense. That's kind of how it's supposed to work. But sometimes the trauma is so great that it appears to overload the—'

'The broccoli.'

'Yes . . . and all the usual social and rational responses to danger are overwhelmed. Now you're in trouble. All you are left with is the alarm bell . . .'

'The panic.'

'Exactly. You lose it. And because the rest of the brain has been overwhelmed, the bell keeps on ringing.' He picked up the potato this time and shook it.

'It's as if the brain had forgotten the code to reset the alarm?' suggested Alex.

'That's perhaps one way of looking at it.' He spoke with the caution of an academic attempting to explain something complex to a layperson. 'Another effect is that in some situations that alarm keeps going off. Even long after the car accident or the rape, it's as if that traumatic incident hasn't actually ended. Those people become stuck in this kind of fight or flight response. People with PTSD carry their trauma with them, as if it's still happening. Some people talk about having lost a sense of time. Something that should be in the past is still firmly in their present.'

Alex realised she was nodding to everything he said.

He stopped. 'You recognise that?'

'Exactly that. When I think of what happened it's not a memory at all. It's now.'

'That's very hard for you.'

'Why doesn't my counsellor tell me any of this?'

'Because it's of no use to them, I suppose. It doesn't solve the problem. Is it of use to you?'

She thought about that for a while. 'I believe it is. It helps me understand what is happening, at least.'

When she told him about what she had done two nights before in the restaurant in Rye, he laughed briefly, stifled it, then apologised. 'I'm sure it probably wasn't funny at the time.'

'We hadn't even started on our main course.'

'How is your daughter coping? The naturalist.'

'She's OK,' she answered.

'Are you sure? It can be very tough on children. They don't always understand why we behave the way we do.'

Alex stood, realising she was irritated by the implication that she was somehow failing her daughter. 'We're fine,' she said. 'We always have been. Look. I should go. I just came because I thought you ought to know . . .'

'Before you go, I need to ask. Do you think someone killed Ayman because of what happened with the money?'

'Revenge, you mean, because they lost their money because of his enthusiasm for Biosfera? It's a possibility.' She peered at him. 'Are you worried you're in some kind of danger too?'

'Constable Ferriter asked me if I'd received any threats.'

'And have you?'

'No. Nothing at all.'

That prickle again, at the back of her neck.

At the front door, she said, 'Thank you for the . . . vegetables. I mean it.'

'Any time. Really.'

She left, glad to be away. It wasn't that she didn't like him; the opposite, in fact.

In the daylight, she cycled home again, via the murder house.

This time it was deserted.

In the daylight, the copse seemed much less sinister.

She found an old rake handle propped against the side of the garage to prod into the vegetation and it took her a couple of minutes to find what she was looking for. It had slipped down onto the dry soil below laurel leaves.

She picked up the black disc she had seen on Saturday night and held it up. It was a lens cap.

TWENTY

Georgia Coaker was a freelance photographer and freelance photographers always need work, so she was easy to track down.

'Oh. It's you.'

'I found something that I think belongs to you.'

The address Georgia Coaker gave turned out to be an old pub. The Prince George Hotel had closed but the ground floor had been taken over by an architectural salvage company. Alex peered inside what had been the lounge bar. It was now crammed with old tables, lamps, electric fans, glass carboys and ship's fittings.

'Can I help you?' A man too young for a beard and wearing tortoiseshell glasses was sanding down a door at the back of the shop. The place smelt of wood dust and old paint. He wore a denim woodworker's apron.

'Just looking.'

The shopkeeper returned to his work. He was sanding by

hand, paper wrapped around a small wooden block. There were machines that did this kind of thing much quicker, thought Alex, suspecting that the activity was intended more for ambience than function.

At the back, she found an old small square sink on a plain white china column. The plughole had been filled and a copper cup-stand, verdigrised and slightly bent, had been fitted with a small feeder, filled with peanuts.

'It's been upcycled into a bird bath,' explained the shop owner. 'Or bird sink, if you prefer.'

And he resumed his sanding.

'How much is it?'

'Two hundred pounds.'

'You're kidding,' she said. 'That's absurd.'

When she had enquired about Georgia Coaker, he had directed her to a door to the right of the pub's side entrance. What had once been hotel rooms for travelling salesmen had been rented out as small flats. Alex checked the number then pressed the bell. The door buzzed.

Georgia lived upstairs in a small one-bedroom apartment whose walls were decorated with black-and-white photographs from the fifties and sixties.

'Tea?'

'Do you have coffee?'

As she waited in the living room, Alex looked at the framed photos crammed onto two of her walls. A couple on a London bus, a woman standing on a wooden roller coaster, her skirt flying up in the wind, two women in a smoke-filled pub arguing.

'Quite a collection,' said Alex.

'I love that stuff. Real people.' The third wall was windows, looking out onto the street. The second was blank; painted white. 'Not just the people in the photos either. Nobody wants to pay for pictures like that any more. I do quite a few like that, street photographs, but these days nobody wants them. I just do them for my Instagram, which is a joke.'

'So you take photos for the scandal sheets instead?'

'Like you love everything about what you do for a living.'

'I didn't mean it to come out like that, I'm sorry.'

Georgia put the coffee down and drew the curtains, turning the room dark, then switched on a projector and Alex realised what that third white wall was for.

They sat together on a big old brown leather sofa that had been covered in blankets. Georgia pulled a laptop towards her. The home screen showed a photograph of her with a young fair-haired man in a wheelchair. She was behind him, smiling.

'That's your brother?'

'Yes.'

She opened up a folder and clicked on a file. Projected onto the wall opposite them, Callum Younis sat in another wheelchair, this one more sophisticated, with big pads for his head and arms. It had been taken on the day when Alex had met Georgia on the footpath that ran alongside Loftingswood Grange. Callum's head was slightly to one side, his hands pressed tightly against his own chest. It was the first time Alex had seen Ayman and Mary Younis's child.

'Are you going to shop me for taking that?'

'Not as long as you don't try to publish it anywhere.'

'Pinkie promise,' Georgia said. 'So he's all right then? Or is he going to have to give up living there now his father's dead?'

'They had insurance, apparently. There's no reason why he can't carry on being cared for there.'

'Bully for him.' She pressed the next photo. A care assistant was sitting beside him in a chair, holding a spoon to his mouth. 'I shouldn't be bitter. It kills my family, paying for care for my brother. Callum's lucky to have rich parents. Or to have had them, at least. It's cleaned us out and I bet we don't pay the half of what they're paying for Callum.'

The photos were all similar. She must have squatted there on the path photographing him for a while before Alex had disturbed her.

'It's not like we're complaining. We're proud to do it. And the carers at his home are just as good.'

'What about the pictures you took at the house in New Romney? From by the garage?'

'How did you know that?'

'I'm a genius.'

'Why do you want to see them? You checking I haven't done anything illegal there too?'

'I'm curious, that's all.' She pulled the lens cap from her pocket. 'It looks like you found yourself a pretty good vantage point.'

'Ah.' Georgia took it from her. 'Yes. As it happens, I did. There's a pathway. You can't really see it from the road. I don't think it's official. There's this homeless guy who's been living in the next field who's obviously been using it to get to his tent.'

'He's the murder suspect.'

'You're shitting me. I was this close to him and I was going to take his photograph but he gave off these vibes . . .'

'I know exactly the vibes you mean,' said Alex. 'I have personal experience.'

'Shit, shit, shit. That photo would have been worth thousands. Where is he now?'

'If only we knew. He's vanished. I wouldn't try to find him either. He's a dangerous man. Show me the pictures then, will you?'

Georgia closed the folder on the laptop, opened another one and brought up a new photo on the wall in front of them.

Alex said, 'Oh.'

'What is it?'

On the screen was a picture of the front door of the Younises' house. Standing just to the left of the doorway was Jill, dressed from head to toe in a white forensic suit. She had her gloved hands to her eyes and was crying.

'Do you know her?'

'Yes. I do.'

There was a male constable, also dressed in overalls, an awkward arm around Jill, presumably trying to comfort her. It was Colin Gilchrist. It was a beautiful image; the tilt of her head caught the summer light, making Jill look like a figure from one of the Raphael paintings Alex's father had taken her to see at the National Gallery when she was young. There was a kind of desperation on Gilchrist's face too; as if he were as concerned for her as he was for the dead people they had discovered in the house. An unexpected tenderness in the young man's face.

'I love this photograph,' said Georgia. 'That police officer is so beautiful. And yet there's something so awful about it. The blood on her clothes.'

It was unmissable; the bright red blood on Jill's coverall. She had been the second person there. She must have tried to check whether the victims were alive or not. Alex knew just how that felt. 'So why didn't you sell this to the papers? You could have made a few quid.'

Georgia closed her laptop. The wall opposite them turned black. 'You can get out now if you want to. I don't have to do this.'

'I'm sorry. My father used to say my mouth runs ahead of me.'

'You think people like me are scum, don't you?'

Alex didn't answer.

'I'm sick of it. I was doing a job. I was earning a living. That doesn't mean I'm a monster.'

'Would you sell it?'

'Of course I would.'

'What was wrong then? Not enough money.'

'It is a great photo. She's a public servant. A policewoman. People think you lot are heartless bastards. There's nothing heartless about her.' She opened her computer again and woke the screen up. 'Look at her. She cares. You can tell she really bloody cares.'

Jill's face again; the trauma of what she had seen was written into her skin too. 'Why didn't you sell it, then?'

Georgia coloured. 'I have my reasons.'

'That officer's feelings not being one of them, presumably?'

'She should be proud of that. She's a hero for going in that house. They all are.'

Outside, gulls squawked angrily. 'This was the Thursday, right?'

'Yes.'

Alex remembered seeing the coveralls in the boot of Jill's car; the haunted look on her face. 'How did you know?'

'How did I know what?'

'How did you know that there had been a murder there? It was on the evening news. This was what, two o'clock in the afternoon? Maybe earlier. Nobody had told the public.'

Georgia shrugged. 'I just saw some police cars. Followed them there.' Alex watched her hands. She had this habit of circling them round each other.

'Right. Just followed a police car.'

'Yeah.'

Alex nodded. 'Show me some more.'

She clicked on. More officers coming and going. Alex recognised them all. She still thought of herself as new around here, but all these were her colleagues, people she had grown to trust. She had once been one of them.

Because of her illness, they had taken her off Serious Crime. When she returned to work next week she would be on what they called 'light duties'. McAdam said they had found something that wouldn't upset her.

Georgia clicked the space bar, scrolling through the pictures. The camera was mostly pointed at people coming and going through the front door. Sometimes she panned a little to the left, as officers seemed to be gathering at the north side of the house.

'I'd found this place under some laurel bushes. It was dark there so they couldn't see me, but I had to be still or they'd notice. So I couldn't really get any other angles. I couldn't move to see what they were doing.'

A gurney appeared in shot, being dragged over the gravel. Even empty, the paramedics seemed to be making heavy work of it. Another photograph of it disappearing round the left-hand corner of the house.

'That's them moving the body. I was thinking they were going to come back right past me, but they went round the far side. There's a stone path there so it would have been easier.' She looked straight at Alex. 'And yes. I would have published it if I'd got the shot. It's public interest.'

The camera moved again, a little to the left. And then back again for the next shots, to the house, to shadowy figures moving on the inside, where Mary Younis's body must have been found, but it was too dark to make anything out in there.

'Go back,' said Alex abruptly.

Georgia flicked at her keyboard.

'Back again. There.'

In her attempt to follow the paramedics she had photographed the garage, a red brick building with a tiled roof at the end of the driveway. The door was open. Alex leaned forward on the sofa.

TWENTY-ONE

Alex stared at the image on the wall for a long time. From the photograph it looked as if no one had parked a car in the garage for a while. It was full of all sorts of junk. After a while, she got up off the sofa and walked closer.

'Anything?'

Alex shook her head slowly.

'You wouldn't tell me anyway, would you?'

She turned and smiled. 'Course not.'

'I can send you that if you want.'

'No charge?'

'Shut the fuck up, will you? I want this person found as much as you do. It's monstrous what they did.'

'Sorry,' said Alex. She reached down, picked up her cup and took a sip of coffee. 'Yes, I would appreciate that. Let me give you my email.' She wrote it on a page in her notebook, tore it out, handed it over.

'Personal email? Shouldn't this have a police address on it?'

'It should, yes. But trust me, OK? I'm not reporting you for invasion of privacy. Give me a bit of rope as well, will you? Did you sell any of these photos at all?'

Georgia clicked through the last few photographs. 'Just the one of the house with the police car outside. You know. Murder house. It was in the locals, the *Mail* and the *Telegraph*.'

'I hope it was worth it.' She replaced the cup on the table. 'Was it Colin?' she asked, watching Georgia's face closely.

Barely a twitch of her face as she asked the question. 'I don't know what you mean.'

'It was Colin who told you about the house, wasn't it? The officer in the photograph, standing behind the woman officer who was crying.'

'No,' Georgia said, a bit too readily. When she'd said the name Colin, she hadn't asked who she was talking about, either.

'That's why you didn't want to sell it, even though it was your best photograph. You didn't want to get him into the shit because he was the one who leaked it to you.'

'I don't even know who Colin is.' Her hands were twisting round in front of her again.

Alex smiled. 'OK.' She stood. That's what it was like around here. Everyone knew everyone else.

Alex was almost home when she saw the two women dragging suitcases from the light-blue shack, down the boardwalk towards the road, bickering as they went.

The honeymoon was over. They had arrived on a Thursday and they were leaving a week later. It wasn't just trauma that affected the sense of how time passed. Without work, the days were formless. It was a surprise to realise that it had been seven days since she had first met them by the railway station cafe, on the day that Frank Hogben's mother had appeared with a knife. Ayman and Mary's killer had not been found. The suspect, the army veteran Robert Glass, seemed to have disappeared.

Stones caught the suitcase's wheels.

'I'm going as fast as I can,' complained Tina.

'You have to lift it.' Stella abandoned her case to help her.

'I'll do it,' Tina snapped.

'Don't be daft. Let me.'

A taxi waited on the road for them, boot open. They would be sweating in this heat with those large bags. The taxi driver, head down looking at something on his phone, made no attempt to help them.

Alex started to trot over towards the newly-weds. 'Hey,' she called out.

They were too busy struggling with the cases to hear her and were already almost at the road when she reached them. 'You're going?'

'Back to normality.' Stella hefted her purple plastic suitcase into the boot. 'Worst luck.'

'Did you have a good time?'

'Next time I get married I'll go to Barcelona,' said Tina.

'Shut up, Tina. We loved it. Best time ever. We said Zoë can come and stay with us in Folkestone any time. Hope that's all right?'

'You did?'

'She's magic.'

'Yes,' said Alex. 'She actually is.'

136

Tina's case was aluminium. Alex watched her as she lifted it, determined to do it on her own to prove a point to Stella, tried to swing it up as high as the boot, and smashed it instead into the back of the car. Her eyes went wide as she realised she had knocked a chip out of the paintwork.

The taxi driver, who had ignored them until now, was out of the car in a second. 'What the bloody hell have you done?'

Stella and Tina looked at each other.

'Look at it, you fucking idiot.'

Stella seemed to grow in size. 'Don't you dare speak to my wife like that.'

The man rolled his eyes. 'Two hundred pounds,' he said.

'If you'd got off your fat arse,' Stella said, her face in his, 'this would never have happened.'

The man seemed to consider the situation. 'Fifty pounds,' he said.

'Let's call another taxi,' said Stella.

The taxi driver picked up the case and threw it into the boot. 'Get in.'

Stella turned and put her arms around Tina. 'See? It's OK,' she said soothingly. 'It's all OK.'

Alex noticed that Tina was rigid; as if her muscles were all working at once to hold her in place. She was staring straight ahead of her, eyes wide.

Stella's voice was low and quiet. 'Are you OK to catch this taxi, or do you need to wait for another one?'

Tina said nothing; it was as if she had somehow become incapable of any thought.

'Come on,' mumbled the driver. 'Let's go.'

'Ssh.' A gentle noise, like one would make to calm a child. Alex realised she was watching Stella deal with something that had happened more than once.

They stood in strange silence for another minute, Stella stroking Tina's hair, the taxi driver standing impatiently beside them, until Tina finally seemed to unwind. She nodded and said, 'Let's go in this car.'

'You sure?'

'Yeah. I'll be OK.' Stella opened the car's rear door and Tina got in. Walking round to the other side of the car Stella paused in front of Alex, leaned forward and kissed her gently on the cheek. 'Look after yourself, copper. You look bloody rough.'

It had been a strange scene. Afterwards, Alex replayed it, over and over in her head, trying to make sense of it.

TWENTY-TWO

Further down the track, next to the Snack Shack, Curly was hauling fish boxes into the back of his Ford Ranger pickup. The smell was heavy in the thick summer air.

Alex walked across the stones to his old truck. 'Had a good day?'

'Not bad.' Curly swept a hand through his hair. 'Not good.'

'Seen Bill?'

'Yeah. Not good.'

This was a small community. Word got around.

'What do we do to help him, Curly?'

He pulled a tin of tobacco out of his pocket. 'Stay out of his way, mostly. He needs to come out the other side of this and be able to look us all in the eye again.'

It was probably true, she thought, but it wouldn't help the fact that he was broke now. 'I was wondering. Do you still fish out of Folkestone?'

He looked at her warily. 'Not often. If one of the boats needs crew, sometimes they ask me.'

'If I wanted to go out on a boat from there . . .'

'Why would you want to do that?'

'I need a career change,' she said.

When Curly laughed it was like sun breaking out behind clouds. 'Seriously. Why?'

'From Monday morning, I'm going to be stuck behind a desk.'

His smile vanished as quickly as it had appeared. 'Is this about Frank Hogben? You were asking Bill about him.'

'Yes. It is.'

'He fell overboard. He wasn't much of a fisherman.'

A gull landed on the cab of Curly's truck, head cocked, one eye on the fish boxes.

'I just want to see.'

'See what?'

'I don't know.'

He thought about this for a while. 'Working boats aren't big. They don't usually take people who aren't crew.'

'I understand.' She stood a little while longer.

A second gull landed on the roof and the two birds started bickering loudly.

'It was just a thought.' She turned and started to walk back to her car.

She was almost at the track when she heard the crackle of tyres behind her. When he was alongside her, he leaned out of the window. 'I could ask around,' he said. 'If that's what you want.'

'I'd appreciate that.'

When he reached the track he floored the accelerator, sending black smoke out of his exhaust. The speed limit around here was twenty miles an hour. Curly had been born here and didn't think regulations like that applied to him.

And then she saw two cars, blue lights flashing, coming down the road towards them and watched Curly slow, as if he thought they were coming for him.

The first car sped to the end of the track, pulling over to park just after the old lighthouse. The second slowed as it approach Alex.

There was a woman she didn't recognise behind the wheel, but Colin Gilchrist was in the passenger seat.

'What's going on?'

'They found signs of someone camping up at the firing ranges. They think it's Robert Glass . . . the suspect. We're heading that way up the beach.'

The army firing ranges were huge, taking up the whole of the north-west of the spit of land up to Camber. Finding someone there would not be easy.

'What's his story? Robert Glass.'

The woman next to him coughed. 'Dunno. Listen. We have to go.'

Alex leaned a little closer. 'By the way, I think we have a mutual acquaintance. Georgia Coaker.'

'Oh,' he said.

She had checked Facebook. Georgia Coaker and Colin Gilchrist had been at primary school together. 'Be careful who you talk to in future, Colin. Do you understand? They could kick you out for that.'

She watched the blush as blood rushed to his neck and ears and thought of Terry Neill and his banana.

She leaned in closer still. 'I won't tell. But I want you do to something for me. OK?'

As she drove off, Alex heard the driver ask, 'What's all that about?'

She watched them drive up the road, park and take their Kevlar jackets out of the boot. A gust of wind blew down the shoreline, shivering the sea kale and sending hair into Alex's eyes.

Far off she saw a figure sitting on the back step of Arum Cottage.

She drove on up the track, turning up towards home, parking outside his house.

Getting out, she opened the boot. Bill South sat with a glass of whisky in his hand.

'I came to say sorry,' she said.

He nodded. 'Not your fault.' He lifted his glass and took a sip. 'Want one?'

'Not much. If it's any consolation, Terry Neill said he was completely taken in too.'

Bill chuckled, took another swig. 'Terry Neill isn't going to miss it, believe me. Have you seen his house?'

'Bitter doesn't suit you, Bill. That house would be a bit flashy for you, I'd have thought.'

Bill nodded. 'Your daughter says we shouldn't need money anyway.'

Alex laughed. 'That's the kind of interesting thing she says.' She held a hand out towards him; he took it with the one he wasn't holding a glass with and gently squeezed it. 'You told her to go away though.'

'I wasn't really in the mood. What are all the coppers doing on the beach?'

'They think a suspect in the Younis case might have been camping rough by the ranges.'

'Bob Glass?'

Alex stared at Bill. 'You know him?'

'He's been around here all summer, living here and there. You never notice anything, do you? So they reckon Bob killed Ayman and Mary Younis?'

'He had been squatting in a field behind their house. They think he argued with Ayman Younis about something. What do you think?'

'He's not a well man. Ex-army. Talks like he was well educated. He was in Afghanistan and Iraq. Saw all his friends blown to bits, I heard.'

'*Kill them all, God will know his own.*'

'What?'

'It's what the killer wrote on the walls in Mary Younis's blood. Maybe that's a man who had seen everyone around him die.'

'It's terrible, the way we throw some men away,' said Bill self-pityingly, and he raised his glass to his lips, though it was empty already. 'Saw you talking to Curly,' he said.

'You don't miss much, even when you're drunk.'

'Good spot, this. You can see most things from here. Some wind coming in tonight.'

'I was asking if he'd get me on one of the fishing boats going out of Folkestone. A ride along, so to speak.'

He dropped her hand. 'What the hell you want to do that for?'

'I'm not sure, Bill. I'm back to work on Monday. Light duties.'

'Bully for you.'

'McAdam has got me seconded to some analyst research project into crime reporting methodology. My life is over, Bill.'

'Speak for yourself.'

She sighed. 'You know I'll give you the money, Bill. Just ask.'

'Nope.'

'I have savings.'

'My own stupid fault I lost the money.'

'The offer stands.'

'Me an ex-cop, and an ex-con, and I fell for it.'

'Don't beat yourself up, Bill. Come here.' She beckoned him. 'I bought you a present to cheer you up.'

He put down his glass and took her hand again, this time so she could pull him up. He was drunker than she had thought, and stumbled a little towards her, ending up with his arms around her. 'Sorry,' he mumbled, stepping back.

'This way,' she said.

He followed, walking around the side of the house until they reached the front, then stopped and stared, swaying slightly.

'What in Jesus Christ's fucking name is that?' The old Northern Ireland accent emerged when he was drunk.

'It's a bird bath, Bill. It's a present.'

And in the pink of the low evening light, she thought it looked pretty magnificent.

'Do you like it?'

On unsteady feet, as if swayed by the wind, he walked around it once, then turned away from the sink and walked back inside his front door without saying another word.

TWENTY-THREE

Saturday night Alex woke, bolt upright and switched the light on. The wind was banging a door somewhere.

Zoë was in the bedroom with her, sitting in the armchair at the bottom of her bed wrapped in a duvet. 'What's wrong? Couldn't sleep?' Alex asked.

Zoë nodded.

Under her duvet, Alex was roasting. Her cotton pyjamas were soaked with sweat. She pushed off her covers and tried to remember what the dream had been. Zoë always looked so small, her bony head poking out of a mass of bedding.

'Want to get in with me?' She moved over, making space. Her teenage daughter inched her way across the room, dragging her heavy duvet with her, then flopped down on the mattress beside her.

'There, there,' Alex said, stroking her daughter's forehead. 'Is everything all right?'

Zoë didn't answer.

'What is it that woke you up?'

But her daughter was already asleep; she lay listening to the soft hum of her breath and remembered the fierce, unexpected love she had felt for her when she was newborn.

And then she was underground again; the earth falling in on her, roots growing around her, trapping her, crushing her chest so tightly she could not breathe. It was terrifying, but also familiar. This was a place she had become used to.

Her job was to disentangle herself, to work her way out of the darkness, but the earth on her chest pressed down so heavily she knew that would be impossible soon.

She wasn't aware of having fallen asleep but when she woke it was bright in her room and someone was shouting. Next to her, her daughter was still asleep, wrapped in that mountainous duvet. Alex stood, opened a crack in the curtains and peered out. Curly was standing out there in a pair of camouflage trousers and a dirty white T-shirt.

She opened the window. He shouted, 'Mate runs a boat called the *Jenny B* out of Folkestone. He's going out on the high tide this afternoon. Want to come?'

'On a Sunday?'

'You're the one who wanted to go out.'

'Mum?' Zoë's voice croaked behind her. 'What are you doing?'

'Curly is taking me out on a trawler.'

'Why?'

She didn't answer. She wasn't sure herself.

'Trawling should be banned,' said Zoë.

Alex looked at her watch and called down to Curly. 'What time will we be back?'

'Three in the morning, maybe four. Best to fish in the dark this time of year. They can't see you coming.'

'I'll be fine,' said Zoë. 'I'll have a party and invite lots of my friends around and we'll all take ketamine.'

'Do you actually have friends?'

'Let me sleep,' said Zoë. She stood, eyes not fully open, and shuffled back to her bedroom, two stick-like legs poking out from under her grubby duvet.

'Just so you know,' said Curly, as he was bumping down the track, too fast as usual. 'Danny Fagg, guy who owns the boat . . . he's Frank's cousin.'

'Oh.'

'Yeah. And he was on the boat the day they lost Frank. So you might want to go a bit easy.'

The weather was overcast but still, the sea calm.

'He was the guy who called it in to the coastguard?'

Curly nodded.

'Did the police ever suspect that it was Danny that pushed Frank into the water?'

'What do you think? Course they did. Interviewed him a few times.' The tree-shaped air freshener dangling from the mirror swung from side to side as he swerved around a pothole.

'Could he have done it?'

'Not a chance. He wouldn't have it in him to do a thing like that. You'll see.' Curly accelerated to make it through an amber traffic light, then slowed again as he rejoined the queue of cars ahead. 'Say he had, though, not saying he had. You'd never be able to prove anything, would you? Two people on a boat.'

'Nope. Not if they never found the body.'

'Well, if it had been me and Frank on the boat, maybe then you'd have a point. Not Danny though.'

'You didn't like Frank much, did you?'

'Nope. Don't know many who did, to be honest.'

'Why not?'

'Bit full of himself, like his father before him. When his father died Frank reckoned he was the big man. Thought he owned the place.'

'But you still worked with him?'

'Sometimes. Beggars and choosers, you know? You don't have to like everyone you work with. It's all about the boats with me. My dad was a fisherman. If I couldn't go out on the boats still, I wouldn't know what I was.'

As long as she lived in Dungeness she had known Curly, though it had never been a friendship. He spent his life on the beach or in the pub. Everybody knew him and he seemed to know everyone's business.

Without indicating, he pulled out to overtake a rubbish truck on the long straight Lydd Road. Coming in the other direction, a Jaguar flashed its lights angrily. Curly laughed.

Folkestone Harbour was an old mess of brick, stone, concrete, steel and wood; a collection of harbour arms, bridges and viaducts. Once, this had been a busy port taking train freight passengers across the Channel. Now they were building apartments where the ships had used to come in.

The trawler was moored in the harbour off The Stade; a fat blue hull, painted with thick white lines, on the bow in big letters designed to be read a long way off, *FE128*. Curly parked the truck outside the Ship Inn, facing the water.

'That's not the same boat . . . ?'

'No. That was *The Hopeful*. She was a much bigger boat than this. *The Hopeful* was fifteen metres. Nobody wants them big boats any more because of the quotas. She was sold after Frank disappeared. His family need the cash.' From the cab of his truck, Curly leaned out of the window, stuck a finger and thumb in his mouth and whistled. On the boat, twenty metres away, a man in a grubby green T-shirt looked up and waved. 'That's Danny. He'll be over to fetch us now.'

In front of them, tourists ambled eating ice cream. Curly pulled overalls and boots from the back of the truck and walked to the metal stairs that had been attached to the old stone quayside.

It was a while before Danny was ready, and when he was, he hopped down into a large tender and rowed towards them, standing up in the boat as he leaned on the oars. A chain ran between the iron post on the edge of the quay. Alex ducked under it and followed Curly down the metal ladder.

Danny was a huge man, arms like pink sausages poking out from the T-shirt that overhung his belly. Curly hopped on board and turned to hold a hand out for Alex.

'Danny. This is Alex, who I told you about.'

Danny nodded. He was a man with a generous smile, younger than Curly, with pale ginger hair and a million freckles. He rowed them across the water, watched by tourists with ice creams.

Alex clambered up the side of the boat onto a broad empty

deck with orange and green nets bundled at one end and a huge winch at the other. As soon as Curly had tied the dinghy onto the mooring, Danny started the diesel, put the engine in reverse and hauled up the anchor.

Inside the wheelhouse, Danny made a place for her to sit.

'She's come to see how the other half lives, Danny.'

Danny nodded nervily, said nothing as the trawler headed down past the harbour arm towards the open water.

'Hold on,' said Danny quietly. 'Gets a bit bumpy, this bit.'

He was right; as they rounded the breakwater the boat lurched up one wave and then banged down onto the next.

Tomorrow she would be back at work behind a desk. The wind had raised a swell. The boat felt suddenly out of place, too heavy for the sea to hold. Always that sense that something bad was going to happen. She tried to push it aside. It was a neuro-dysfunction, Terry Neill had told her; bad things happened, but not just because she believed they would. Nothing bad would happen here.

TWENTY-FOUR

The boat started to roll the moment it left harbour. When they were clear, Danny turned the boat south-east and headed along the coast.

'What was the weather like, that day seven years ago, when Frank disappeared?'

'Pretty heavy weather. A good deal worse than this, wouldn't you say, Danny?'

Danny nodded.

'There was a north-easterly moving up the Channel, so coming back, the boat was heading right into the waves.'

'A lot of up and down?'

'You could call it that. Pitching.' Curly motioned with his hands.

Another smaller boat was approaching from the bow, heading in to Folkestone as they headed out. It was stacked with lobster pots, marker buoys adorned with blue and red flags that flapped in the headwind like heraldic banners. One man stood at the wheel, another on deck, beside the wheelhouse, waving.

A few seconds later, the radio crackled. 'Got new crew, Danny?' a man's voice called.

Danny flushed. A giggle escaped him.

Curly picked up the handset. 'What's it to you, mate?'

'There's someone better-looking than either of you on board.'

'Don't understand what you're saying, bro. We're all beautiful on this boat,' Curly said.

'Woman aboard a trawler,' explained Curly. 'Always gets the lads excited.'

'I thought we were bad luck.'

'She thinks we're all pagans who believe in mermaids, Danny,' said Curly.

Danny snickered.

'Course, we'll blame you if Danny doesn't catch nothing, won't we?'

She was used to seeing Curly in the bar, or on the beach, endlessly tinkering with his own boat. On land he was a man with a half-full glass. She had never seen him on the water. Out here, he seemed to become somebody much more confident. This was his element, she realised; he had come alive. She watched him, eyes fixed on the horizon as Danny steered.

Alex checked her phone for any messages from Zoë. The signal was still strong, but there was nothing. She checked in her email too to see if there were any messages from Jill – there weren't – then went on to the local news site to see if there had been any developments in the Younis case, which there also hadn't been.

It was a mistake, looking at a small screen as the boat rocked. She felt a sudden thickness in her chest, nausea rising.

'OK?' Curly was frowning at her.

'Fine.' She put her phone away and looked out at the horizon instead, not wanting to seem weak.

It was an hour before Danny slowed the engine and went back with Curly to prepare the nets, then Alex watched the green and orange nylon playing out from the rear of the boat as Danny pulled the boat forwards. There were three sets of nets; each needed to be dropped separately. Then the boat moved more slowly, pulling the gear along the bottom.

'Too light yet to catch much,' said Danny.

'Never know. That wind last night stirred it up a bit.'

The fish would see the net coming, they explained, unless it was dark or the water murky.

The wind was warm. It was about an hour into the first trawl when she started throwing up over the side.

'Some people get it worse than others,' said Danny, with a sympathetic smile. 'It's not even that rough today. Think how much worse it would be if the wind came up.'

'Thank you.'

'Welcome.'

Crouched against the gunwale, she watched her sick splashing down the blue hull of the boat. She felt rotten and wished she had not come out here. It was stupid. For some reason, in her head, she had imagined she would be good at this, but she wasn't. She didn't know what she had expected to learn; but all that she was learning was that she could never do this job.

Some time later, they started the winch and hauled the first net back up. To Alex the nylon seemed full of shiny wriggling fish, mouths poking between the holes, gasping for water.

Danny's face showed no particular emotion, but Curly looked contemptuous. 'Rubbish,' Curly said, tugging at the opening at the bottom of the net.

Fish and crabs poured out like a thick liquid onto the deck. She watched them disentangling the struggling creatures from the ragged net, bodies flashing silver in the dull afternoon light. Small dogfish, black-eyed and pale, writhed in their death throes, mouths opening and closing slowly. When the other two nets had been dragged up, Danny and Curly stood over them, dividing them between white plastic crates. The dogfish went into one. Crabs thunked into another, crawling slowly over each other to try and escape. Plaice and turbot went into a third, while a single skate went into the fourth; white sides up, their gasping mouths looking unsettlingly human to her.

Gulls gathered behind them, hoping to catch anything thrown back overboard.

They worked quickly, clearing the deck of what they had dragged up. For the first time, watching him pick out the fish, she noticed Danny had only three fingers on his right hand. 'What happened to your hand, Danny?'

His face flushed. 'Accident.'

'He caught it in the winch, didn't you, Danny?'

Bile rose in her throat again.

'I'll make tea,' she suggested.

'Best stay out here,' said Danny.

She was going to object, but Curly added, 'Going inside will make you sick again.' And on cue, she retched again, though her stomach was empty now.

It took them the best part of an hour to sort the fish and

sluice the decks, and then they set about dropping the nets for a second haul.

She joined the men in the wheelhouse, standing in the glow of the screen that showed the map of the seabed beneath them, and the line of the course they were travelling. They were approaching a strange black T-shape. 'Is that a wreck?'

'Plane,' said Danny. 'That one's a Dornier.'

Looking closer, she could see it was a tiny symbol of an aeroplane.

'See that one there?' He pointed to another one further ahead that they would also pass close to. 'Spitfire. I pulled up a window from that one in the net. It had bullet holes in the glass.' He grinned.

'Danny knows where they all are like nobody else does. Anyone different comes trawling round here and the chances are they'll snag their nets on them.'

'So this is his territory?'

'Pretty much,' said Curly.

'You were on *The Hopeful*, the day Frank Hogben disappeared,' she said to Danny.

She caught Danny giving Curly a glance, a roll of the eyes. 'Yep.'

'What were you doing?'

'Sleeping.' He pointed to the opening at the front of the wheelhouse. Steep wooden steps descended to a cramped cabin in the 'V' of the bow. There were two small bunks in there. 'I'd been asleep for half an hour, forty minutes maybe. Woke up, he was gone. Just me on the boat. That's all.'

Alex watched him look over towards Curly, as if for help. '*The Hopeful* was on autopilot,' Curly joined in. 'Maybe he was having a piss over the side and fell in. Maybe he just tripped. Frank never kept a tidy boat.'

'Wouldn't he have shouted?'

'Might have. No way you'd have heard him down below. And *The Hopeful* was a bigger boat than this. Once you're overboard, you're gone.'

Danny spoke again. 'Then I called up the coastguard. That's all.' He was staring straight ahead at the horizon as if concentrating on something he had spotted there, but when Alex looked there was nothing at all she could see.

It was starting to get dark now. Dungeness lighthouse flashed ahead of them. Only the rectangular bulk of the power station interrupted the otherwise flat horizon.

It was midnight when they dropped the nets for the last time. Away to the south, somewhere over France, there was a thunderstorm lighting the horizon in bursts of yellow. Alex had recovered, though she was hungry now and tired. Danny had offered to share a pale ham sandwich, but fearing it would set her off again, Alex turned it down. She moved to the back of the boat to watch as Danny played out the net. Curly stood by the other side, keeping an eye. It was mesmerising, watching the net disappear into the black water.

'What about his father?'

'Max Hogben? Why you asking about him?'

'Did you ever know him, Danny?'

Danny nodded. 'Got killed in his car, did Max. That red thing.'

156

'Beautiful thing, that was.' Curly shouted above the noise of the winch. 'German engine. Went like the clappers.' Curly knew about cars, loving them almost as much as he did boats.

'I heard that Frank Hogben used to drive it around after his father died in it.'

Curly said, 'That's how it was. Think about it. Pretty bloody weird. Imagine driving round, sitting in the very seat your father died in. You don't have to be Sigmund Freud to figure that one out, do you, Danny?'

'Nope.'

'Hated his father. Can't say I blame him either. Everyone hated Max Hogben. Whole family did. Even Mandy hated him.'

'From what I heard, no one really liked Frank much either.'

Danny said, 'Can't say I really felt warm towards him.'

Curly said nothing at all.

The net was all out now and the winch was suddenly quiet, the noise replaced by the slapping of water against the hull of the trawler. Glancing at her, Curly and Danny seemed to be conferring about something in low voices.

Cautiously, she went to stand at the back of the boat, looking over the metal edge and down at the water. The cold depth beneath them made her suddenly shiver, and she had a vision of herself, drowned, half underwater. Shocked at how real the premonition felt, she straightened abruptly, turned . . .

Danny was right behind her, inches away, hands out.

The jolt made her feet slip on the wet metal and she lost her balance. Throwing out her hand to catch hold of the ropes above her, she missed, and started her fall. For a second she thought she was going into the net, to be pulled down into the cold water with it, but a big hand had shot out already and grabbed her by the upper arm, yanking her back into the boat.

She looked up at Danny, heart thumping. 'What the fuck were you doing, creeping up behind me?'

He had been standing so close, as if ready to push her into the water. Danny looked down at the deck, not answering. She turned towards Curly, but he had disappeared into the wheel-house.

TWENTY-FIVE

She scrabbled back towards the wheelhouse and stayed inside as a thin grey rain fell. The sky darkened behind the grey drizzle and the distant outline of the white cliffs vanished.

They motored on for almost two more hours on autopilot while Danny and Curly gutted plaice with little scoops of their knives and cut the flesh from skates. The boat was a ball of light in a black landscape, illuminating the white gulls that crowded towards them. Alex stayed in the dry. Nobody talked much.

Back in the harbour, Curly ran the tender alongside the ramp so that she could get back onto dry land.

'I'll be a while helping Danny finish up with the catch and tidying up the boat,' said Curly. 'It'll be an hour yet. Wait in the truck.'

'Was that how it happened – what happened to me? Danny was there, ready to push me.'

'Don't be daft. If he hadn't been there, you'd have gone straight in. He was looking out for you. Dangerous places, trawlers.'

'Seriously?'

He shrugged. 'I'll take you home in a bit.'

'I'll catch a cab. I need some sleep. I have to work in the morning.'

The little boat accelerated away from the dockside, back to the trawler. She stood on the dock a long time, waiting for a taxi. It was gone two in the morning by the time a car arrived. In just a few hours she would be back at a desk for the first time in weeks.

'Light duties'. No phrase had ever left a heart so heavy.

She was to work alongside two data analysts, on loan from the Performance section, and an IT specialist seconded from Sussex Police. They had been given a two-month project to devise and test a new system for reporting and categorising data for various crimes of violence that would satisfy new criteria that had been handed down from Her Majesty's Inspectorate of Constabulary. She walked into the small room in the modern outbuilding behind the main HQ building, and three men looked round, warily.

'Kill me now,' she muttered quietly.

Here, crime would manifest itself only as numbers, to be subjected to quantitative or qualitative analysis. There was nothing triggering about working at this desk, and that was entirely the point.

'How is it?' Jill called her from the incident room after she'd been at her desk for the first hour.

Alex closed the door to her small, bare room. 'My initial analysis is that the workforce are a hundred per cent men,' she said.

'Good-looking men?'

'Sixty-six per cent bearded.'

'Are you going to be OK, Alex? Are you going to have enough to do? I know what you're like.'

'Thirty-three per cent with personal odour problems,' said Alex.

'You crack me up. This is going to be good for you, Alex. Change is the law of life.'

'You talk such utter bollocks sometimes, Jill.'

Jill laughed that high, tinkly laugh that would normally bug the hell out of Alex when she was trying to work. Now she missed it. 'They seem nice enough, to be honest. One of them even told me a joke this morning.' Alex could hear the hubbub in the background of Jill's room. People were chattering, swapping jokes and information. Her workplace was silent.

'McAdam is next to me. He sends his regards. Do you want a word?'

'Tell him I'm fine. Thank him for getting me back to work, I suppose.'

'It's OK. You're safe. He's gone now. So. What's the joke?'

Alex pulled open an empty drawer and closed it again. 'How do you kill a data analyst?'

'I don't know. How do you kill a data analyst?'

'You don't have to. They just get broken down by age and sex.'

Jill's laugh was as high and piercing as the last. Alex held her phone a little further from her head.

'They sound like a great bunch,' enthused Jill. 'You should look on this as an opportunity. Maybe it's a perfect fit for you and where you are now.'

Alex didn't answer.

'Buy some new clothes. Get some new trainers instead of those beaten-up ones you always wear. Or wear heels to the office for a change. Shock me.'

'That's your answer to everything, isn't it, Jill?'

'Because it *is* the answer to everything.' She sighed. Her voice lowered. 'Listen. I thought you should know. They've made an arrest in the Younis case.'

Alex sat up. 'Who?'

'Robert Glass. The ex-squaddie. You know what? They found him living not far from the Younises' house. He had a little tent set up in the corner of a field there where no one could see him. Found it after we saw him but he'd scarpered. Left surveillance on it. Turned up back there last night. It took fifteen people to bring him in. He ran and climbed a tree. They had to call fire services to get him down and he put one of our guys in hospital on the way, apparently.'

'Did they find a gun?'

'No. Turns out he's an evangelical Christian, though, if that counts as a smoking gun. He doesn't talk much at all, apparently. They're interviewing him this afternoon.'

Alex was puzzled. 'Do you want to have a coffee or something?'

'Yeah. Course.'

'Later today?'

Jill hesitated. 'I don't know. Up to my bloody eyeballs today with Bob Glass. I'll see what I can do.'

She had a proper job, thought Alex. Her duties were not at all light. Afterwards, Alex, alone in her office, laid her head down on her empty desk and stayed like that for some time as minutes passed, and was still like that when one of the bearded men entered her office. He coughed several times, politely, before she lifted her head.

Tomorrow she was scheduled to attend a meeting in the Deputy Chief Constable's office. The DCC was concerned that the proposed new methodology might lead to violent incidents of domestic abuse being under-reported by officers because of the complexity of the proposed reporting methodology. The non-bearded member of the team had already spelled out the answer in broad terms. 'Yes. The probability is that there would be some under-reporting, but a more robust system might also identify incidents which had been ignored in the past.'

This was going to be her life. She raised her head from the table, stood and went to the next room. 'Coffee, anyone?'

They turned from their screens and looked at her, puzzled, as if no one had ever asked them this question before. When she returned to the office having dished out drinks to her team, she closed the door and opened up Google. She started with the search term 'ex-military ptsd'.

TWENTY-SIX

Violence was a virus. It infected all the stories she found. One ex-Afghanistan soldier had joined G4S security and shot two colleagues dead for no apparent reason. Another ex-army man who had been a victim of a roadside bomb on active service had beaten a friend to death with a scaffolding pole, simply after hearing a loud bang. Afterwards, he told investigators, he had no memory at all of committing the murder. When he was released from jail after nine years he killed another man with a lump hammer. His family said he had been a quiet child before his time in the army. There were ex-servicemen and -women who had left their families, become alcohol and drug dependent, creating havoc around them. The strange make-up of the brain allowed violence to self-replicate. Misery could be passed from parents on to children. Abuse and brutality rippled outwards. She descended into a dark hole, reading these accounts, taking notes in a pad on her desk.

At one point, one of the men knocked on her door, looking apprehensive.

'What?'

'Coffee? You made one for us, so we thought we'd offer to make one for you.'

'I think we've found common ground,' she said. 'Flat white please.'

He smiled nervously back.

At ten to five, Jill cancelled:

Sorry. Stuck in meetings all day. Tomorrow morning? Promise xxxxx

These were meetings she would have been in. The urgency of life in Serious Crime seemed very appealing.

That evening she went for a long bike ride out into the marshes, up Midley Wall to the flat road that ran along White Kemp Sewer. It was almost dark by the time she got back. She knocked on Bill's door to check up on him but Arum Cottage was dark. The curtains were all still open. She carried on home.

When she got out of the shower, she switched on the news. '*It's understood,*' said the young, fair-haired woman on the local news, dropping her perky smile for this item, '*that the accused, Robert Glass, is a former army officer who had been living in the New Romney area for over a year.*'

Zoë looked up from the computer on her lap. When Alex caught her eye, she realised that it was her she was looking at, not the TV screen.

Alex pretended not to look interested. The item changed to a dispute over farm waste that was polluting a local water-course.

★

The next morning the police canteen was quiet. She found Jill alone at a table with a cup of herb tea, looking through a pile of papers. 'Can't stay long,' she said, looking up as Alex put down her coffee cup. 'Got an evidence assessment meeting in fifteen minutes. It's doing my head in.'

'You look tired.'

'Miss you on the team. There's a load of shit to get through, you know?'

'God, yes. Sounds absolutely bloody great.'

Jill laughed, then stopped. 'I know what you want to say. You're sure it's not Bob Glass as well, aren't you? Because frankly, I'm nervous about this.'

'Absolutely sure.'

'I know. I can't see it. It was a murder that was planned to look chaotic, rather than a chaotic murder, you're bang on there. But McAdam is convinced of it right now. He thinks the Ocado order was just a coincidence. He's going to be charging him this afternoon.'

'I think you're walking into something you'll regret.'

'You're best out of it, Alex. It's wrong.'

'So they think he was the man the postman heard arguing with Ayman Younis?'

'He denies it.'

'They ever find the gun?'

'Nope.'

'Or the knife?'

'Maybe. I mean, the man had a whole bunch of knives. His tent was like Freddie Krueger. He was, like, preparing for the End Times or something. They're all being tested for matches now.'

Alex picked up the salt cellar and poured a little onto the table.

'What about the fraud investigation? They any nearer finding out where the money went?'

Jill picked a pinch of the salt and threw it backwards over her shoulder. 'Alex. Leave this alone.'

Alex said, 'Oh, go on.'

'It's going nowhere, Alex. They'll never get that money back. We've pretty much been told that now. It's layers within layers.' She leaned forward and kissed Alex on the forehead. 'I have to run,' said Jill, standing. 'It's bonkers right now.'

Alex scowled. She sat on her own, finishing her coffee, then stood, and was about to return to her office on the other side of the wide car park when she paused, returned to the countertop, and ordered three cups of take-out coffee to take to her team.

That afternoon she came out of the meeting with the DCC with a headache and a sense that she had prepared for completely different questions from the ones she had been asked and a sense that the metrics her project was intended to produce were less about fighting crime than about justifying spending and applying for future funding. She had always done her best to avoid dipping into police bureaucracy, but in this new role she was swimming deep into it.

The meeting had been in the main HQ – that solid 1950s red neo-classical architecture that spoke of an era when the police went about their business unquestioned. It felt strange being in there now. She already felt like an exile. And then, descending the stairs towards the front door, she ran into DI McAdam coming the other way.

He looked up at her and smiled. 'Glad to see you back here, Alex. How's the new job?'

She clutched her folder. 'Dull.'

'Excellent. Exactly what the doctor ordered.'

'And how's it going with the Younis case? How did the interview with Bob Glass go?'

Toby McAdam crossed his arms; as close an expression of disapproval as he ever gave. 'You shouldn't even be asking about this stuff, Alex.'

'Did he actually confess before you charged him?'

He looked a little uncomfortable. 'No.'

They had stopped in one of the busiest places in the building. People continued around them, walking up and down the stairs. 'I didn't think he would. And you have him in the location that night?'

'Of course. Multiple witnesses saw him in the area. And we have him arguing with Ayman Younis on several occasions, and one particular occasion in which threatening words appear to have been used.'

'You have a witness who saw that?'

McAdam hesitated. 'Overheard.'

She turned and walked on down the stairs.

She had made it to the floor below before he finally leaned over the banister and said, 'Why are you asking me this?'

She called up. 'Because he didn't do it. You do know that, don't you? He's mentally ill.'

She was outside onto the path at the front of the building by the time he caught up with her.

'We're aware of his mental health issues.'

'It wasn't the work of a madman.'

'You've been talking to Jill, then?' His face hardened. 'I know she's your friend, but I'm going to have to ask her not to discuss the details of this case with you. It's for your own good, you know, Alex. We all care a great deal about you.'

He stood looking at her for a full thirty seconds. People passed around them, busy with their own work. 'I am aware of Jill's theory, but it doesn't stand up. We've checked the IP address. The email came from the household's own address. It was a coincidence that they ordered so little, that's all. Not everyone is logical all the time. Not every person suffering from delusions is illogical either.'

They stood awkwardly.

'I miss you, Alex. You ask the right questions. But this is not the time. You need to get better first. Leave it to us now. For your own good.'

'Right.'

'Are you looking after yourself? You and Zoë? Perhaps you should come round for dinner some time?'

DI McAdam's wife Colette was a brittle woman who made Alex feel anxious whenever she was around her.

'Yes, that would be lovely,' she said, and turned away before he could start suggesting diary dates.

Work finished earlier than she was used to. On the kitchen table, a note. *Gone to Folkestone. Z. Xxx.*

Without Zoë in the house she could eat meat. She cooked some sausages, looked at them on the plate for a while without touching them, then opened up her laptop and scrolled through emails until she found the one from Georgia Coaker. She clicked on the photograph, peered at it, zooming in until the shapes dissolved into pixels, trying to understand what she was looking at.

After a few minutes, she put the cooked sausages back into the fridge and pulled her car keys out of her bag.

Ten minutes later, Terry Neill was opening his front door in shorts and a blue T-shirt.

'This is a surprise,' he said.

'You said you went to his birthday.'

'What?' He blinked at her, confused, then opened the door wide for her to come in.

TWENTY-SEVEN

'Were there balloons?' she demanded.

'What?'

'When you went to Callum's twenty-first-birthday party at Loftingswood Grange, did Ayman and Mary bring balloons?'

He looked at her with a bemused look. 'You don't know how pleased I am to see you. Would you like a glass of wine? I've already had more than I should.'

He led her through to the back of his house again. 'Shit day?' she asked.

'I'm on my third glass,' he said. 'Alcohol releases dopamine and serotonin. None of that is having the desired effect right now. Would you . . . ?'

'I'll be glad to help you in your research. Just one, though.'

'The thing about alcohol is it's supposed to increase the release of gamma-aminobutyric acid, which is an inhibitor. That's why you drink to blot things out. Alcohol can literally do that. Only it's not really working yet.'

She stopped. 'You heard the latest about Ayman and Mary then?'

'Yes. They've arrested the man who murdered them. There was stuff on the news. It's all a bit raw.' He made an attempt at a smile but it was less than convincing.

'Sorry. I should have been more thoughtful. I didn't mean to butt in.' For once she held her thoughts in her head; now was not the time to suggest to him that they had arrested the wrong man.

'No, no,' he said. 'It's fine. I'm glad of company.' He poured Zinfandel into a mammoth glass. 'What was it you were saying about his birthday?'

'I wanted to know if they brought balloons.'

'Balloons?'

'Yes.'

'That's a weird question. Yes. They did. He blew them up himself. He brought all the gear with them in the boot of his car. A cylinder of gas. They loved that boy a great deal. Was that it?'

'That's all.'

'Why balloons? What's all this about?'

She ignored him and looked out towards the grass that grew between them and the sand. 'I've been thinking a lot about what you told me about vigilance. I thought someone was trying to kill me on Sunday by pushing me off a boat. I'm still not sure if they were, or whether it was just my brain imagining it.'

'Just because you're paranoid doesn't mean they're not out to get you?'

'Sort of. I want to know more about this. I need something rational to hold on to right now. Are there books you can recommend?'

He took a while to answer. 'Can I give you a bit of advice?' he said. 'I'm a scientist, Alex. Like you, I tend to think if I understand the mechanisms behind things, then I am in control. Trauma isn't like that. There's a danger you're using science to push away the unpleasantness of it rather than dealing with the problem itself. Your brain has rewired itself in a way that is harming you. It's one thing to know that, it's another to deal with it. I'm a big believer in counsellors. You should talk to him about this.'

'That's what my daughter says.'

He raised his glass. 'Here's to her. I would like to meet her properly one day. How was her starfish dissection?'

'Utterly gross.'

'Good. What about her father? Where is he?'

Always beware men who ask your marital status, she thought. 'Amicably divorced. He lives in Cornwall.'

'Why doesn't Zoë live with him?'

'I used to think that she stayed with me because she liked me more, or that she didn't like his wife, which wouldn't have surprised me at all. His wife runs a business making handmade herbal beauty products. But now I realise that she stays with me because she thinks she has to look after me.'

He whistled. 'Self-pity?'

'I'm not sure I am capable of it. Maybe she just prefers it here. He's a university lecturer at Falmouth.'

'Poor bastard.'

'Because he has a wife who makes herbal beauty products?'

'Because he's a university lecturer. Universities are doomed. I'm lucky to be out with a pension.'

'You're young. I thought university people stayed in the job until they died. How come you got out?'

He smiled a little sadly again. 'It was not a choice I made. They asked me to retire, if I'm honest.'

'Oh.'

He put down the wine and interlocked his fingers. 'I had a problem with drugs. I don't try and keep it a secret. It became an issue. We worked out a severance package and though I thought I'd be miserable, the change made me happier than you can imagine. I'm clean now, by the way. Alcohol is still a vice, obviously.'

'That's why you're a fan of counsellors?' She heard crickets in the marram grass.

'Everything I knew about the physiology of addiction was just an excuse not to quit. But yes, I had a good counsellor. In fact, one of the things he encouraged me to do was to take some exercise. I took up golf. You should try it.'

'God, no. So you shifted one addiction for another?'

'Exactly so. And Ayman took me under his wing here. He was kind to me when I needed it the most. He helped teach me. And he was genuinely delighted when I started to beat him at the game. And I am obsessed, now, unfortunately, though very healthy.'

Other people's lives were always so various and strange, she thought to herself. 'I have a question. It's about Ayman. Do you mind if I ask? Did you ever hear about Ayman arguing with anyone?'

'No . . . Your colleague asked me that. They say he argued with the homeless man who killed him.'

174

'But you never heard about it. He never talked about it?'

He shook his head. 'No.' Another smile. 'I'm glad you came, actually. I was hoping to invite you round. I'm quite a good cook,' he said.

'I bet you say that to all of the lady golfers.'

'Most of them. Look, I know I'm sounding like a bit of an arse, but cut me a little slack.'

'You're desperate?'

He nodded. 'I suppose I am, really. How would tomorrow be?'

She stood. 'No. I'm sorry. I actually have to be somewhere tomorrow evening.' Tomorrow evening it would be two weeks exactly since the deaths of Ayman and Mary Younis.

'But another day then. Saturday?'

'I don't think so, Terry. I'm not really in the right place for this.'

'What about the weekend after?' he asked.

Irritated at his persistence, she replied, 'I'll promise to think about it. OK?' in a tone that was supposed to imply 'no'.

On the way home she passed Bill's house and noticed there were no lights on again, and she realised, with a start, that she had not talked to Bill at all this week. In fact, she thought, she had not even seen him. They were friends; they might not talk to each other every day, but she was normally conscious of his presence, and yet she had been so wrapped up with disliking her new job that she hadn't reached out to him once.

She stopped the car, got out and banged on the door. There was no answer.

She walked around the back in case he was there, but the

bench was empty, so she peered in through the rear window into the main room. The place was deserted.

She dug out her phone and called Zoë in Folkestone. The first time she didn't answer. The second time she picked up. Alex could hear music in the background.

'Did Bill say he was going away anywhere?'

'Not as far as I know.'

'Think. Are you sure?'

'Quite sure, Mum.'

'Have you seen anything of him?'

'No. Not for a few days in fact.'

'Me neither.' She was suddenly worried. 'Do you think something might have happened to him?'

In the background she heard Stella and Tina's chattering. Some laughter. 'Maybe he's trying to get away from that bird bath,' joked Zoë.

'He liked it.'

'So you say.'

'I'm serious. Do you think something happened to him? I'm worried, Zoë.'

Zoë sounded suddenly concerned too. 'Are you all right, Mum? Do you want me to come home?'

'I'm fine,' she said, making an effort to sound less anxious.

'I mean, I can. If you want. I don't mind.'

'It's OK. It sounds like you're having fun.' She changed the subject. 'I wanted to ask, are you volunteering at the Wildlife Centre tomorrow?'

'I'll wear suntan lotion, Mum, I promise. And a hat.'

'I want you to do me a favour,' Alex said casually.

'What?'

'I want you to tell Kenny Abel to meet me for a drink. Tomorrow at half past nine. At the pub.' As she said it, she opened the lid of Bill South's bin and peered in. It was completely empty.

'What?'

So was the recycling box. But the refuse lorries had only come on Monday so maybe there was nothing out of the ordinary about that.

'Mum? Are you still there?'

She would stop by again in the morning. There would be a simple explanation for his absence, she assured herself.

TWENTY-EIGHT

Each minute ticked past more slowly.

At her desk first thing on Wednesday, Alex left four messages for Bill South; there had been no sign of him when she left for work this morning, either. She called Jill three times and each time it went to voicemail. And the work was not enough to hold her attention. She spent the afternoon distractedly learning how to explore the granularity of the crime data they compiled, looking at it by date and location, trying to see what the men in the room next to hers were seeing in it. She was used to crime as unfolding narrative, not as plain numbers. She was logging off her computer when Jill finally called back, apologising.

'Can you help me do something tonight?'

'What?'

'It's about the Younis killings.'

She heard her friend sigh. 'Whatever it is, no.'

'Please. It's important. I think I've got something major.'

'Even if I didn't have a Bumble date tonight with a very nice-looking man in the Ashford Fire Service, I can't, Alex. McAdam has had a word with us. He knows you're . . . kind of interested in the murders and he's told us all to avoid talking to you about them.'

'He what?'

'I'm sorry, Alex. He says it's for your own good. I mean . . . I can see that, too. Besides, it's operational stuff. I can't share it with you.'

She thought of how she had told off Colin Gilchrist for leaking details of the case; it came as a shock to realise how much on the outside of this she was now. Like Georgia Coaker, she was someone who didn't have the right to know all the facts. 'Right,' she said. 'I get it.'

She wished Jill luck on her date, because despite being young and beautiful and clever, she never seemed to have any, and ended the call.

'Everything all right?' asked one of the beards, popping his head around the door before he left for the day.

'Peachy,' she said.

At half past nine, Kenny Abel was there, standing outside the Romney Hotel looking apprehensive.

'And you want me to look and see . . . you know. If I see souls again?'

Alex checked her watch. 'I'll buy you that drink.'

The bar was surprisingly empty. It was a hot night. Everyone was outside in the beer garden at the back. She ordered an alcohol-free lager because she needed a clear head; he asked for a pint of Bishop's Finger. 'Was that what you were drinking on the night?'

'What is this? A crime scene re-creation?'

'Just it's pretty strong.' She checked the pump clip. 'Five-point-four per cent.'

'I know exactly what I saw.' When the drinks were poured, she led him out to the back of the pub. A summer weekend had started; the working week was over and the beer garden was packed. The air was thick with smoke and the scent of barbecues. Sleepy-looking children sat with Cokes and crisps while their parents chatted and joked. The multiple murder that had shocked everyone a fortnight ago seemed to have been forgotten. Other people reverted to normal so easily, she thought; unlike herself.

There was nowhere to sit, so they stood at the far end of the garden, looking north, towards the Younises' house, obscured by a line of trees.

'Mind if I smoke?'

'That's what you were doing a week ago . . . Go ahead.'

He put his drink down on a nearby table and pulled out a tobacco tin.

'I doubt you know it, but your daughter knows more about the wildlife round here than most people twice her age.'

'It's nothing she gets from me.'

'I don't know,' he said. 'You seem pretty obsessional too.'

A group of young men in brightly coloured rugby shirts, white collars all turned up, laughed abruptly at something. 'Is that what I am?'

'Don't take offence. Nothing would happen in this world if it weren't for people like you and her.'

'Halfway through the dullest week of my life, I suppose that's a nice thing to hear.'

'You'll miss her when she's gone, I expect.'

Alex turned to him. 'What do you mean, gone?'

A blush rose in his face. 'Nothing,' he mumbled.

'She's been talking to you about leaving home, hasn't she?'

'I'm just guessing,' he said, but too hurriedly. 'I mean. She's eighteen in a while. She'll probably want a place of her own.'

She turned her head away. 'Of course,' she said, though the thought of her daughter wanting to leave and live on her own had never entered her head before. 'What has she been saying?'

He shook his head. 'Bits, you know. Just chat.' He pulled out an orange plastic lighter and lit the cigarette. Alex was stung. It was not just that her daughter had wanted to leave home; it was that she would discuss it with this man, rather than with her.

'You've been ill then, I heard,' he said.

Again she turned to him; she could feel his nervousness under her glare. 'She talks about that, then, too? I suppose she said she's worried about me and won't leave until I'm better.'

He fell silent now.

'I'm fine now, as a matter of fact. I'm feeling much better. I'm back at work.'

Kenny nodded. 'Right.'

'She's a sweet girl,' said Alex. 'But sometimes she gets things out of proportion.'

Kenny raised his eyebrows, but said nothing. Alex felt suddenly sad. She had never spent any time thinking what it would be like to live on her own. Of course, she had known that Zoë would leave at some point, just as she had left her own mother and father, but she had never imagined that it might happen so soon. Because she had chosen, against Alex's advice, not to go to university, Alex had imagined they would have been together longer. There was no reason why Zoë shouldn't live on her own. She was capable of it. It smarted too to realise that Zoë would probably be perfectly happy without her.

Alex checked her watch and tried to picture herself living on her own in the house by the nuclear reactor.

'You know Bill South, right?' she asked.

'Sure. Everyone knows Bill.'

'You haven't seen anything of him, have you?'

She watched Kenny frown. 'Actually, no. Not for a few days, now you mention it.'

'I think he's disappeared. He hasn't been in his house for days.'

'He's almost like Zoë's dad, isn't he, Bill? She hangs out with him a lot.'

She nodded.

'Maybe he's off visiting friends or relations?'

He doesn't have any relations, she thought to herself. 'Almost five past. Keep looking.'

Kenny lifted his pint to his lips and drank; then drew on his cigarette. 'I don't know what precisely you're expecting me to see,' he said.

'Was this what it was like two Wednesdays ago?'

'Warmer tonight maybe. Few more people out here.'

'What about the sunset?'

He looked around the sky. To the north, where they were gazing, the azure deepened to dark blue. Stars were appearing low on the horizon. Above the Younises' house, a dim cluster of stars were brightening, shaped in a flat W. 'Pretty much the same.'

She checked her watch again, then tilted her head up again. 'Keep looking,' she said.

The minutes ticked by.

Beside her, Kenny gasped. Raised his arm and pointed. 'There,' he said.

A streak of light floating upwards at speed, only visible for seconds, and then it was lost in the growing darkness. An unearthly silver streak, rising rapidly against dark sky.

'That's what you saw?'

He had spilled what was left of his pint on the grass at his feet. He looked at her, bug-eyed.

TWENTY-NINE

'Finish your pint,' said Alex. 'I need to show you something.'

Glass in one hand, cigarette in the other, Kenny was still having trouble understanding what he had just seen. He gulped the last of the brown liquid down and put the glass onto a crowded picnic table, then stared once more out towards the north horizon where the streak of light had been. Nobody else in the pub garden seemed to have noticed anything.

'Was that just the same as before?'

He nodded.

Kenny was a little like her daughter. Like Zoë, Kenny had trained himself to notice the world around him; naturalists were like that. Like good police officers, they trained themselves to spot unseen patterns, to be always alert to anomalies.

'Come with me,' Alex said again.

He snapped out of it and followed her. 'Where are we going?'

'To the Younises' house.'

'Why?' He sounded afraid.

'I want to show you something.'

Headlights on in the darkening evening, they drove the short distance down the lane.

She tucked her car by the gate and untied the piece of cord that had been there. Zoë was sitting on the steps in the gloom. 'Did I do it right?' she asked.

'Perfectly.' She leaned forward and kissed her daughter's forehead.

'I wasn't sure I should do it at all,' said Zoë, looking at Kenny as if she expected him to be angry with her.

Kenny said, 'No. Whatever it is . . . it's cool.'

'There may have been souls rising up from here last week, but that's not what you saw.' Alex pointed at the open garage door and the cylinder of helium that she had seen in Georgia Coaker's photograph. 'I found a pack of four silver weather balloons in there. Two had already been used. Ayman Younis probably used one as a test and a second on the night. That's what you saw.'

'A weather balloon?'

She had inflated the third balloon, tied it to the Younises' front gate, and asked Zoë to cut the cord at exactly seven minutes past ten. 'They're large and silver. At this time of night I figured you'd probably just get a glimpse of the shine of it as it was shooting up.'

Poor Kenny seemed lost. 'Someone was getting killed here and Ayman Younis was letting off balloons? That's the craziest thing I've ever heard. Are you going to explain it to me?'

'No. Sorry. Not really.'

'It was Ayman Younis who released the balloon? Before he was killed?'

'Kind of,' said Alex. 'Look, Kenny. I'd really appreciate it if you didn't talk about what you'd seen, about coming here, to anybody at all.'

'Not even your daughter?' He looked at Zoë.

'Jesus, no. Especially not my daughter.'

Zoë said, 'I didn't do it to make you feel like an idiot, Kenny. She asked me to, just at the last minute.'

'Course you didn't.'

'I didn't want to do it at all.'

'It's OK. It was like an experiment, wasn't it?'

'Do you still believe in souls?' she asked. ''Cause I do.'

Kenny smiled. 'Course I do. I was wrong this time though, that's all.'

Zoë looked relieved.

After she'd dropped Kenny at his house, they drove back to Dungeness in the dark.

Zoë remained a dark bundle of silent anger in the passenger seat next to her.

'I'm sorry,' said Alex. 'We had to do it, though. I would have asked Bill, but he's not here. I asked Jill but she's . . . busy.'

'Why? Because you wanted to prove a point?'

'No. Because there's a man being held on a charge of murder who shouldn't be. He's ill, a bit like me, I think. Only, what he has is much worse. I think he must be very confused and scared. I am pretty sure that it can't have been him. So thank you for helping,' she said. 'I'm sorry I had to, but there was no one else I could ask.'

The headlights swept up the track towards Arum Cottage; it was still dark. Neither made mention of it.

Neither was ready to sleep. After visiting the Younises' house, they both felt jumpy and strange.

In the kitchen, Zoë was making herself a cup of mint tea. 'I had to sit in the dark next to that creepy house where two people were murdered.'

'I'm sorry.'

'You have to tell me why you made me let off the balloon. It's not fair if you don't.'

Alex nodded. The kettle clicked. 'Is it true you're thinking of leaving home?'

Zoë's jaw dropped. 'Did Kenny tell you that? He had no right,' she said angrily.

Alex put her hand on her daughter's. 'He kind of let it slip by accident. It's not really his fault. Is it true?'

'Maybe.' She sniffed. 'I don't know. I just thought I could live in a caravan somewhere. There are loads for rent. I asked him if he knew anyone with one, that's all. He wasn't supposed to say anything at all.' She poured the hot water and stood for a while, dipping the tea bag in and out of the cup.

'I think it's a great idea,' said Alex.

Zoë kept her eyes fixed on her cup. 'Maybe in a little while. When . . . you know. It's a bit easier.'

Alex nodded.

'So? The balloon?'

Alex sighed.'Do you want to hear this, Zoë? It's pretty gruesome.'

'It always is, Mum.'

'You're seventeen.'

'You seen the stuff we can actually see on YouTube?' She picked up her cup and cradled it in both hands.

They went to sit on the living-room sofa together, side by side, and as she talked, her daughter leaned in close, laying her head against her shoulder, and it felt like the first time they had been like that for months, together and close; and it made Alex sad to think that she might soon be gone.

On Thursday she called DI McAdam at his desk, but there was no answer. When she tried Jill's number, Jill said he had gone to a conference in Maidstone and wouldn't be in until tomorrow. 'I can prove that Robert Glass is innocent,' she said.

'I'm not supposed to talk to you about this,' said Jill miserably. 'I told you. He gave me orders.'

'Who else can I speak to?'

Jill lowered her voice. 'Like I said, he's told everybody they shouldn't discuss it with you. Only because he's worried about you. You know that, don't you?'

Alex returned home after work, still angry. Even Zoë noticed. 'What's wrong, Mum?'

'You don't mind if I go out tonight, do you?'

Zoë shrugged.

It was a new detached house in a perfectly maintained garden with close-cut grass and neat borders. There were two cars on the driveway, his and hers, so she parked hers on the narrow verge and walked up to the large blue door surrounded by yellow roses. A security light blinked on as she approached.

She had only just rung the bell when DI Toby McAdam answered, yanking the door back with a loud 'Ta-da!'

He was wearing a red sequinned dress that stopped mid-thigh.

THIRTY

DI Toby McAdam's grin vanished. 'Oh. I wasn't expecting . . .'

'Clearly not,' said Alex. He was wearing eyeshadow too; it made him look unexpectedly good. She tilted her head to one side. 'Sorry. Am I interrupting something?'

'Toby?' A voice from inside the house.

'No. Wait,' said Toby, beneath the arch of yellow roses. 'I'd better explain . . .'

'Are they here?' Inside the house, Colette McAdam, Toby's wife, was calling to him. 'I need to pin the back properly first.'

'I need to talk.'

'It's for a play,' her senior officer explained. '*What the Butler Saw*. The local am-dram. We're doing a costume-fitting.'

Colette appeared around the door. 'Oh.' She looked Alex up and down. 'It's you.' She gave a tight, small smile. 'Work, is it?'

'Kind of.'

Colette sighed. 'Could you be a dear and come back later? The director was going to come here to check on Toby's costume?

Oh. Here he is now.' A man with an exuberance of grey hair and a paisley shirt had arrived on foot with a paper folder under his arm. Colette paused, looking from her husband to Alex, and back again. 'I suppose you'd better all come in then,' Colette said. 'You can wait until they're done.'

The McAdams lived on the edge of one of those downland villages that were now full of couples, one of whom usually working in London, the other raising the kids. They were hamlets full of community spirit.

'There was a part for a policeman who wears a dress. I thought it would be hilarious if Toby did it,' Colette explained, unsmiling. 'After all, he never does anything else, apart from work.'

Alex waited in the kitchen while the amateur-dramatics director and the costume maker worked on Toby's dress. She heard occasional gales of laughter. The fitting seemed to take an age and then the director stayed for a glass of Picpoul. In his boomy voice he announced he thought it absolutely hilarious that his actor had opened the door to a police officer, dressed in his wife's party dress. 'I'm sorry. I expect you're here on important business.'

'At nine o'clock in the evening,' said Colette McAdam.

'Priceless,' the director declared, when he finally left. 'Absolutely priceless. You will come and see the show, won't you?'

'I'm just going upstairs to put some clothes on,' Toby called as the man left.

Alex was finally allowed into the living room. 'Toby says you've been ill,' Colette said. 'He said you've had some mental health issues.'

'Did he?'

191

'He's been very worried about you, actually.' Colette McAdam was a tight-wound woman, who sent her husband to work each day with neatly made packs of sandwiches. 'Are you on the mend?' she asked.

'Yes.' Alex smiled brightly, her jaw clenching. 'Much better.'

'Really?' Colette smiled.

Toby McAdam bounded down the stairs. He had quickly changed into sweatpants and a T-shirt; almost as if he had been reluctant to leave the two women alone together for too long. 'I suppose you'll tell everyone at work that you saw me wearing a dress?'

'Of course.'

'Oh God. How much do I have to pay you?'

She knew, though, that Toby McAdam would be disappointed if she didn't. Police officers loved to tell stories about each other and if nobody told stories about you, you barely existed in the force. 'To be fair,' she said, 'I've seen worse-looking people in dresses like that.'

'So? What are you here for?'

'I think I have just worked out who killed Ayman Younis and his wife. And it's not Bob Glass.'

He exhaled; walked to the living-room door and closed it so no one could overhear. 'I don't think it's appropriate to discuss this with you, Alex. You do understand why, don't you?'

'You think you're trying to help me, don't you?'

He frowned. 'Of course.'

'If you don't listen to me now you are going to end up in the shit. You have an innocent man in custody. Five minutes. Please.'

He looked at her, moving his head slightly to one side, as if trying to judge if she was crazy or not, then said, 'OK. We'd better sit down then.'

He took her to his study, a room at the front of the house, and he sat and listened, while she told him about the balloon and the flash of silver light that Kenny Abel had seen, which he thought had been carrying souls up to heaven.

'What's this about? I don't get it, Alex.'

'You never found the gun that Bob Glass is supposed to have killed Ayman Younis with, did you?'

He looked irritated by the question. 'He had plenty of time to dispose of it.'

She looked at the silver-framed photos on his desk of Colette and the boy and the girl whose name she could not remember. 'He didn't dispose of it. Ayman Younis did.'

'But . . .' Some time in the last year he had developed crow's feet at the side of his eyes. You could only see them when he smiled or frowned.

'Did he have life insurance?'

'Yes.'

'Then it wasn't a murder. It was a murder suicide. Ayman Younis had money saved up to look after his son, Callum. I'm guessing that the money he lost in the Biosfera scam was pretty much everything he had in that pot. Maybe he wanted to increase it. Maybe he was just being greedy. But either way, he lost it all, and with it the prospect that his child would be cared for privately.'

McAdam said nothing, just narrowed his eyes a little more.

'And because of that, maybe he was too ashamed to admit it

to his wife. He wanted a perfect life, and while it may not have been perfect, what they had was being taken away from them. From what I gather they were a couple who kept up appearances. Ayman did, that's for sure. I think he gambled that and lost, and rather than face up to the humiliation, he tore it all down instead. Some men are like that. I don't know. But I do know that he had life insurance. If he just killed himself, Callum wouldn't get anything at all. But if he made it look like murder, Callum would have enough money to last him a lifetime.

'So,' she continued, 'he killed Mary by cutting her throat. He put the body downstairs so the delivery woman would find her the next morning. Made it look like the work of a madman. Then he went outside and shot himself with a gun tied to a weather balloon. There was a north-west wind that day. I checked. Nobody found the gun because it's probably somewhere at the bottom of the Channel. I presume the knife was on there too. He ordered a pack of four balloons. There were two left. One would have been a test run, to see how much a balloon would carry. The second was outside, holding the gun to his head.'

Cradled against her last night, Zoë had been silent as she had explained this. Alex had known why; her teenage daughter would have been imagining the dead hand slipping off the trigger, the silver ball full of helium rising upwards with the deadly metal cargo beneath it, thinking about the knife and the gun floating away on the night air, falling somewhere indeterminate, far away from here.

'And that's what this man saw? The balloon?' said McAdam incredulously.

'That's why there are no fingerprints of anyone else at the

house,' she said. 'Because there never was anyone else there anyway.'

She recognised the look of apprehension on his face as she talked. He had locked up an innocent man who was mentally ill on a charge of murder. There would be repercussions for him.

'It gets worse,' said Alex.

McAdam's face tightened.

'I don't know for sure, I'm guessing now, but I think this is what happened. Ayman Younis was so ashamed of losing the money they had saved for their son that he killed his own wife rather than tell her. Her pacemaker said she died at four minutes past ten, right? To the exact minute. He shot himself at about seven minutes past ten, because that's when the balloon went up. We know he cut her throat on the bed upstairs. He probably thought he had killed her then. He thought she was dead when he arranged her body at the bottom of the stairs to make it look like the work of a madman. And he killed both of their dogs too. He wrote the message on the mirror and then cleaned the place up. Three minutes was not enough time for him to do all that.'

He had his hand in front of his mouth now.

'How long would that have taken? Twenty, thirty minutes? Longer?'

'And you're saying she was alive all that time?'

'Yes. She died where you found her at the bottom of the stairs. Everybody talks about what a nice man Ayman Younis was. How much he cared for his son. He may have thought he had killed her, but she was not dead. Her own husband. You have to hope that she wasn't conscious.'

★

195

When she got back home afterwards she was utterly exhausted. Zoë had gone out somewhere. Normally Alex would have wandered up the road and talked to Bill about what had happened; that helped sometimes. Instead, she lay on the couch alone, numb. Bob Glass would be released soon, at least.

Moths had gathered on the window, drawn by the light. More arrived, banging against it. The air seemed full of them.

'But you know what you've just done, don't you?' her daughter had said when she'd told her the story.

'Hopefully, I've found a way to get an innocent man out of custody.'

'Yes. And now the insurance aren't going to pay for Callum Younis's care any more because you've proved it wasn't a murder. Finding this out means he won't get any money, just like with Bill.'

The moths seemed to multiply on the window. Those that didn't settle knocked against the glass, over and over, the sound of a gloved knuckle gently tapping. There seemed to be hundreds of them there. Alex shivered.

THIRTY-ONE

The weekend came and went, with still no sign of Bill. Alex waited for news about the Younis case but heard nothing.

On Monday, for the first time, on Jill's advice, she tried heels, to mark her first week back at work. Low ones.

'Really, Mum?' said Zoë.

'I'm just trying them. You're the one who wants me to change, after all.'

'They just look wrong on you, that's all. I prefer your dykey look.'

'My what?'

'Seriously, Mum. I'm glad you're doing this. Even if you're dressing funny.'

Alex leaned forward for a kiss. Zoë jerked her head backwards, laughing.

At work there was coffee, at least. The one without the beard had brought in his own beans and made the coffee on an AeroPress.

Alex smelt it, took a sip and looked up. 'This is actually amazing,' she said.

'I roast them in a popcorn popper,' he said shyly.

She looked at him. 'Married or single?' she asked.

He blushed.

'I'm kidding,' she said. 'Anyway, I'm half lesbian, according to my daughter. It's just I don't want to accept that I actually like you guys,' she said. 'I might get stuck here.'

The man retreated, backing out of the door.

'Wait,' she said, calling him back. 'That data you are putting together on domestic violence. Is it anonymised?'

'Of course.'

'Before you get hold of it?'

'Yes. Why?'

'I want to look at historical clusters of domestic abuse.'

'Fine.'

'Particularly in Folkestone.'

He hesitated. 'Folkestone?'

'Yes. Between say, seven and nine years ago. Can we do that?'

A look of concern crossed his face. 'That's a very specific data set. You might not be able to learn much from such a small sample.'

She took another sip from her cup and smiled. 'That's a risk I'm willing to take. Will it take long?'

He blinked. He thinks I don't understand anything he does here, she thought.

'About the same time as it takes to make a cup of coffee.'

Five minutes later an email pinged in: *Is this what you need?*

She opened the link. There was a graph and a click-through to a map, created from the data she had requested. She zoomed in on it until it showed a small selection of streets in the north side of the town. A slider at the bottom allowed her to move through the dates, starting with the oldest. As she moved through the dates, a large blue blob appeared on the screen, first in early 2010, then it faded. It was back in the following summer and again that autumn. A blue blob indicating a roughly anonymised area of town that included the street that Tina Hogben had lived in with her husband Frank. She zoomed in closer. The blob hung over the bottom end of Broadmead Road.

She called through the door. 'Can you help me with this?'

His head appeared around the door and edged around to her side of the desk. She ran through the dates over again. 'What would explain that kind of pattern?'

The man peered at the screen. 'I would assume that to be a single household, with multiple call-outs over that period.'

As she slid through the dates, she watched the blob bloom from some time in 2011 and disappear around a month before Frank Hogben disappeared.

'Call-outs from that address?'

'Yes.' He hesitated, then changed his mind. 'Not necessarily from the address. Just as likely the neighbours calling it in. You can't tell from that data which address it is, but it's very localised. So whether it's someone calling from that address or people calling in a problem about that address . . .'

'People who hear stuff and make the call?'

'Yes . . . Is that all?'

When he'd closed the door, she thought for a while, then took out her phone and texted Zoë.

Do you have Stella's number?

At lunch she arranged to meet Jill on the recreation ground at the back of the HQ; on hot summer days, they weren't the only people who took their lunch out here. Jill was sitting under the shade of a horse chestnut. She had several plastic pots around her containing brownish dips, and vegetables carefully cut into fingers. Alex had bought an egg sandwich from the canteen and wolfed it down faster than she should have.

'Look at you,' said Jill, looking approvingly at her shoes.

'Bog off.'

Jill grinned. 'And what about Bob Glass? We were right all along. They released him. Apparently we're looking at a possible murder suicide. Did you hear?'

Alex said nothing.

'Which is totally weird, isn't it? If they'd actually listened to what we were saying . . . DI McAdam says he thinks it was all so the Younises could get insurance for their son on account of Ayman losing all that money.'

'Really?'

'You should do something about your hair too.'

'Will you leave it alone?' said Alex, but she didn't mean it. Maybe she should look after herself a little better, she thought.

'We are in such shit. Did you see the papers this morning? They mentioned DI McAdam by name as the one who'd cocked it up.'

Alex lay on the warm grass, feeling like a woman with

superpowers again. The Younis murder was a big lie. She had figured it out, all by herself. Sometimes she felt strong enough to handle anything.

That afternoon she left work two hours early. 'I have to see my counsellor,' she said.

The men nodded. They knew why she was on light duties. Nobody seemed to mind. She drove south towards the coast. At Folkestone, instead of going south to The Leas, where her counsellor's office was, she turned east. This part of the coast made her glad to live at Dungeness. So much of the Kent coast was occupied by lines of dull bungalows facing the sea.

The road rose up above the town. The Battle of Britain war memorial had been built on a stretch of green that lay between the row of houses and the escarpment that looked out over the Channel. She had moved to Kent two years ago but had never once visited here. She wasn't sure why; she approved of remembering the dead, after all.

On a weekday, the car park was almost empty. She left her car at the far side of it, tucked close to the hedge in the hope that it would shade the Yaris, and walked down the slope towards the main memorial. The summer grass was parched brown. Gulls swooped over the slopes towards a sea that was bluer here than she ever saw it on the spit where she lived.

Carved out of Portland Stone, a lone airman sat facing the Channel, as if waiting for the signal to scramble. He wore a thick flying jacket; he would feel hot on a day like this, thought Alex. Far behind him, carved into black marble, were lists of names. She looked around, checked her watch. She was early.

THIRTY-TWO

London was a place with open arms; this was a place that was used to defending itself. The monument was surrounded by ramparts; a green circular bank of earth that reminded her of the circle around her house. A small notice confirmed that this site, too, had been a wartime gun battery.

Her father had been an Irishman with little interest or respect for English martial pride, but she found it moving, thinking of the names of hundreds of men, little older than Zoë, behind her who had died fighting for this place. She thought of the plane wrecks below the sea; the metal that Danny's nets dodged.

She checked her watch, looked around. An elderly man was walking down the path towards her. She stepped away from the memorial to let him have his time alone.

Just as she was about to give up and go home, she saw a familiar, tall woman striding towards her, smiling. Stella was wearing red shorts and a big white T-shirt with the word *Arizona* on it. When she was close enough, she stopped and called her over. 'I usually sit over here. I brought coffee.' Two benches had been erected facing the black wall of marble. Stella sat on one of them and waited for Alex to join her.

'Come here often?'

'That's my great-grandad,' she said, pointing to the wall. 'Flying Officer James Godden. He was twenty-two. Since they built it, my mum comes up here all the time. Ironic, really, because I used to come up here all the time when I was, like, nineteen, twenty, before they built it. It was a good place to get wasted.'

Alex looked at the memorial; the lists of names picked out in gold. 'Did you tell Tina you were coming here?'

'No. But I don't like keeping secrets from Tina. What is it you want to say?'

'You told me you knew her when she was still with Frank.'

She nodded. 'Course I did. Yeah.'

'And you talked about how Frank disappeared.'

'Yeah?' she said blithely, as if it were nothing to her. 'Coffee?' Stella took a metal thermos from her backpack and laid two stainless steel mugs beside her.

Alex waited until she was pouring the first cup before asking, 'Now tell me about how Frank treated Tina.'

A dribble spilled down the side of the cup onto the ground, just a small, tell-tale shake of her hands. Coolly, Stella completed filling the cup and passed it to her. 'Who said?'

Alex shrugged. 'Does that matter? It's true, isn't it?'

She had thought about the look on Tina's face the day the taxi driver shouted at her and she realised she had recognised something in it; she had remembered what Terry Neill had said about the amygdala being like an alarm bell and about how some traumatised people just freeze up when that bell starts sounding.

'No,' said Stella flatly. 'Course it's not.'

Alex had seen the blue circle on the map; the pulse of reports of domestic abuse incidents. 'She was living with an abusive man, wasn't she? Someone who probably didn't like the idea that his wife was having an affair with another woman.'

Stella poured a cup for herself and said, 'I don't know what you're digging at here, but Frank never knew nothing about Tina and me. We were absolutely one hundred per cent sure on that. She didn't want to hurt him. She didn't want to hurt anybody; she never has. She was discreet. And so, believe it or not, was I, though the effort almost bloody killed me.'

'It would give someone a motive for killing Frank, though, wouldn't it?'

Stella looked up at the wall of men's names and said, 'Oh Jesus. You're nuts.'

'People tell me that all the time.'

'Is that why you wanted to talk?'

'I wanted to find out what you thought.'

'No. I'll tell you what I really think. Listen to this, right?'

'OK.'

She looked Alex right in the eye. 'I came out when I was just fifteen. My family was all straight, you know? They were Seventh Day Adventists and all that shit. I thought I was a complete freak. I was some total weirdo, you know? They didn't like me. I didn't like me either. So I hung out with everyone else who was different . . . I used to hang out with all the drinkers and druggies. Classic behaviour, you know?'

She stood and pointed over the cliff behind them. 'Down there, in the Warren. We used to come up here too, before all this was built. Cider. Drugs. Anything we could lay our hands on. Glue. Heroin. Pills. I got chucked out of school, used to rough-sleep in empty houses. My parents tried to look after me, but I hated them so much back then. Stupid, really. They weren't that bad. Half the people I called friends were much worse than my mum and dad ever were. Before I knew it, I was in my late twenties, going absolutely fucking nowhere. People used to cross the street to avoid me, you know? Anyway.'

She stopped, opened a tin and pulled out a pre-rolled cigarette, then lit it. 'So. One day in summer I was coming down from something, I don't remember what, and I'd been on whatever it was a couple of days and I realised I was starving. Literally starving. Probably filthy, too, but I knew I had to get something to eat, so on my way back into town from somewhere round here, I stopped into the fish bar down on The Stade and Tina was there behind the counter, and I must have looked like shit on a stick. I said, "Sorry. Got no money but I could kill for some of your chips." And she gave me this look. And it was . . . Fucking hell. What a smile! I was expecting pity. It was like a really sexy little smile. And I looked like hell and was probably stinking but it was . . . wow, you know? She was a married woman as far as I knew . . . and one of the Hogbens, and if you grew up where I did, you never messed with the Hogbens. But that's the kind of smile a woman gives another woman . . .'

She grinned, looked back down at Alex. 'Has anyone ever given you a smile like that? You know . . . I bet they probably have. Anyway. I cleaned up basically because I wanted her after that. I knew there was absolutely no way she'd let me near her looking the way I did.' She turned and dropped back down onto the bench, head turned towards Alex. 'So what I'm saying is, she saved me. Totally saved me. Tina is the kind of person who saves people. Even a wretch like me. And in return, I kind of saved her.'

'Nice,' said Alex.

'Isn't it? Smoke still. Drink too much, but you can't have it all.'

Stella finished her cigarette, stubbing it out in the lid of her tin and carefully putting the remains into her jacket pocket.

'You didn't tell me about Frank assaulting Tina.'

'No,' Stella said. 'I bloody didn't. Because, like I said. You're barking up the wrong bloody whatsit.' She picked up her flask and put it in the backpack, slung it onto her back and said, 'I'll tell Tina you said hi, shall I?'

Halfway down the slope, she climbed up the steps in front of the memorial statue of the waiting airman, leaned forward and kissed him on the lips. Then she walked off down the sloping grass, the way she had come, without looking back.

Alex had to get to her appointment. She was not supposed to be here.

She walked back to her Yaris, alone at the far side of the car park. Her pace quickened as she saw something white under the wiper. A parking ticket was her first thought. In her hurry to get to the monument she had forgotten to check whether there were any parking restrictions; now she looked around and saw a pay-station by the main building.

The closer she got, though, the more she realised it was nothing of the sort. It was a plain piece of paper torn out from a notebook, folded over, and tucked under the arm of the wiper.

Before picking it out, she looked around. On first view, the car park was deserted.

She lifted it out.

In big biro capitals: *PLEASE LEAVE ME ALONE. STOP ASKING ABOUT ME. YOU WILL MESS UP EVERYTHING.*

Underneath that, the name: *FRANCIS HOGBEN.*

She read it twice, just to make sure. Again, she looked around. On the north side, facing the road, the car park was surrounded by a thick old hedge, mostly hawthorn. Through the hedge beyond the bonnet of her car, she could see a silhouette. There was someone on the other side, watching her.

'You,' she called.

The figure didn't move.

'Wait. I'm coming round. Don't go.'

With a crackling of branches, the figure disentangled limbs from the hedge and set off running.

Alex set off sprinting towards the exit, twenty metres away. Stupid office bloody heels.

THIRTY-THREE

She made it to the gap in the hedge but it was too late. She had already heard the car door slam and the engine start. All she saw was a red car roaring away loudly down the hill at speed, round the curve of the road out of sight.

Sure that whoever had been peering through the hedge at her had been the same person who had placed the note on her windscreen, the same one she had seen driving away, she turned and ran as fast as she could back to the Yaris, turned the ignition and reversed away from the hedge, skidding on the tarmac.

They would have a head start, but a bright red car was easy to spot.

At the exit, the road was clear. She pressed hard on the accelerator but the car stalled. Her first thought was that she should have had it serviced. She restarted.

The car spluttered, coughed and stalled a second time.

Third time it wouldn't even start. The starter motor just ground away to itself. Again she turned off, turned on again, pumping the accelerator.

'Shit.'

Behind her, a car honked.

Angrily she waved it past her and laid her head on the steering wheel.

Getting out, she looked around for any CCTV cameras, but saw nothing, so there would be no record of who had left the note. Checking her watch, she saw she needed to be at her counsellor's in five minutes. She would have to apologise for being late.

In the end, she pushed the car to a corner, sweating like a fool. She left another note on the windscreen saying *Broken down*.

The only person she could think of who could help right now was Curly. She called him. 'I thought you weren't speaking to me,' he said.

'I'm not. Except I'm in need of a favour.'

'What was the make of Max Hogben's car again?'

'What are you on about, Alex?'

'Remind me.'

'Ford Escort RS 1600-i. Kind of like an early boy racer classic.' She didn't know what an RS 1600-i looked like but she guessed it was probably quite like what she had just seen disappearing down the New Dover Road.

'Red, right?'

'Very.'

She left the keys on the front tyre. The Uber was late picking her up and by the time she got to the counsellor's office, down on The Leas, she was half an hour behind schedule.

— Don't worry. It's your time.

— I don't feel great, to be honest. You want to know why I'm late? I'm late because I met a ghost.

— Ah. So we're back to that, are we, Alexandra?

The session was exhausting. He had asked her, yet again, about the days that people had died; all the things she had witnessed and done. The stories came out exactly the same. Nothing changed. The endings were just as bad as they had been before.

Her Yaris was outside the back of the house when another taxi finally dropped her home after the session. Curly's pickup was there, too. After her time on the trawler, she was not sure she could cope with Curly.

Here he was now, inside, sitting at the kitchen table, eating a giant bowl of brown vegan bean stew that Zoë had made. The hand he held his spoon with was still covered in smudges of oil, black in the cracks of his skin.

'Somebody don't like you,' he said, mouth full.

'Just the one?' said Zoë.

Alex was not sure what she felt about Curly being in her house right now, but Zoë must have invited him in when he had arrived towing her dead car. 'What do you mean?'

Curly wiped his mouth with the back of his hand. 'Someone gone and put a gallon of water into your petrol tank. That's why you broke down.'

'Deliberately?'

'Well, I don't know how else it would have got in there.'

Alex frowned. 'When? Could they have put it in a few days ago?'

Curly pushed his spoon slowly around the bowl. 'Nah. Water's heavier than petrol. Goes straight to the fuel line. You'd have noticed it pretty quick.'

'So someone would have done it in the car park where I left my car?'

'Most likely.'

'I've got a question for you . . . You told me that Frank was on *The Hopeful* when he fell off the back.'

Curly scowled. 'Not this again.'

'Mum,' wailed Zoë. 'I thought you were done with all that.'

'Listen to your daughter, Alex.' Curly tipped the bowl and scooped up the last mouthful of stew. He took a glass of water and drained it, then stood up.

'Could he have survived? You a hundred per cent sure he's dead?'

Curly just looked at her evenly and said, 'You'll want a new engine. Better still a new car. A total fresh start. That one is pretty much only good for scrap now. Want me to tow it?'

'Jesus. We have no car?'

'Nope.'

'We don't need a car, Mum.'

Alex looked at her daughter like she was mad. 'We live out here on the edge of the world. How am I supposed to get to work every day?'

Zoë shrugged. 'We're all going to have to give up cars soon anyway.'

'How much do I owe you?'

Curly shook his head. 'You're OK, Alex. You're a friend.'

'Nope,' she said. 'Definitely not.' Alex picked up her bag and started digging around trying to find her wallet. She pulled out ten-pound notes and started counting them out.

'No need for that, Alex,' said Curly. 'Honest to God. We look after each other, round here.'

'I'm still a police officer, Curly. In case you hadn't noticed.'

Curly looked a little hurt but didn't stop her adding cash. When the pile reached £70 he said, 'That'll do it,' folded the notes in two and put them into the back pocket of his oily jeans.

When he'd gone, and Zoë had disappeared upstairs, she made herself a coffee, though the counsellor had suggested she avoid them – especially in the evenings.

Zoë had left the cooker in a mess. The dirt had burned on. It was going to take an age to clean that.

In the morning, she had felt superhuman. Now she took her coffee to the living room and sat down alone, drained and miserable. The room was stuffy and hot. She noticed dust on the picture frames. In her bag was a note from a man who had been dead for seven years. Bill South was still missing, and maybe he had gone for ever. Jill was working so hard, she barely saw her any more. A man had killed his wife in horrible circumstances, and then murdered himself, because he had been cheated. An awfully traumatised man had been arrested, charged with a murder he had not committed. Though he had now been released, there would only have been the usual apology and nothing more. He would be back out there on his own.

After a minute, she stood again, closed the curtains. The bright sunshine outside was too much; there was something malevolent about its brightness. The light seemed to press on her chest, like a weight. She sat back down on the couch and closed her eyes.

Now they were closed, she was suddenly sure that if she opened them, she would find blood all around her, soaking into the fibres of the carpet, though in her rational mind she knew there was nothing there at all. And now there was a smell of earth in the room.

'Mum?' Zoë's voice was suddenly loud right next to her. 'Are you OK?'

'I don't think I am,' she said, eyes still shut. 'I think I'm having what's called a panic attack.'

THIRTY-FOUR

There was a large bouquet of flowers lying on the kitchen work surface. Zoë must have been at home when they had been delivered, but she had not thought to put them in water because she didn't really approve of cut flowers.

There was a note: *Sorry to hear you're not well. Get well soon.* It was signed, *2 Men with beards, one without.*

Zoë had called a doctor, and had also called Jill; Jill had called DI McAdam. On Tuesday McAdam had signed her off light duties for another week. If she wasn't mad already, she would be soon.

The week dragged. Instead of going to the Visitor Centre to do volunteer work, Zoë hung around the house, offering cups of herb tea at regular intervals.

'You don't have to watch me,' said Alex. 'I'm not going to do anything stupid.'

'I know that.'

'I hate being looked after,' she said.

'Obviously I have figured that out, too.'

On the Wednesday, after she'd divided the bouquet into two bunches, Alex put one on the living-room mantelpiece, and wrapped the second in polythene.

'Where are you going with them?' Zoë asked, when she was halfway out of the door.

Alex knocked on the door of Bill's house, and when no one answered, she let herself in with the spare key. The house was tidy, as it always was. He was a neat man. The bed was made and unslept in. She checked the fridge for anything that might have gone off, but it was empty. Arranging the flowers in a glass jug, she put them on the table by the back window and sat on one of the chairs for a while, looking out at the view, where she knew he often sat.

'We could go for a bike ride together or something?' Zoë suggested.

That afternoon they rode together out through the marshes and had hummus sandwiches in a field on the banks of Puddledock Sewer, by St Thomas à Becket Church. Alex pointed to a red car that had pulled up on the narrow road, a couple of hundred metres away. 'Do you recognise that car?'

'Why? Should I?'

'I thought I'd seen it before somewhere.'

The driver seemed to be looking out of the window towards them, but when Alex stood, the driver moved on, driving slowly at first, but then, passing the farmhouse where the church key was kept, it roared loudly up the road.

'What, Mum?'

Alex sat down again.

The August days seemed too long and shapeless. Jill called every day, but Alex could tell she was distracted, weighed down by work that was too involved and complex to explain to someone who wasn't part of it any more. The local free newspaper had a headline on page 5: *Concerns Over Mentally Ill Ex-Soldier*. Residents in Littlestone had complained about the homeless man who had been spotted living rough in the area. Before the arrest he had been anonymous. People knew who Bob Glass was now. He was an ex-murder suspect.

On Thursday Alex began trawling the internet, looking for another car to replace her Yaris. 'I'm feeling much better, honestly, love,' she told her daughter.

'Is it OK if I go out? I'll only be a couple of hours?'

'Of course.' Alex kissed her. 'Where you going?'

Zoë hesitated a second before she said, 'Nowhere special.' Alex watched her cycling away, tatty backpack on her shoulders. As she watched, the red Post Office van approached in the opposite direction. It parked at the end of the row of houses. Alex emerged from her front door in time to see a woman in a pale-blue top and shorts walking towards her carrying a single large brown envelope. 'Saves me trying to push it through your letter box,' the postwoman said.

Inside, she opened it. A bundle of photocopied pages with a single handwritten one on top: *Our secret. PS hope you're feeling better*. It was signed, *Colin*.

On the Friday Zoë said, 'What if I was to go to the Wildlife Centre on Saturday? I'd be there all day.'

'Great,' said Alex. 'You'd enjoy that, wouldn't you?' It had been excruciating watching her hanging around the house all week to keep an eye on her. Her daughter was like a caged bird.

Zoë was already gone when Alex woke on Saturday morning. There was a note on the fridge: *Call me if you need ANYTHING!!! Z x.*

Terry Neill texted at around midday after she'd showered, when she was out strolling along the high tide line:

What about dinner tonight?

She sat down on the beach and called him back. 'I'm sorry, Terry,' she said. 'I don't think I'm really up for any of this.'

It was curious how disappointed he sounded. 'No, no. I understand.'

They stayed on the phone talking for a while. He asked if anything had set her back. She told him about her car, and the panic attack on Monday. 'I thought I was better than I was. It's kind of dawning on me . . .'

'The cracks run deep sometimes,' he said. 'But you're doing the right thing. You have to stick with it.'

'And how are you doing?' she asked, when she realised uncomfortably they had spent minutes just talking about her.

She could hear a sigh in his voice when he said, 'Now they're saying they think that Ayman killed Mary. Is that right?'

'That must be hard to hear.'

'It is true, then?'

'I don't think we'll ever know for sure . . . but it's likely. He seems to have planned it all.'

'He was a very methodical man. I don't know how to feel about that. I thought he was a good person. I can't imagine what was going through his head. I feel it's my fault. I feel I let him down very badly.'

She turned towards the land. When you were close to the waterline, the chalets and shacks were all hidden behind the rise of ochre stones. 'Yes,' she said. 'I let people down too.'

'Look. I'm not your therapist, but I think we're both pretty low. You shouldn't be home, brooding on things. This isn't just a way of trying to persuade you to come out for a meal, but you should find something outside yourself. The offer still stands, though I totally understand if you just want to stay home and watch box sets.'

So, walking back up the beach, along the path of one of the old crooked rail tracks that fishermen had once used to haul their boats on, rusted now, turning the stones a darker brown, she called Zoë to say she would be out tonight. The call went to voicemail. She left a couple of messages, but by the time she'd reached the road, Zoë hadn't answered, so she tried the Wildlife Trust centre instead. A woman was in the office, pecking at the keyboard of a computer. 'No, there are no volunteers in today.'

'Sorry? Are you sure? You must be wrong. She definitely said she was coming over there.'

'I know Zoë,' the woman said. 'The very serious one? No, she's definitely not here today.'

Anxious now, she texted Zoë again:

Where are you, love? Called the WT. You're not there. Are you OK?

From where she stood now on the curve of the beach, only the masts of boats were visible, triangles of sail moving parallel to the shore. She lay down on the shingle by the Snack Shack, concentrating on slow breaths as her counsellor had told her to; in through the nose, out through the mouth.

Sat at a table, having lunch with her family, a four-year-old said loudly, 'Is that lady sleeping?'

When her phone finally rang, she sat up and grabbed it. 'Sorry. I got the day wrong,' Zoë was saying, 'I'm not at the Wildlife Trust.'

'So where are you?'

'I got the bus into Folkestone instead. I'm fine, Mum. Sorry. Were you worried?'

Alex exhaled. 'You went all the way to the Visitor Centre, discovered it wasn't a volunteer day, then went on to Folkestone?'

'Yeah, Mum. I know. You're not the only crazy one in the house. Sorry. Bad joke.'

When Alex told her about the meal, Zoë said incredulously, 'Is that like a date?'

'No. He's just a friend.'

'It sounds like a date.'

'He's just a nice man and he's feeling a bit low too.'

'You should go. You should definitely go, Mum.'

'But I'll be out. Will you be OK?'

'Course I bloody will, Mum. I'll stay over with Stella and Tina. They'll be fine about it.'

'Will they?'

Alex stood and went to the hut that sold fish and looked at the rows of lobsters lined up on the table. She texted Terry:

I'll bring fish.

'Two plaice,' she said to the rosy-cheeked boy behind the counter in the little hut. Then she had an afterthought. 'And a mackerel. Can you wrap it separately?'

THIRTY-FIVE

Instead of cycling straight to Greatstone, Alex took the long way round, via the Younises' house. The windows looked dusty. The grass had grown unruly since she was last here; the petals on the rose bushes had browned and the beds were full of weeds. She locked the bike to the gate, then fought her way into the copse.

In the evening light, the footpath Georgia Coaker had talked about was visible; young plants had been trampled. It had been recently used.

The summer heat hung heavily. Small black bugs filled the air. The shaded earth seemed to give off a thicker smell. Someone had tugged down the barbed wire of the fence at the north side of the wooden brake to make crossing easier. She stepped over it and into a hay field.

The tent was still there, as Georgia had described it, lurking under the low trees about a hundred metres away.

There were sheep. Instead of scattering at her approach,

they just stood staring at her. Maybe they had become used to humans, or maybe they were just too hot to run.

The smell of an old fire gave him away as she approached. She was right. He was still living here; he must have returned here last week. 'Mr Glass? Is that you?'

The site was tidy, as she'd expect from a military man, whatever his mental state. There was a small wooden cross driven into the ground by the front end of the tent. She could tell that the tent's flap was open, but it was pitched with the entrance up towards the hedge, so she couldn't see inside.

She lowered her voice; she spoke as softly as she could. 'Hello? I don't want to disturb you. Please don't be afraid. My name is Alexandra Cupidi. I want to apologise to you.'

There was no reaction from inside the khaki canvas.

'Mr Glass. Are you in there?'

She was sure he was. It was a small tent. When she stepped closer, seeing the far side of the canvas for the first time, there was a tell-tale bulge in the cloth.

He was lying still, hoping she would go away. He was not used to people. He didn't like or trust them. But she heard a small rustling from inside – as if he were searching for a stick or a knife, she thought.

'Don't worry.' She kept her voice low; almost a whisper. There was just canvas and air between them. 'I mean you no harm, I promise. I just want to say that I'm sorry. I feel bad that you were arrested for the murder of Ayman Younis. I think that was my fault. If I hadn't come across you that night and given a description, you would never have been a suspect. I knew it wasn't you, though, all along. I tried to tell them.'

221

She waited and listened. Inside the tent she heard him turn. Sure that she had his attention now, she said, 'You don't have to say anything.'

The hum of summer reasserted itself in the air around them.

'It's just that I think I understand a tiny amount of what you've been through,' she said. 'I've been diagnosed with post-traumatic stress disorder myself. Some stuff I've been through. Obviously nothing like . . .'

The evening bird song was loud. She never had the patience to learn which bird was which. Zoë had told her which the one that sounded like a squeaky bicycle pump was, the one that said '*A-little-bit-of-bread-and-no-cheese*', but never paid enough attention at the right time.

'You were in Iraq and Afghanistan. I saw your records. I know I haven't been through the half of it compared to you, but sometimes I think I've been going mad with it – making bad decisions, pushing the people away from me.'

She thought she could hear Bob Glass breathing now as he listened; a low, nervous scraping sound. So she continued: 'I'm lucky. It must be very hard if you're alone. This sense of the past always being alive in the present – that's what it's like, isn't it? You carry it all with you. And feeling that something just as terrible is always about to happen again.'

He had not moved or shouted back at her.

'Sorry. I know you don't want to talk. I know you just want to be on your own. I just wanted to say this: if you ever need any help, I'd like to try and make it up to you.'

He didn't answer.

'One thing, though. I would like to ask you a question. You

don't have to say anything at all, but if it wasn't you who argued with Ayman Younis a few nights before he killed himself, I wondered . . . do you know who it was?'

No answer.

'I figure that camping here, you're not far from the house. You would have heard it.'

Again, nothing at all from inside the tent.

'OK. I'm leaving a card. It has a phone number on it. And I brought you some fresh fish. I don't know if you like it, but it was caught this morning.'

Still nothing.

'I'm just coming closer so I can leave it in the cool, OK? Then I'll leave you alone.'

She waited a second, then stepped forward. As she did so, a gentle breeze blew towards her and within a second, her skin was suddenly cold and her breath was gone. Before she had even understood it, she knew something was very wrong and she turned to run.

She forced her lungs to fill, ordering herself to stay calm, to stay in the present, to quietly absorb what was happening to her instead of running. It took her another couple of seconds to realise what it was that had triggered that desire to run away screaming. The air around her carried a faint but familiar scent of something very bad.

'Bob? Are you OK? Do you need help?'

As she stepped forward now, dropping the fish, the tent jerked. She ignored the impulse to run.

'I'm a police officer,' she said, loudly now. 'Who's there?'

The whole tent convulsed violently, as if it were being shaken by something invisible.

THIRTY-SIX

Something dark crashed out of the tent, wide and low.

It took her another second to realise what she had just seen. She had watched these creatures often enough now, in the late evenings and early mornings when she couldn't sleep. There had been a badger in Bob Glass's tent, rustling around, probably stealing his food. It was the badger's raspy breath she had been listening to, hiding in there. Terrified of being captured, it had burst through the hedge beyond the tent to escape. She laughed out loud at her own stupidity.

With comic timing, a cuckoo called, somewhere far beyond the Younises' house.

But when she bent to pick up the dead mackerel, sprung from its newspaper, it seemed to stare right back at her with its dead eye. Inside the tent, she heard flies buzzing against the nylon.

She remembered something Bill South had once told her on one of those early summer evenings when they had lain on the ground together, binoculars at the ready. 'Badgers will eat anything at all. They don't care.'

She stayed in the dimming light until the officers had arrived to secure the site, and then, because she had stood crouched at the entrance of the tent, too, for the crime scene manager to arrive so she could record Alex as having been present at the site. **I am going to be late**, she texted Terry Neill, not knowing what else to say.

She had looked inside the tent. The badger had eaten what he could get at easily. The skin from Bob Glass's face was gone.

'You look like hell. What's wrong?' was the first thing he said when she finally arrived.

And when she had told him, he had put down a glass of wine, put his arms around her and hugged her, which was, right then, exactly what she had needed. When he finally released her, he said, 'I don't suppose you really feel like eating now.'

'I left the fish behind anyway,' she said.

'No loss then. What about a drink instead?'

And when she woke in the morning, and found herself on his sheets, looking out onto the pale sand beach where browned grass was swaying in a light breeze, she was somehow not surprised.

It had been a very long time since she had slept with anyone.

She was alone. She could hear Terry downstairs. The view from his bedroom was better than hers. She looked out on a nuclear power station; he looked out onto a wide sea and sky.

After a few minutes, he arrived, impressively naked and with coffee. He was older than her; she wondered if he felt it important to show how well-kept his body was.

'You talk in your sleep,' he said, putting the wooden tray on the bed. 'A lot.'

'So my daughter tells me.' She was surprised she had slept at all. He had fallen asleep immediately afterwards. She had lain awake watching the stars moving through the half-open blinds, her mind still racing. 'How long have you lived here?'

'Seven years. No, eight. I lived in Folkestone for a while, but didn't like the gentrification.'

'Whereas here it's much more ghetto.'

He laughed. 'Here I can ignore every else. I needed to be away from all temptation. What are your plans? If you aren't doing anything, I'd love to teach you golf.'

'That is never going to happen,' she said.

Still undressed, he pulled up Venetian blinds and the sunlight streamed into the window. It felt like anyone who was on the beach would be able to see this man she had just slept with.

'You drunk, last night?' she said.

'I was. You were in shock.'

'We probably shouldn't have done that, then.'

'No,' he said. 'We probably shouldn't. I don't regret it for a second, though. Do you?'

At that point her stomach rebelled. 'Excuse me,' she said, standing.

'What's wrong?'

She got up and went to the toilet and threw the coffee she had just drunk straight back up again.

When she returned to the bedroom he was wearing a blue towelling robe and a concerned expression on his face. 'Are you OK?'

'Sorry. Flashbacks.' When she had been younger, sex had been a way of forgetting things. That no longer seemed to apply. The vision of Bob Glass's faceless face had haunted her through the night, and continued to do so now. 'It was pretty horrid, what I saw.'

He nodded. 'I'm sorry. I feel like a shit now. As if I'd somehow taken advantage of you.'

She laughed. 'How very fucking gallant of you.' He looked stung. 'You were the one who was drunk, Terry. I knew exactly what I was doing, and no, I don't have any regrets.'

He looked relieved. Her mouth tasted vile. 'Do you have a toothbrush I can borrow?'

'Of course.' He went to the bathroom and returned with a bamboo one, still in its box. She raised her eyebrows at him as he handed it over. 'I know what you're thinking. I am not a saint. You are not the first woman I've slept with here, but no, I don't keep a special supply of toothbrushes just in case. I buy them for myself in packs of four.'

She showered, then returned to the bedroom and held the toothbrush out to him.

'I'll keep it in the drawer. For next time.'

'Next time?' she said.

'It's an aspiration, not an assumption.'

'You could write my name on it, to make sure it doesn't get mixed up with any of the other ones from the other ladies who visit.'

He took it. 'I'll be sure to do that. After all, there must be hundreds of brushes with names on it in a drawer in that bathroom now.'

She laughed. 'Hundreds, I'm sure of it.'

'I hope there is a next time, that's all.'

She didn't answer. 'Do you believe in ghosts, Terry?'

'No. Why do you ask?'

'You lived in Folkestone. Did you ever go and buy fish at The Stade?'

'All the time. I still do.'

'Do you remember a story about a fisherman called Frank Hogben? He disappeared at sea.'

'The trawler guy? The family had that chip shop?'

Alex nodded.

'I remember Frank Hogben, yes. That was a story. They had a picture of him in the shop for ages, with flowers and everything. I remember. God, yes. I used to buy fish from him. And . . .'

'And what?'

'Oh, you know . . .' His voice went quieter now. 'Other things.'

'Did you? What things?' she asked, checking her phone for messages from Zoë.

'You're a police officer. The kind of things you shouldn't talk to police officers about.'

She looked at him. There was an anxiety in his expression that she hadn't noticed before. 'Oh. I see.' She put two and two together. 'The drugs, you mean?'

He looked down, put his hands in his pockets.

'He was your drug dealer?'

'*A* drug dealer, not *my* drug dealer. I had a few. I am just trying to be honest with you.'

'Frank Hogben was a drug dealer?' She frowned. 'Heroin?'

'That's right. Are you OK?'

She nodded slowly, still processing what she had heard.

'What do you want to do today?'

She pulled on her trousers. 'I'm sorry. I have to go somewhere.'

'What if we met later? We could go to a nice restaurant somewhere? Zoë could come.'

'I don't have a good record with restaurants.'

'No. Maybe not. Maybe just get together some other time?'

'Maybe, Terry. Maybe. Is it OK if I leave my bike here?' She was already dialling an Uber.

THIRTY-SEVEN

It was one of the two-storey terraced houses in Albion Road; an unprepossessing building with a green bin outside and a bay window that had sagged towards the pavement over the years. There were streets like this in every English town; the ones built right onto the pavement, without the fancy Victorian terracotta or brickwork, render streaked with rust from old satellite dishes.

Alex rang the bell, hearing a buzz somewhere inside the house.

Tina emerged dressed in a black top and skirt, smiled, then called back down the hall. 'Zoë. It's your mother.' Then, 'How are you? Zoë says you've been having hard times.'

'Where's Stella?'

'Gone to her shop. Why?'

'I wanted to ask you something, Tina. About your husband.'

Her eyes flickered down towards the pavement.

'You were asking Stella about him, weren't you?' Her voice was paper-thin.

'What if he didn't die on the boat?'

She remained, staring at her own feet. 'I don't know what you're talking about. He went missing.'

'Tina. There's something wrong here. I know there is.'

Tina raised her head and looked Alex uncertainly in the eye. 'Why?'

'What did you know about your husband selling drugs?'

She said nothing, shook her head gently.

'You see, I think it was convenient for him to disappear.'

'No comment,' she whispered.

'This isn't a cross-examination, Tina. I'm not trying to get you into trouble. Exactly the opposite, I promise.'

'What are you on about, Mum?' Zoë emerged from down the hallway in the same shorts and baggy T-shirt she had been wearing the day before.

'I was just asking if you'd been any trouble,' said Alex smoothly.

'Why would I be trouble?'

'She's welcome here any time,' said Tina.

Zoë put her arms around Tina and hugged her, then stepped past her onto the street. 'Oh. I forgot we didn't have a car. How are we getting home, Mum?'

'Go on out. I just need to have a private word with Tina.'

'What about? Are you talking about me? They don't mind me here, honest – do you, Tina?'

'She's a delight,' said Tina.

'Two minutes.'

Zoë walked a little way down the street, then leaned against a telegraph pole, looking back with accusing eyes.

Tina was still at her doorway, apprehensive, not meeting Alex's gaze. Alex went up close to her and said, very quietly, 'Look, Tina. I know your husband assaulted you.' A nervous flicker of eyelids. 'All I want to know is the truth.'

'I don't want to talk to you any more,' she said, with sudden anger, and stepped inside the door. 'I would like you to go away, please.'

Before Alex could say any more, she closed the door hard, forcing Alex backwards onto the pavement.

'Oh God. What was that, Mum? What were you saying to her? Were you talking about me?'

'No. It was nothing to do with you.'

'They're my friends, Mum. What is it you're so worried about? They're lesbians? You always pretend to be better than that.'

'That's not what any of this is about.'

They were walking back towards the town now. 'What then?'

They had nowhere to be but both were stamping along like they were in some crazy hurry to get down the hill and into town. 'I can't tell you.'

'Brilliant,' said Zoë.

Alex stopped. 'Let's call a cab.'

Zoë scuffed her heels on the pavement. 'You're not going to spoil all this for me, are you?'

'No. No I'm not. I'm glad. Anything planned for the rest of the day?'

Her daughter stuffed her hands into her pockets, shrugged. 'Just stuff.'

When, finally, they emerged from the taxi, Alex noticed there were three text messages on her phone. **Really enjoyed last night and I'd love to do it again**; the second read, **Are we**

OK? and the third was a JPEG of a bamboo toothbrush with *ALEX* written on the handle in biro.

She was in the front room when she saw the bicycle disappearing down the track towards the lighthouses. Zoë, head down, backpack on, cycling into the breeze.

In the heat of the afternoon, she walked down the track to Bill South's empty bungalow. The bird bath was dry. She looked around for something to fill it with and found a black rubber bucket by his back door. She filled it at the outside tap close by and was carrying it round to the front when she saw the car pull up.

'You know, I was expecting you,' she said as Jill got out.

Jill was dressed for work. A blue cotton suit, trousers that ended above bare ankles and a plain white T-shirt. 'Matter of fact, I called round last night after work, after, you know . . . I heard all about Bob Glass, obviously. Apparently he wasn't very pretty when you found him.'

'No. Poor bastard. He wasn't.'

She looked around. 'Bill not turned up yet?'

'No.'

Jill nodded, smiled sympathetically, as if she knew how much Bill meant to her and Zoë. 'He'll turn up soon. I know he will. You'd have heard by now if anything had happened to him. I need to ask you this . . . Why did you go looking for Bob Glass?'

'I wanted to say sorry.'

'It wasn't your fault this happened.'

'Not my fault, but I always knew it wasn't him. And I felt sorry. He had PTSD. That's why he was there. He did his training around here. It's like he was still in the army. He could never move on.'

'That's not your fault. You didn't make him go to Afghanistan.' Jill stood, hands on her hips, looking down at her feet. 'You've got to stop all this, Alex. You know that, don't you?'

'You want to know the reason I wasn't in last night, Jill? I had a date.'

'A *date* date?'

'Yes.'

Jill's mouth dropped. 'No way. No bloody way. With a man?'

'Yes, with a man.'

'Go, Alex!'

Alex mimed zipping her lips, and then told her who the man was. Jill whistled. 'Terry Neill? I was in his house yesterday to let him know about Biosfera. Was that where you . . . ?'

Alex nodded.

'Jesus. Seriously lovely property.'

'You don't have to sound so surprised. It's not a thing. It was just, nice, that's all. I was in shock. How was your fireman from Bumble?'

'Recently divorced. Spent a long time talking about his custody battle for the kids and by the main course I was already on his wife's side.' Jill stopped. 'Wait. This was just after you'd found Bob Glass?'

Alex nodded.

'Oh. Right. Yeah. I do things like that, too.'

'What? End up sleeping with men because you've had a really shitty day?'

'Kind of. Yeah.'

★

It was a summer evening. They walked a little way down the track and sat on the mound of shingle to the north of the Coast-guard Cottages and talked, watching kites flying above the beach. From a long way off Alex saw a bicycle coming back down the road; a familiar small figure, spinning along, pushed by the same breeze that was lifting the kites into the air.

'That argument where people heard Ayman Younis shouting. Bob Glass denied it was him, didn't he, Jill?'

'Yes.'

'Thing is, Bob Glass only ever told you the truth. Even when people didn't believe him. Why would he have lied about that?'

'I don't know. Maybe because he knew if he'd been arguing, we'd have been more likely to believe it was him that killed the Younises.'

'Possibly. But what if it wasn't him? What if someone else was arguing with Ayman Younis?'

'I thought you just proved Ayman Younis had committed suicide, so why does it matter who he was arguing with?'

'Because there's a reason why he killed himself. Someone stole his money. I went there because I wanted to apologise, but I also wanted to ask Bob if he was telling the truth.'

'And if he was sleeping in the next field . . . maybe he had heard the argument?'

'Exactly.'

Zoë was on the approach road now coming towards them. She stopped when she saw Jill, smiled and waved.

Alex stood and walked down the slope towards her. 'Where have you been, then?' she asked. 'Looking for caravans to rent?'

'None of your business,' her daughter replied, then pedalled past her towards the back of the houses.

Jill was still teetering her way down the shingle slope in her work shoes. 'Has she got a boyfriend, then?'

'Or a girlfriend . . .' said Alex.

'You reckon?'

Alex changed the subject. 'Any cause of death for Bob Glass yet?'

'Stop it, Alex.'

'Sorry. I genuinely can't help it.'

'Did you have sex with him?'

'Yes.'

'You slag.' She laughed. 'There was a bottle of what seems to have been methadone in the tent. Wasn't prescription. Looks like something he bought on the street. May not have even been methadone. People are selling it cut with all sorts of stuff these days. So right now we assume it's an accidental OD.'

'Poor bloody man.'

Jill nodded. 'So if he had heard an argument between Ayman Younis and your mystery man, we'll never know now anyway, will we? I better go.'

Alex walked her back to her car, still parked outside Bill's. 'Did he have a history of drug abuse?'

'Homeless, wasn't he? Loads of them do.'

'Exactly.'

Jill looked at her, puzzled. Alex said nothing; waved at her as she drove back to the world of work. When she got back home, the house still smelt of the flowers she had put into a vase earlier that week.

Zoë was in the shower. Alex sat at the top of the stairs, thinking. When she emerged, one towel wrapped around her body, another round her head, Alex said, 'Right. I think it's high time you told me where William South is.'

Zoë walked straight past her to her bedroom without saying anything and closed the door behind her. Alex heard her turn the key.

THIRTY-EIGHT

At one in the morning, Alex noticed the light still on under her daughter's door. She knocked gently. 'You awake?'

After a few seconds, her daughter's voice: 'What is it?'

'I really need to know about Bill.'

Zoë opened her door, her forehead tilted forward aggressively, like she was readying herself for a blow, but she was wearing one of her dad's old Tribe Called Quest T-shirts and it looked so huge on her it undercut any attempt at looking fierce. 'I can't tell you, Mum.'

'I won't make you. Did Bill South make you promise not to say where he was?'

'Yes.'

Alex had to pause before opening her mouth again because hearing that hurt.

'He's somewhere safe, Mum. Don't try and find him, please. OK?'

'What about the drinking?'

The teenager blushed. Whatever it was, it would have to be bad if it made Zoë blush these days.

'Oh God. He's still drinking?'

'No. Don't worry, Mum. He's fine. Totally fine. He's safe. He hasn't drunk for days. I'm not saying anything else, OK?'

She laid her hand on her daughter's arm and said, 'You're a good friend to him, aren't you?'

Zoë's shrug was a minimal jerk of her shoulders.

'Will you pass him a message then? Tell him I think I know what really happened on *The Hopeful*. So there's no point in him hiding any more. And I really, really need to talk to him about it. For his own good. It's really important.'

Zoë frowned. 'What?'

Alex dropped her hand. 'He'll understand. Just tell him next time you see him. Will you do that?'

'Night. Mum,' she said, and pushed the door closed on her mother.

She woke in darkness underground again, the smell of earth around her once more, the pressure of roots gripping her chest, her face wet from sweat and tears.

And then it wasn't just a ceiling that had fallen on her. Now, instead of damp soil, there was the scent of cold metal and oil. She was no longer in the cellar, and a red car had dropped on her and the weight of it was crushing her, making it impossible to breathe.

'Ssh,' a voice beside her whispered. A cool hand on her forehead. 'It's OK. Go back to sleep now.'

★

In the morning when she woke, skin clammy, Zoë had gone out. She tried to remember her dream but it had gone.

There was a note by the toaster: *We need more oat milk and tahini. Out all day. Love you. x.* She was still in her pyjamas when her phone rang at eleven. 'Which house are you in?'

'Why?'

'Because I'm outside.'

She opened the kitchen door and Terry was there in his open-top Mini and a blue baseball cap. 'Not dressed yet?'

'I'm off sick,' she said. 'It's allowed.'

'Get some clothes on and fetch your passport. I'm taking you for lunch. Or do you have a better offer?'

'I told you about me and restaurants. I don't get on well with them.'

'That's why. I'm taking you. You'll be fine with me.'

'Did you say passport?' she asked.

He drove her to his house on Greatstone beach, where another car with a driver was waiting, uniformed, with a cap. 'Fancy,' she said.

'That way I can have a drink. I'm treating myself.'

They made the ferry with twenty minutes to spare.

'What if I'd said no?'

'I'd have gone alone. Plus, there's thirty per cent off ferry crossings today so it wasn't too big a risk.'

The ferry juddered as its thrusters pushed the stern off the pontoon at Dover. Foreign travel always had a smell to it; airports smelt of concrete and kerosene, ferries were fresh paint, salt and diesel. She leaned over the handrail, breathed it all in and watched the milky blue water churn under them.

The ferry was called *The Pride of Kent*. Why had she never done this trip before, she wondered? Her daughter disapproved of all air travel, but they lived so close to France. She blamed herself for being so self-absorbed. They had not taken holidays at all.

'Penny for them?'

'This is good. Thank you for doing this.'

'I don't like to sound smug, but I thought so.' The ferry nosed its way through the harbour entrance as the white cliffs unfolded themselves to the east. The top of South Foreland Lighthouse shone brilliant in the ridiculous sun.

She took a photograph of herself against the southern fringe of England and sent it to Zoë:

Bill's not the only one running away from home x

Her phone buzzed a second later:

?????

I'm on a day trip to France. Back this p.m. Remember to tell BS what I said. I love you xxx

She waited for another message, but there was nothing.

'Texting your boyfriend?'

'My daughter.'

'Starfish girl. I'd like to get to know her.'

She raised her eyebrows; he raised his hands, in mock self-defence.

'It doesn't mean I'm asking you to move in with me.'

'I'm not sure I like the view from your house, anyway.'

'You prefer a nuclear power station?'

'You barely notice it,' she said.

He laughed.

They found a place out of the sun and sat together in the shade. 'It's good to see you smiling,' he said.

'I sometimes wonder if I'm ever coming out of this.'

'You will,' he said. 'It's just about allowing your brain to put things back where they ought to be.'

'You make it sound like I've just put my socks away in the wrong drawer.'

At the ferry terminal they picked up another taxi. The ferry was half empty and they didn't have to wait long, but the drive was disappointing. The Calais seafront was flat, cluttered with bland post-war concrete flats that looked out over half-hearted post-industrial spaces. They pulled up in front of an unprepossessing apartment block that looked much like the one Jill lived in in Ashford.

'Is this it?' She peered sceptically up at the cream-painted block.

'This, believe it or not, is one of the best seafood restaurants on this coast.'

'You recall that last time I was at a restaurant I had a total meltdown.'

'And this time you will be fine. You'll see.'

She offered to pay for the taxi, though she had no euros. He said, 'It's my treat.'

'The car was your treat. And the ferry.' How long, she wondered, had he been planning this?

'You pay for the meal, then,' he said.

'Expensive is it?'

'*Très.*'

They caught the lift to the fourth floor. Terry's French was shaky, but at least he tried. '*La table pour Monsieur Neill.*'

The maître d' pronounced his name 'Nile', but led him to a table by the windows that looked out over the Channel. They sat either side of a crisp tablecloth and looked at the menu. He had booked tickets and a table for her without asking; she was unsure how she felt about it. She tried to remember the last time she had gone out with a man who had behaved like this. Her ex, Zoë's father, had never planned anything at all. She had had a long affair with a senior officer in London; he was married. In many ways, that had been her most successful relationship. What she had enjoyed about it was the lack of commitment; nothing had ever been planned. It had all been about snatched moments. They had slept with each other whenever chance had provided the opportunity. Since moving to Kent, between her daughter and her new job, she had never had time for men. Now here was a man who had organised everything. When he had asked her out it had felt spontaneous, but the longer she was with him the less comfortable she felt. She imagined telling Jill about it, complaining that he picked a restaurant without consulting her. Jill would think her unease ridiculous. Jill loved men who bought her stuff.

She looked up at him, frowning at the menu. 'The lobster casserole is supposed to be amazing,' he said.

She looked down the '*Plats*' menu and found *cocotte de homard*.

'Now I said I'm paying, you're getting the most expensive thing on the menu?'

'Naturally.'

When the sommelier arrived Terry asked, 'Red or white?'

When she said red, he ordered a Pic Saint-Loup, and only after the waiter had gone said, 'Is that all right?' She tried not to mind. She should be enjoying herself. When the waiter approached she wondered what she would do if he tried to choose food for her too, but he didn't. She ordered in French, picking the monkfish and bass tagine.

She should relax, she told herself. He was controlling, but weren't most men? It was lovely to be somewhere completely different.

'Why the police?' he asked, out of the blue, settling back in his chair.

'My dad was a copper. Sweetest man you'd ever meet. I idolised him. My counsellor would say I was still probably trying to get his attention.'

'My father was a surgeon,' he said. 'Probably the same.'

The wine came. It was delicious. The entrées arrived after the first glass and they were exceptional too. She had scallops, which Zoë would have disapproved of, and enjoyed every soft mouthful. As they ate, looking over the water at the ferries that came and went from the port, the day turned a rich hazy grey.

He talked about university politics and how he'd been glad to escape them. She began to relax. The wine helped. She talked about Zoë, how she said she didn't want to go to university because she could learn everything she needed on a computer these days and she didn't want to end up fifty thousand in debt.

'Wise girl.'

'I worry about her. She can't seem to make friends with people her own age.'

'People her own age are overrated. I used to teach them.'

'And you don't miss it at all?'

'God, no. You do, though, don't you? Miss your job.'

She didn't answer.

'You should learn to miss it less. That way happiness lies. That's what I found.'

When the monkfish came, she ate it in silence, watching the ships.

'Did I say something wrong?'

She shook her head. The tagine was rich and full of subtle flavour, and she tried hard to enjoy it.

The waiter approached, asked them in English whether the meal was OK.

'Are you sure nothing's wrong? You're very quiet.'

'I'm sorry.' She put down her fork. 'I just don't react very well to people telling me what I should and shouldn't do.'

The alcohol was in Terry's veins now. He leaned forward. 'All I said was that you are too involved, sometimes. It's not good for you, considering what you've been through. You need to take time off too. You're not recognising the trauma. It must have been awful for you, seeing that man, dead. And now you're back there in your mind, aren't you?' He laid down his fork, reached out his arm across the small table, and put it on top of hers.

Terry was just a thoughtful man. He had been through bad things himself. And he was only trying to help, she told herself.

THIRTY-NINE

Despite that, there was a kind of stiffness to the rest of the meal. They stuck to safe topics; which TV shows they liked, the best gigs they had been to. He had seen Nirvana at Reading; she said Soul II Soul at Brixton Academy. For dessert he ordered a sorbet with genever. When she said she didn't want anything, he ordered two spoons and pushed one across the table towards her, so she pecked at his with her spoon, eating most of it though she hadn't wanted it, trying to lighten the mood.

'Quite a place, isn't it? Enjoying yourself?'

'I am,' she said, 'Yes.' They ordered coffee. '*Décaféiné*,' Alex added. The restaurant was in a dull part of the town, so there was no point suggesting a walk. She felt trapped in there with him until the time came to take the ferry home, feeling like she had ruined his treat. When the bill came, he tried to pull out his wallet again in a show of gallantry, but she paid.

On the ferry home she stood on the starboard deck and

looked north. The lights of a container ship came on, blaring on the horizon.

Under the overcast sky, the Dover Strait had turned grey. She thought of Frank Hogben. In Curly's boat she had been down in among the waves; up on the deck of this big blue and white car park of a ship, they felt a long way below her.

And just as she was thinking about Frank Hogben, trying to puzzle things out, her phone came back in range and beeped with a message from Zoë:

Hope u r having a good time. Staying with T & S tonight. Will you be OK on yr own??? x

As she was looking at it, another pinged in from an unrecognised number:

Z says you want to meet. Will message you tomorrow at 9.

She broke out into a grin.

Terry noticed. 'News?'

'Just an old friend who I haven't heard from in a while.'

She replaced the phone in her bag and stared a little longer at the dark sea. 'Tell me about your addiction,' she said.

'Really?'

'Go on. You know everything about my catastrophes now.' She looked up from the sea below and looked straight at him. 'Even things up a bit.'

'I don't really talk about all that that much.' For the first time, he looked less sure of himself. 'I was never actually a junkie. I was an addict. I had enough money to fund the habit and so I managed it. There's such a cliché about addiction; I was nothing like that.'

'God forbid you are a cliché,' she said.

His grin was not so bad, she thought. 'It was a bit like that, to be honest. I would have rather died than look like a junkie. I kind of organised myself around my needs. I'm quite an organised, single-minded person.'

'I can see that.'

'I made sure I did my job properly so I would have time to take drugs. It made life extremely simple. It gave me priorities. Unfortunately, the biggest priority was buying and taking drugs, which meant I couldn't sustain a relationship. I had occasional girlfriends, but never for very long because I always had to lie to them about my life and they always played second fiddle to . . . the other thing.'

He looked at her, and there was something very direct about his gaze.

'It's one of the things that made me want to change, if I'm honest.'

When they called for foot passengers to disembark she was oddly relieved to be in England again. In the queue for passport control he said, 'Will you come back to my place, for a drink?'

Her daughter would not be home. There was no reason to say no. 'OK. Just a quick one.'

She flicked through her passport. In the last few years she had only used it to apply for bank accounts. It would expire in a year. She examined the photograph in the back, taken when she was still working in London and when Zoë had still been in primary school. It was a picture of a woman who seemed a lot younger and a lot more carefree who stared back at the camera.

Her hair was shorter; maybe she should try that again. She had no memory at all of the blue top she was wearing.

'Show me your passport photograph,' she said.

'Why?'

'I'll show you mine if you show me yours.'

He turned away from her, facing in the direction of the slowly moving queue. 'We'll be there in a minute,' he said.

'Go on. Show me it. Or is that awful?'

He ignored her, looking ahead. Showing each other your passport photos was one of the things you did, wasn't it? Like squeezing into photo booths together.

'Show me it,' she insisted, laughing. 'It can't be that bad.'

'OK,' he said tightly, pulling the passport from the inside pocket of his pale-blue jacket. He flicked through it and opened it at his photo and held it out towards her. 'There. OK?'

She looked at it. From a distance it appeared to be a perfectly ordinary photograph of Terry, hair a little longer perhaps but there was nothing to be embarrassed about.

She reached out to take it, but he pulled it back and put it into his pocket.

When they approached the immigration officer, he said, 'You go first.'

When she was waved on, she turned and watched him take the passport out again, hand it to the woman. The moment she gave it back, he tucked it swiftly inside his jacket again.

The same driver who had taken them there was waiting on the Dover tarmac. 'Nice day?'

'Yes,' she said. 'It was, actually.'

In the car back Terry was talkative, jolly, telling the driver and her anecdotes about his former students. An English public school boy whom he caught cheating in exams who was now a minister in government. A Scottish girl who vomited with nerves whenever she sat an exam.

Alex was distracted, looking out of the window, deep in thought. It was a long drive home. The car smelt of leather. There was a copy of the *Financial Times* tucked in the seat back in front of her. Everything Terry did was like this, she thought. A little too much on the flashy side.

'Unfortunately I was invigilating that day and before I knew, she'd thrown up all over me . . .'

Alex wondered if it had been a good idea to agree to go back to his house. 'What?'

'You weren't listening, were you?'

'Sorry. Not really.'

He laughed. 'Don't worry. It was a pretty dull story.'

When they arrived at his house he paid off the driver, took out his keys and opened the front door. She waited on the step until he had switched off the alarm, then followed him in. When he took off his jacket and hung it up on a hanger in the hallway, she took her own jacket off and put it over his. 'Gin?' he asked.

He led her upstairs and opened the patio doors, lit candles on the balcony, then returned a few minute later with two glasses and a bowl of olives.

They sat on the balcony outside, overlooking the beach below and watched the sky darken.

'A lot of junkies I know can't drink,' she said.

'As I said, I was never a junkie,' he answered, and raised his glass.

She took a sip from her glass, then excused herself and went to the bathroom. 'I just need to wash up a little.'

Behind the locked door she opened the cabinet and checked through its contents; then opened his washbag and looked through it.

By the time she got back he had almost finished his glass. Hers was still there, barely touched.

'You were a long time.'

'You missed me?'

He looked at her. 'Did you find anything interesting?'

She shook her head. 'Nothing I could arrest you for, anyway.'

He nodded. He knew precisely what she had been doing. 'I understand. You don't trust me,' he said.

She felt a heaviness in her chest. 'I'm sorry. I find all this hard.'

'Yes. You do.'

'I should go home, I suppose.'

He stepped forward and took both of her hands. 'I understand. It's OK. We can go easy, if you prefer. But you know I really like you.'

'It's been a lovely day and it's done me good, but yes. Maybe it's for the best if I go home now.'

He nodded. 'I'll call you a taxi,' he said.

While his back was turned, she reached for her jacket, and while she was doing so, slipped her hand inside the pocket of Terry's blue jacket. The inside pocket was empty; the passport was not there.

FORTY

That night she didn't dare sleep. Her brain felt like it was on fire.

Instead, she took a blanket and cycled out to Lydd and sat on the scrubland where Zoë and Bill had showed her badgers.

In the darkness she thought she saw shapes moving, but she could not be sure. She heard cracks of sticks and the rustling of dry leaves. Everything that had happened in the last few weeks lay around her like patterns and shapes that she could see and hear, but only obscurely.

At around one in the morning it started to rain; a light drizzle falling out of the darkness. She had not brought waterproofs, so she let the blanket soak up the water.

At around two in the morning, two men came, tramping across the path that crossed the patch of land. They caught her in their torch beams. 'You all right, love?' one of them asked. When he lowered the torch and approached, she saw a man in his sixties dressed in waterproofs and waders. They must have been night-fishing in the marshes somewhere. The man who had spoken put down his kit bag, lay the torch on the ground and squatted down next to her.

'Are you OK, darling? Want us to give you a lift somewhere?'

'I'm local. It's fine.'

'What the heck are you doing out here then?' The other man said, his face hidden in the darkness.

In a more kindly voice, the man beside her said, 'You're shivering. You should get inside.'

She nodded, but didn't move.

'Is she crying? Is she on something?' the other man muttered. 'You get all sorts out here.'

'I'm fine, honestly. I just don't want to go to sleep tonight.'

The man beside her stood again, took an umbrella out of his bag and opened it. 'Something bad happened?'

'Pretty bad.'

'What you doing?' demanded the other man. 'That's my umbrella. It's not yours to just give away.'

The gentler of the two men set it over her. Now rain pattered softly onto the nylon above her head.

'Thank you,' she said. 'That's very good of you.'

'It's OK, love. Drop it into the Dolphin Inn next time you're down there,' said the man. 'Hope everything's all right, love.'

As they left, she heard the second man saying, 'That's the last I see of that, then.'

She sat, still thinking about how everything was not all right at all.

The nights were short at this time of year, but it seemed a long time before first light.

When the first rays finally warmed her, she stood, limbs stiff and cramped, folded her damp blanket and furled the umbrella, strapped it to her backpack and set off home.

The cold had made her hungry. After she'd plugged in her phone to charge, she fried two eggs and ate them on toast, washed down with strong coffee, then sat, watching the screen of her phone until, just after nine, it pinged. The message was a postcode. TN29 0DU. That was enough. She found the location on Google maps. It was just over ten miles away.

With no car she had only her bike, so she packed a thermos with more coffee, and two chocolate bars, and set off on the bike. Her limbs should have been tired, but they weren't. She was itchy with energy.

On a bike around here it was like you floated above the land. The roads she cycled on had once just been banks, raised centuries ago to keep the water out of fields as the marsh grew, one field at a time. Over time they had turned into pathways, then tracks, then roads. It took her less than an hour riding from Denge Marsh, through Walland Marsh, into the oldest part of the landscape; what the locals called Romney Marsh Proper.

Midweek there were a few tents in the field. She looked around, wondering if he was in one of them. She wheeled the bike into the field, rattling it over a cattle grid, then walked towards them.

A European couple listening to music on their phone looked up and smiled. '*God dag*,' they said.

She was approaching the next tent when she heard a cough behind her and turned, and there he was. Bill South had grown a beard. It was greyer than she wanted it to be.

She nodded, opened her arms wide and put them around him and hugged him tightly. 'Stupid arse,' she said.

He nodded.

'You look a bit shit,' he told her.

'Yes. I probably do,' she said. She reached out and pulled his beard. 'You look worse.'

He had been staying in a wooden shepherd's hut tucked into a corner of the next field. It was not one of the new ones, the caravans for the middle classes; it was an old one with a pitch-black corrugated iron roof and greying timbers, slightly askew on its base. 'I know the farmer. I told her I needed a place to, you know . . .'

'Hide,' supplied Alex.

Bill nodded. 'Yes. And she said I could have this for as long as I needed it.'

He opened the door. It felt even smaller inside; whitewashed wood, a pair of tiny casement windows, one on each side, fringed by faded curtains. A pile of clothes lay on the bed, neatly folded. There was no room for a chair. Stepping inside, he lit the gas hob under the kettle.

She looked around for empty bottles but saw none. 'You still drinking?'

He shook his head. 'Zoë told me she wouldn't visit me if I carried on, so I stopped.'

'Good girl.'

'Isn't she? She's been coming to see you every day?'

'Most days.'

'How come you told her where you were and not me?'

He pulled two tea bags from a box and dropped them into a teapot. He knew Alex didn't like tea, but that had never stopped him making it for her, as if he believed not liking it was just some kind of Londoner's affectation. 'Because I knew she would have been worried if she hadn't known where I was.'

'Like I wasn't.'

'It was you I was disappearing from. You know that, though, don't you?'

'I know,' she said. 'Yes.'

He nodded. 'I was worried you would figure out what had happened on *The Hopeful*. Thing is,' he said without smiling, 'you generally do.'

'I found out you were on the docks when *The Hopeful* came in. You were the one who reported Frank Hogben missing all those years ago. You were in on it all along.' She had asked Colin to send her the reports on Frank Hogben's disappearance. It had been there on the printed sheets. Constable William South had been there on the dockside to take a statement from Daniel Fagg and the other crewmen.

He nodded. 'Question is, what are you going to do about it? Same as last time?'

'Frank wasn't on board because he wasn't ever on board. You made sure you were there that night so that it was you who made the report that he had disappeared. So you disappeared, because seven years ago you were part of the conspiracy to make *him* disappear.'

He looked at her oddly. He handed her the cup, and she took it and followed him onto the steps which were just wide enough to sit on, side by side. 'Did he have something on you, Bill?'

Bill looked shocked. 'What?'

'You let him get away with it. You were the one who let him disappear. There has to be a reason for that.'

'What do you mean, get away with it?'

'I'm not sure entirely he's even dead, Bill. I think I may have seen him. I think you arranged for him to disappear so that he would never be prosecuted for running drugs. In return he had to leave Tina alone. That was the deal. You did it to save her life. I understand. That was a good thing. But to do it, you let him get away. You, Curly and Danny concocted that whole charade of the search for his body but he was never on that boat.'

'Jesus,' he said.

'Sorry, Bill. You're a good man. A much better person than me.'

On the step beside her, he turned towards her. 'Jesus,' he said again. 'You'll be telling me you believe in all sorts now, Alex. Frank Hogben is alive, you reckon?'

His laughter grew until she thought she felt the whole hut behind them rattling with it as she sat there, bewildered.

FORTY-ONE

'I thought you were the copper who got everything right, Alex,' he said, when he'd finally got his breath back. 'What went wrong?'

She frowned.

'Frank Hogben definitely didn't get away. I saw him dead with my own eyes. And he has been for seven years. No question.'

She frowned. 'You saw him dead? You did? You never reported that.'

'The reason I ran away is because if you knew the truth, it would result in good people going to prison. You have form on that. But here you are again, like a bad penny.'

'Here I am,' she said, with a small smile. 'A bad penny. I can't help myself. Tell me, then, Bill.'

He nodded. 'I'm sorry I tried to keep this from you. I have reasons. But you're here now, so it's your call what you do with it now.'

'I never wanted to send you to prison, Bill, back then. You know that.'

'Here we go again, then,' he said, and the laughter stopped and his voice was serious again.

There was the sense of time moving on now. The bright greens of midsummer were fading. The grass around them was flecked with pale seed heads. The alders by the ditches were looking dry. The two of them sat on the bed, side by side, looking out of the square white window and the flat fields, and he talked and she listened, asking occasional questions, making the odd comment.

'Beginning at the start. Everyone knew the Hogbens. Frank's father, Max, was the big man in town. He drove a souped-up Ford Escort with all the trimmings.'

'Sunburst red,' she said.

'Sunburst red. Yes. You heard about him, then? Fast car. A real people's car. Know what I mean? Him and his mates used to race rallies, all around these lanes. Terrified people. Only, Max died in a stupid accident in that car and Frank inherited his father's reputation, and the car.'

Alex shifted with impatience. 'Frank Hogben was a drug dealer. Tell me about that.'

'Wait now. Be patient for once.'

'Sorry. Go on.'

'But you found that out too, then? Yes. Frank was a drug dealer. Right under everyone's noses.'

'You knew that?'

'God, no. Not at the time. I only found out after he was dead. I'll tell you, Alex, if you'll only be quiet for a minute.'

'Right,' she said. 'Right.' And waited what seemed like an age for him to begin.

'Frank wanted to be the big man,' Bill said eventually, 'just like everyone said his dad had been. Max Hogben was a violent man. Always punchy, you know what I mean? I think he used to beat up everyone. Not just enemies either. We had Max a few times on assault charges, but nothing stuck. Like father, like son, it turned out. Frank was one of those who we suspected was up to stuff, but we didn't know what, exactly. Found out later that Curly used to crew with Frank on *The Hopeful* and that's where it all went on.'

He had a way of telling stories that made her want to scream, she thought.

'What I found out after was Frank had been using the trawler to meet a Spanish boat in the Channel and bring back drugs. It started off as just a bit of marijuana but it grew into something pretty big. Curly turned a blind eye and then Frank kept giving him a bit of money to do exactly that. That way everybody kept quiet about it. I think it crept up on Curly. No harm in it at the start, he thought. Then, the bigger it got, the unhappier Curly was.'

'Curly was in on all that too?'

'Insofar as he was on the boat, yes. Frank had learned the value of scaring people from his dad. He threatened Curly. Told him to keep working and keep his mouth shut. Curly didn't even want the money. Never spent a penny. It came to thousands of pounds in the end, and he never never once spent a single cent. He just kept it in a tin under his bed. Lucky for him he didn't.'

'Why was it lucky?'

'I'll get to that, for pity's sake, Alex. Almost fifteen grand by the end of it.'

'Jesus. It was a big operation.'

'Not at first. Not big enough to get too much attention. Not big enough to get noticed by the bigger gangs either, who'd have wanted part of it. Just steady, over the years. I know. Either way it couldn't last. They were bringing in up to almost a hundred kilos of heroin a trip by the end of it, Curly says. That's industrial quantities. I believe Curly must have been terrified about what would happen if they were caught and just as scared about what would happen if they weren't. Give it a couple of years, and Frank Hogben would have been a full-on don himself, you know. Or they'd all have been dead.'

'You knew Curly and you had no idea any of this was going on?'

He sipped his tea. 'I had a good idea that Frank Hogben was a self-centred bastard. I had a good idea that people were scared of him. But nobody dared peach. You have to understand what Frank was like. There was a man killed in The Grenadier eight years ago in a fight; we found his body in the toilets. He'd been beaten and kicked to death. Rumour was Frank had done it, but nobody would come forward. Everybody swore he wasn't even there, though we know from CCTV outside the pub that his Escort was. Tina said he was at home with her, and she stuck with that, so there was nothing we could do. There was nothing on him.'

'He was beating her up too.'

'You found that out as well?'

'She still wears it. I think you can see it in her face. I guessed it from the way she behaves, and I took a chance and looked at the domestic abuse stats in East Folkestone. Around the same time you're talking about there were multiple reports of domestics taking place at the bottom end of Broadmead Road. That was all Frank and her, wasn't it?'

He looked at the bare pine floor; the curve of planks where the softer parts had worn, leaving knots and the grain. 'I remember all that. Neighbours said they heard fights but nobody named names, you know? They were afraid, too. Without Tina saying it, we couldn't do a thing about it. The neighbourhood team up there knocked on doors to see if everything was OK, but Tina always told them she was fine.'

Alex nodded.

'I've known Tina all my life. She's not a bad girl. She just ended up in the wrong place. I went down to the docks, saw *The Hopeful* leave, and once I knew it was out of the way I would drive up to their house, knock on the door. I said, "Tina. Tell me the truth." She wouldn't say anything, even to me . . .'

'Stella told me I was barking up the wrong tree with that angle. Why would she do that?'

He said, 'We'll come to that, OK?'

He stood, opened a drawer under the cooker ring, took out a packet of digestives. He offered her one, then took one out of the packet for himself and lowered it carefully into the cup. Before the wet biscuit could disintegrate, she watched him pop it whole into his mouth and then chew. 'I knew Curly was the one who went out on *The Hopeful* with Frank Hogben. I came across him one day out on the beach at Dungeness and asked him straight out if he thought Frank was assaulting Tina. Like everyone, Curly said he knew nothing at all about it. I reckon he suspected all along, just like we had. Hearing it from me was confirmation; Frank was beating his wife. Know what? Curly never went out on *The Hopeful* again with Frank. Refused point-blank. Frank wasn't happy at all, roughed Curly up pretty bad, but Curly wouldn't shift so nothing he could do about it. Curly said he wanted to give all that money he'd been given back to him. Frank just laughed at him. Know what Frank said?'

Alex shook her head.

'"Chuck it in the bin," Frank told Curly. "Half of it was forged anyway." When Frank was starting out, he sold on drugs to another dealer and got paid out forged notes. That's what Frank was paying people off in to get rid of them. A cold bastard in every way. And that's when he started taking poor Danny Fagg out instead.'

'His cousin?'

'That's right? You met him?'

'I went out on his boat.'

'You notice his hand?'

'One finger of his right hand was missing.' She remembered the flush in the big, shy man's face as she had asked him about his missing finger.

'Frank did that. Danny wasn't much keener than Curly to do any of this. They had an argument about it one day, Frank held his hand on the winch so the cable cut the finger right off. Crushed it. That's the kind of man Frank was. An angry little bastard, all the time. You can say it was all his dad's fault but – know what? – you don't have to turn out like your father.'

'No, Bill. You don't.'

Bill paused to pick up his tea and drink. 'And now, every time Frank went out, Curly would go round to check on her.

Neighbours probably thought they were having an affair. It used to happen all the time, with the boats. Curly tried to look after her. He did his best.'

There was a knock at the door. Bill stood and went to it. A woman in her fifties was there; face brown from the sun. She looked disapprovingly at Alex. 'Is everything OK, Bill?'

'Not really.'

'That's her, is it?' demanded the woman. Alex guessed the woman in khaki dungarees was the smallholder.

'Yep.'

'She found you, then?'

'Yes. She did.'

She looked at Alex, unsmiling. 'Please be nice to him.'

'I will try.'

'Not like the last time.' The farmer held her gaze for a second, then turned and disappeared.

'This is her place. She lets me stay here for nothing.'

'She knows about me, then? And she doesn't like me much.'

'Nope.'

Alex said, 'Good for her. I don't like me much right now, either.' She took a gulp of her tea. It wasn't so bad. 'Go on, Bill.'

'And so it went on. Of all people, I ought to understand why women who are being beaten up by their husbands just carry on through it all and don't tell anyone.'

'You didn't turn out like your dad, Bill.'

Bill nodded. 'Just the same. That's what it was. I looked at Tina standing there on her doorstep at Broadmead Road and I saw my own mother. All she needed to do was to tell us and we'd have arrested him, and he would have been out of her life, but she never would.'

'People like Frank control every aspect of a woman's life.'

'I know all that.' He sighed deeply. 'I know everything about that, believe me. So I waited to hear from her and I never did. Until one day, a little over seven years ago, when Curly called me up and told me Frank was dead.'

'Oh my God.' Alex slammed her tea down onto the step, splashing tea. 'It was Curly that killed him?'

'I got a phone call in the middle of night. Curly told me to come urgently because something terrible had happened. My first thought was that Tina had been attacked by Frank again and that he'd finally done it. I told him to call the police. But he said no, she was safe. But he wanted me to come to her house because he had something he needed to show me. Well . . . not even the house. He told me to come to Frank's garage. Broadmead Road is one of those Victorian streets with workshops at the back, built against the railway line. Half of the Hogbens' house was above the old archway you had to go through to get there.'

'I know. I went there.'

'Of course you did. You would do that, wouldn't you?' A breeze rustled the wheat in the next field; a pale shiver of silver passed across the brown. 'So it was two in the morning or something. When I got there, I could see the light was on, so I knocked on the door. One of those big old wooden doors with a smaller little door in it. Curly opened up the wee one and let me in. At first all I could see was Frank Hogben's Ford Escort. His dad's old car.'

'Sunburst red.'

265

'His pride and joy. The car his father had died in. That's another story.'

She nodded. 'I've heard it.'

'Of course you have. It was the car that killed his father. What you didn't know is it killed the son too. I saw two feet sticking out of it.'

'Oh God.'

'That's right. He had been changing the gearbox, Curly said. Great cars for being able to tinker with, those old Escorts. Curly said Tina had found him like that a little earlier and had called him in a panic, not knowing what to do about it. It fell on his chest and crushed the life out of him. Alex?' Bill looked at her, suddenly anxious. 'Are you OK?'

FORTY-TWO

'You look like you've seen a ghost.' Bill said.

Alex realised she had her arms pressed against her chest; she felt as if someone were pulling a strap tight around her. 'I don't know what it is,' she whispered. 'Do you think I'm getting asthma?'

'You're sweating,' he said.

'It's the weather. It's close.'

She was panting like a dog in a hot car. Bill put his arm around her with a tenderness that she was not used to from him. 'Take some more deep breaths.'

When she had calmed enough, he stood and returned with an earthenware jug of water, which he poured for her. It wasn't cold, but he had put a sprig of mint in it to freshen it.

'Better?'

'I have these dreams. I don't really remember them. But I just wake up feeling really short of breath. A little like that.'

He nodded.

'Like a weight is pressing down on me.'

'Poor girl,' said Bill.

Lambs almost as big as their mothers were bleating, demanding milk. A breeze blew dandelion seed into the sunlight.

'Go on then. Tell me what happened, Bill.'

He waited until she'd drunk all the water. 'You sleeping badly?'

'Yep.'

'Drinking too much?'

'Rich, coming from you, Bill.'

And now a pair of lambs, foreheads thick with new wool, approached to inspect them, sniffing Alex's trainers. When she stretched out a hand towards them they skittered away. 'Get on with it. Tell me, Bill, please. I can't bear it.'

He settled himself on the wooden steps. 'Frank Hogben hadn't died straight away. I could see that. His shins were covered in blood from where he'd been kicking up at the car's sills. He must have been doing it quite a while.'

'What made you realise it was murder?'

He turned towards her. 'Why do you say that?'

'Because if it was just an accident it would have been simple and you'd have just called it in. You obviously didn't.'

He ran his hand through his hair, then put his elbows back on the step above. 'I could see that right away. There were two heavy-duty jacks taking the weight under the engine. Both had been let down. You might get one jack failing, but not two.'

'Someone let the car down on top of him deliberately and crushed him slowly to death. But you still didn't call it in as murder?'

'No.' He sat up again, plucked a long stem of grass that was growing up through the steps. 'Of course, she said she didn't do it. She just called when she found him there. Claimed she wasn't even there.'

'Why didn't she call the police, then?'

'Well, exactly. And Curly told her to call me. Because we were friends.'

'She might have got away with it. History of domestic abuse. Juries are getting more lenient about that.'

He shook his head. 'Given the method of murder, I much doubt it. He was still kicking when the second one came down on him. However much he deserved it, that was absolutely pre-meditated. She would have gone down for a while. What would you have done, Alex?'

'You know what I would have done.'

He nodded. 'Oh yes. I know. But I'm not you and I was there, thinking, what shall I do? That's when Curly told me about the drugs and how he'd intimidated half the neighbourhood.'

The lambs were back again, still curious.

'And so you took it on yourself to make sure she walked?'

'Yep. Nobody was going to accuse Danny Fagg of doing it. And there were plenty of people who turned up at the inquest and swore blind they had seen Frank get on *The Hopeful* the day he disappeared. Curly had seen to that. Even if people thought there might be more to him disappearing, there was nothing for them to go on.'

'You helped her get rid of the body? Where is it then?'

He looked at her with sadness. 'I know we're different, you and me, Alex. I know you do what you feel you have to do now.'

She nodded.

269

'I don't mind going back to jail. I've lost all my bloody money, anyway,' he said with a small laugh.

'How will you manage?'

'I'll manage. It's Curly and Tina who I worry about. They'll go down too, won't they?'

'What happened to the money?' she asked. 'Frank must have had loads. It has never turned up – if it had, they might have figured out that Frank Hogben had been dealing drugs all this time. You got rid of that as well?'

'We hid all the money, forged or not; Frank's and Curly's, same place we hid Frank. It's somewhere nobody's ever going to find it. I told Tina and Curly that I'd help Frank disappear, but they had to promise they would never touch any of the money they'd got from all that. Know what? I don't think either of them really wanted it anyway. They just wanted him gone so badly. That's all either of them ever wanted.'

'What about you? Did you ever want the money?'

He was a man who had worked all his life and who was now sitting on the bare step of a dwelling that was no more than a few square feet. 'I don't mind saying it's been on my mind, recently.'

'I bet it has. You are flat broke, is what I hear.'

'You don't think I haven't considered taking a few to tide me over?'

'You wouldn't do that, Bill.'

'Says you.'

'Not that you don't deserve it, Bill.'

'Life's not fair, Alex.'

She stood and turned to face him. 'What did you do with the body, Bill?'

'Secret,' he said.

'Last time I arrested you, I remember I cried,' she said. 'I couldn't even get the proper bloody words out.' She leaned forward and kissed him on the cheek.

'It's OK. Somebody has to believe in all this stuff. It might as well be you.'

She sat next to him for a long while, and eventually said, 'Can you get us a ride home, Bill? I'm done in. I'm too tired to cycle.'

He looked confused. 'Aren't you arresting me now?'

She stood. 'Not today, Bill. Maybe another day.'

'I don't get it,' he said.

'Nor do I, really, but there's something important I have to do first.'

She shook her head, then reached her hand out to him to help him stand.

FORTY-THREE

They rode home together in the farmer's Land Rover pickup, Alex's bike in the back.

Bill got out at Arum Cottage. 'I've been keeping the bird bath topped up for you,' she said.

'Bloody thing. You know you're going to have to do that when I'm back inside?'

'Sure.' He turned and sighed. After the farmer had said her goodbyes, Alex wheeled her bike up the track, leaving him alone. Zoë was at the house when she let herself in.

'How was Tina?'

'I like her. She's nice.'

Alex thought of the way Tina had let down the jacks, one after the other, on top of her husband. Not nice, perhaps, but understandable. Frank Hogben's mother had been right all along. Tina had been a murderer. Alex had figured out who had killed Mary Younis; now she knew who had killed Frank Hogben. She should be satisfied with the way she had made something of vague shapes in the dark.

'You look done in, Mum.'

'Yeah. I am.'

'What about Bill? Did you find out why he's hiding from you?'

'As a matter of fact I did. Did you?'

'No. He never told me. He just asked me to trust him.'

'And you've been seeing him every day?'

'Some days. I took him food and stuff. Is he back?'

Zoë's grin was pure and uncomplicated. And she was running out of the door to welcome him back before her mother could say anything else.

At eleven Zoë was not back. She would be staying over at Bill's, which was good.

The curtains in Terry Neill's bedroom were open, but there was no moon tonight, and the tides were getting higher. The new moon was bringing a seven-metre tide with it. A low pressure system was moving down the North Sea. The summer weather was about to end and the pumps out on the marsh would be working hard again soon.

She could hear the waves from up here; the small thump as the water fell, the regular, gentle hiss as it retreated. At around one she heard a car pull up outside, then the key in the door, and finally the feet on the stairs.

When the light came on, it was absurdly bright. She was blinking when Terry exclaimed, 'What the hell—?'

'I let myself in,' she said.

'Obviously.' He stood at the top of the stairs at the end of the house that faced the road.

She sat at the opposite end, on the window seat. 'I couldn't sleep.'

'What a lovely surprise, to find a gorgeous woman waiting for me in my bedroom.'

'Creep.'

'It's the truth, Alex. Can I ask how you managed to get in?'

'I'm a police officer – allegedly, at least. I saw where you leave your spare. Your alarm code is 1974, which I saw you enter last time you brought me back here and which is also confirmed as your date of birth as displayed in your passport.' She held it up.

The smile left his face. 'Ah.'

'I had already guessed why you were hiding it from me on the boat trip. I just wanted to be sure.'

He walked a few more paces into the room. 'Drink? Wine?'

'I'm fine.'

'Something stronger?'

'No thanks.'

'Coffee maybe? You look tired.'

'Yes, I am. I'm very tired indeed. More tired than you would ever bloody believe.' She flicked through the passport. She had found it in a drawer of his desk downstairs. 'Five trips to Guatemala in the last three years.'

He approached her. 'Are police officers allowed to go rummaging through people's drawers? I could make a complaint.'

'You invited me into your house, Terry. I was just acting like a suspicious lover. You could try complaining but it wouldn't stand up. You're a cold one, aren't you?'

He shrugged. 'You've got me wrong.'

'I believe I did get you wrong, yes. You called Ayman Younis your best friend.'

He pouted slightly. 'And he was.'

'But you didn't mind defrauding him of over four hundred thousand pounds for a forestry project in Guatemala that doesn't even exist. It was the money he had saved for his son.'

He kept a straight face. 'What makes you think it was me?'

'Of course it was you. How else do you live like this?' She waved her arm around the house. 'Don't tell me that this is all your pension. I looked into that, too. You were asked to leave your university under a cloud after several warnings about your drug use. I doubt your pension was stellar.'

'Maybe I had a big inheritance.'

'Maybe you did. Or maybe you are the con man.'

He frowned. 'Even if it was true, which it isn't, you wouldn't be able to prove anything. Hypothetically speaking, obviously.'

Alex sat there for a while looking at him. 'Are you sure about that?'

For just a second he looked nervous, his head jerking back a fraction, and she knew right then absolutely that she had been right.

'Fairly confident,' he said eventually. He was right about that too, unfortunately. She had spoken to an old friend at the Met who specialised in this kind of crime. That was how these scams worked. There would be no trail at all that led back to Terry Neill. He was not listed among the benefactors of Biosfera. He had used Ayman Younis as the conduit for the cash from all the other so-called friends at the golf club. He had set Ayman up to be the one who told everyone else how great the investment would be. By now all the money would be lying in some obscure account in the Caribbean where Terry Neill could access it whenever he wanted. As long as he wasn't too greedy and didn't move too large a sum in any single transaction, nobody would be able to prove anything.

'How low does this all go, Terry? Did you invite me out because you wanted to know how the case was going, as well?'

He shook his head. 'Nope. All that was sincere, I promise.'

'Nothing you say is reliable. You're a con man.'

'Are you fishing for compliments? You want me to tell you I asked you for a date because you were intelligent and good-looking?'

'I'm just trying to figure out how exploited I was.'

'I promise you it was not about that. If it was, it was a ghastly mistake, because here you are, breaking into my house, with all these . . . allegations.'

'You're not denying any of it?'

'Nor am I admitting any of it. It was Ayman Younis who invested the money. Not me.' He turned. 'Look. I need a drink, even if you don't. Are you sure?'

'A hundred per cent.'

When he was gone, she sat still, looking over at the neatly made bed they had slept in.

He returned with whisky and sat on the end of the Egyptian cotton duvet, looking at her. 'Well, this is awkward,' he said and took a gulp.

'Give the money back.'

'You're joking, obviously.'

'No. Absolutely not. Do the decent thing and give the money back. You don't need it.'

He said nothing.

'I'm ashamed to have known you.'

'I'm sorry about that.'

'Give the money back.'

'Or else what?'

She stood. 'I guess I should be going.'

'I'll change the alarm code just in case you try coming back.'

'Don't worry. I won't.'

She was just at the end of his bed when she stopped. 'You took money from Bill South, too, didn't you?'

'No comment. Isn't that what people say? Besides, as I said, it was Ayman Younis who took the money.'

'Bill is a friend of mine. He's had a shit life and it's probably about to get a great deal worse. That was his savings. It wasn't a lot, but it was all he had.'

'Some people make poor investment decisions. It's not my fault.'

'Thirteen thousand pounds. You could afford to give the money back.'

He squinted at her. 'You're kidding me, aren't you?'

'Please.'

'This is ridiculous.'

'I don't like to beg, Terry, but he deserves something, at least.'

'I think you said you're leaving.'

She nodded and walked to the end of the room and down the stairs. 'Close the door on the way out,' he said.

The hot summer rain started on the way home, soaking her through; headlights glared off the wet road. It was a twenty-minute ride home. At home she yanked off the soaked clothes, showered, then lay on her bed listening to the sound of water.

FORTY-FOUR

The next day, Alex travelled to London to see her mother. It had been too long.

Helen lived alone in Stoke Newington in a house that was far too big for her. She let herself in; sometimes her mother didn't answer the doorbell because she was playing music too loud.

The bed in the front room was new. Her mother was in the kitchen, sitting at the kitchen table playing patience, listening to music on the radio. There was a pile of washing-up in the sink and knickers drying on the back of the chair.

'Oh,' she said as Alex walked in. 'It's you. No Zoë?'

'There's a bed in the front room,' Alex said.

'Yes,' her mother answered. 'Put the kettle on, love.'

'That's where you're sleeping now? In the front room?'

'I can't be bothered going up and down the stairs,' she said.

She walked up to her mother and gave her a kiss. Her mother tolerated the embrace. When her father was alive, the house was

278

spotless. He had done most of the housework. Her mother was never really much concerned about that kind of thing. 'Come on, get your coat on. I promised to take you for lunch.'

'You look very tired,' Helen said. 'Are you ill?'

Alex laughed. 'Yes. I think I am. I just broke up with a man.'

'Good for you.'

While her mother was getting ready to go out, Alex washed up the dishes in the sink and told her about Zoë's starfish in the fridge, which made her laugh. 'I miss that girl,' her mother said. On the 73 bus, Helen said, 'Seriously, love. Are you all right? You look unwell. Zoë says you've been seeing a counsellor.'

'Yes.'

Her mother made a face.

'It's because of work and stress. It's been good, I think. I found myself talking about you and Dad a bit.'

'Oh dear,' said Helen. 'That's the trouble with all that stuff. It's always our fault. *They fuck you up, your mum and dad.*'

'Maybe you do.' Her parents had both been police officers. Her mother quit when she became pregnant with Alex, but her father spent his working life in the Metropolitan Police. 'What I've been thinking about is that maybe I've been trying too hard to live up to Dad.'

'Maybe you have. He wore me out with it, that's for sure.'

'He never let it get to him,' said Alex. 'I wonder if we're just weaker than your generation. He never suffered from stress.'

Her mother snorted.

'What?'

'What do you mean, he never let it get to him? That stuff you do. It eats away at you. It ate away at him, too.'

279

Alex blinked. 'Really? He always seemed so calm and on top of everything.'

Her mother stood and took hold of one of the yellow grab rails near the door; they were almost there now. 'You see what you want to in your parents. You always adored him. You didn't see him some nights after the lights went out. Terrible nightmares sometimes. It passed in the end, but there were a couple of years when he was a wreck.'

'I never knew.'

'You built him up,' her mother said. 'You're still trying to live up to him. Maybe that's your problem.'

'I don't really see that as a problem,' said Alex.

'Suit yourself,' said her mother.

They ate at a gastropub in Islington, sitting at a table outside so her mother could smoke. 'Was he nice, the man you broke up with?'

'Absolute scum of the earth.'

Her mother smiled. 'Life's a lot better without men, sometimes, I find.' That stung a little. Alex still resented it – how much her mother seemed to enjoy life now her father was gone. She had some financial business she had to discuss with her mother. Her mother never liked talking money, but Alex forced her to do it. She took out documents and a pen, and watched as her mother signed them.

'Are you sure you're going to be all right, Alex? You're worrying me, you know.'

A busker was setting up a pitch close to where they were eating. He had a large, green metal frame with a small seat on it.

'Don't get me wrong. Your father was a very good man. But he wasn't perfect all the time. He just hid that part well.'

Alex reached out and put her hand over her mother's.

'Is there any wine left in the carafe?' Helen stared at her daughter. 'You shouldn't measure yourself against your father all the time. I know how much you two had this thing together. I was always a bit jealous of it, you and him. He was a good, kind man, and I suppose I was lucky with him, but sometimes I wish he'd have taken the stick out of his arse, know what I mean? You're your own person, Alex.'

Helen picked up her wine glass and took a decent gulp.

'It's so easy to pull the wool over people's eyes when you just show them what they want to see, isn't it?'

For a second Alex thought she was still talking about her father and was about to start an argument, then she realised that her mother was not looking at her at all but at the busker. He had hauled himself up onto the metal chair, a metre above the ground, and tugged a Yoda mask over his face, then pulled on green rubber hands and rested one on the pole that held the chair. With the cloak falling around him it looked like he was floating in the air. Within a minute, the coins started falling into a copper pot he had left on the ground in front of him.

'It's just a trick,' said Helen. 'People are so stupid.'

'That's what it all is,' said Alex, smiling at her mother. 'A very neat trick.'

Afterwards, she made it down to Waterloo and caught the train back to Kent. She was trying to think things through, over and over, but she kept getting distracted by a young couple who were taking photographs of each other with an old Nikon camera, laughing. And then, before she realised she had fallen asleep, the girl with the camera was shaking her awake, saying, 'Is this your stop?'

The train was at Folkestone. She had meant to get off at Ashford. She had barely time to leap up, disoriented, thank the girl, and jump out of the door before the train started moving again. On the platform she looked at her phone:

Where are you?

Are you OK????

Jill had been waiting at Ashford station to pick her up and drive her home. Alex called her. 'I'm sorry. I don't sleep that well, and I'm tired all the time now . . .'

'Wait there. Don't go anywhere. I'll be there in thirty.'

But with half an hour to kill in Folkestone, she took the opportunity to walk up the hill to the east of the station. She found the house again, and emerged through the arch into the space behind the old houses, where old street cobbles showed beneath worn tarmac. It was quiet. There was nobody around.

Lining the far side of the yard were several old workshops, most of them disused. From Bill's description it was easy to see which the Hogbens' lock-up had been. It still had the big wooden door, but there was a fat padlock on it and no way to get in.

She walked up to it, bending down to try and see in through the crack between the smaller door and its frame, but though she caught the whiff of old oil, it was too dark inside to make out anything inside.

'And what do you presume you're doing?'

Alex stood up and looked round. The woman she had disarmed at the Light Railway Cafe in Dungeness stood behind her, hands in the pockets of a faded purple housecoat.

'Mrs Hogben,' Alex said.

'Do I know you?' The woman leaned forward a little. There was a blob of spittle on her lip. From the puzzled expression on her face, it seemed she didn't even remember the encounter they had had at Dungeness.

'You live here still?'

'Why not? It's my fucking house. My son doesn't need it any more.'

'What about this lock-up?' Alex asked, gesturing behind her.

'That's my son's. Used to be his father's. Both fucking dead now.' She swore as old people do sometimes, when the fabric of their minds is worn too thin to hold the words in check.

'Who uses it now?'

Mandy Hogben shook her head. 'It's that woman's. She kept it.'

'Tina's? Do you know what's in there?'

'That bloody car.'

'A Ford Escort?'

'Yeah. Max loved that car more than he ever loved me. Same with Frank. Little bastards, both of them. Stupid car.'

Alex nodded. If she was right, the car that had killed Frank Hogben was still in there. 'I've a question for you, Mrs Hogben. Have you seen her using it recently?'

'Who?'

'Tina. Your daughter-in-law.'

'Ex-daughter-in-law, thank fuck. No. She'd never bloody dare come round here. She hasn't been back since he disappeared. She fucking killed my Frank.'

'You think she did, don't you?'

'Killed him,' the woman said. 'Yeah.'

'Can I ask something? How do you know that?'

The woman leaned in a little again. 'Do I know you?' she asked again.

'How do you know she killed your son, Mrs Hogben?'

'Stands to reason.'

Alex nodded. This woman had dementia, but she was right. It stood to reason. Alex looked around. 'Has anybody else been here?'

The woman took her hands out of her pockets, looked down at them for a little while, and put them back again. 'Apart from that boy?'

The wind blew rubbish up into the air behind the houses. A yellow sweet wrapper floated in the air for a second, then sank back down. 'What boy?'

'Hangs round with Tina and that lesbo. I told them it's my Max's car. They've no right to it.'

'A friend of Stella's?'

'Her brother, I think. Looks like her. I don't know. Sometimes at night, he comes here. I can see him.' She pointed to a window at the back of the house.

'Do they ever take the car out?'

'You smoke?'

'No.'

The woman looked disappointed. 'Who are you, anyway, snooping around here?'

'What's he look like, Stella's brother?' asked Alex.

The woman sniffed the air. 'You smell like a copper. You're a copper, aren't you?'

The back door to the Hogbens' house opened and a young woman with a cheery smile came out dressed in a blue nylon top; a carer on a home visit.

'Is she bothering you?'

'Not at all,' answered Alex.

'Well, she's bothering me,' muttered Mandy Hogben, and turned away, leaving Alex on her own.

Alex didn't need an answer, anyway. She had a pretty good idea of what Stella's brother looked like; she was pretty sure it was him she had seen up at the memorial.

She had plenty of time to get back to the station and wait on the bench, eating sandwiches from the newsagent, before Jill's mint-green Fiat pulled up outside.

Alex folded herself into the passenger seat for the first question. 'How was your mum?'

'Drinking and smoking like a good 'un. Tell me. Have you made any progress on who the con man was at the golf club?'

'Jesus. You don't bloody give it a rest, do you? Not our department any more, but no. We've passed that one on to another team now. Good luck to them with that.'

The traffic was heavy going through Hythe. The queue of cars waiting to get into Waitrose had backed out into the main road.

'We're used to winning,' Alex said.

'What?'

'Murder's simple most of the time. We're used to getting

convictions. Financial fraud is so much more complex. People get away with absolute murder there.'

Jill scowled. 'What if I come round tonight? Stay over, drink some pink wine, and you tell me about your love life and talk about nothing else to do with murder or money. 'Cause there's nothing going on in mine.'

'Not tonight, Jill. I'm too tired.'

Jill indicated and pulled out, past the queue of cars, foot working the accelerator hard. They drove past Bill South's little house; a *For Sale* sign had gone up. There was an estate agent's Mini outside, and a new Audi. The only people who could afford to live around here these days were the ones rich enough to have two homes. 'Is he selling?'

'He says he needs the money.'

'That's bloody awful. Oh, Jesus.'

'I know.'

When Jill dropped her outside her house, she said, 'Sorry. You know. I just need a little more time to myself.'

'Fine,' said Jill, though Alex could tell she was hurt.

And it wasn't true either. Because that evening, instead of going to bed early like she should have done, she put on a little make-up, a nice black shirt and trousers, did her hair, and booked an Uber.

FORTY-FIVE

The look on Terry's face when she came into the bar was worth much more than the price of her wine. At first puzzled, then anxious, and then angry too. She liked to see the way his head jerked around the room to see who else was in here.

He ordered himself a gin. When the barman's back was turned, he muttered, 'I didn't really expect to see you here.'

'I don't suppose you did,' she said.

When the barman came back with Terry's drink, she held out a note to him. 'My treat,' she said. 'I insist.'

Holding out his card, Terry hesitated, then brought his eyebrows together in a way that she would have once thought attractive. 'Well. OK then.' The barman took her note instead and returned with change.

'I want to talk,' she said.

'No comment.'

'Just ten minutes of your time. Then I'll leave you alone.'

He looked around. It was a weekday evening. The bar was

fairly quiet, at least. 'Over there,' he said. To one side of the old fireplace there was a small round table, beneath a wall of photographs of men and women holding trophies. It was far enough away from the bar for them to talk in private. Ever the gent, in appearance at least, he took both glasses and put them on the table.

'It's about Bill South,' she said when they were sitting down. 'He's in a bad way. Like I said, I want to help him.'

'You're a good woman. I appreciate that.'

'You took his money. I am asking you again. I want you to give it back to him.'

He looked up towards the whitewashed ceiling. 'I don't have it. How many times do I have to tell you that?'

'As a favour. Please. Just give him the money. Just tell him that you, or Ayman, hadn't had time to invest it yet. Or put it into his bank account anonymously, no questions asked.'

His smile was full of condescension. 'If I did, which I can't, it would be an admission that I had somehow taken the money from him. Which, obviously, I haven't.'

She paused, took a deep breath. 'OK. Listen to this. What about if I give you the money, will you give it to him?'

He laughed. 'What?'

'He's a good friend. He's desperate. He has no money now. He's going to have to sell his house. I'm the one who lost him his pension. This is your fault, but some of it is my fault, too. I am trying to heal wounds. I feel like unless I do something about this . . . I'm kind of lost here, Terry.'

'This is your kind of penance, you mean?'

'I don't really go for the religious thing, but yes, in a way.'

288

He thought for a minute. 'Find another way. I don't want to be part of this.'

'Think of it as a favour. I won't tell anyone what you did. Just do this and I'm gone from your life.'

'You want to give me thirteen thousand pounds, and for me to give it to him?'

She didn't answer.

'Why would I do that?'

'For me. Just as a last favour.'

He finished his glass; squinted at her. 'If I was to do that, it wouldn't prove anything at all. Just that I'd pretended to be someone who knew where his money was.'

'There's nothing at all linking you to the money, for better or worse. But he'd believe it was you because you are from the golf club. You knew Ayman. I believe it's you. He would too.'

He shrugged. 'He's not stupid.'

'No. He's not. But I think he'd actually believe it. The thing about Bill is that unlike me, he always thinks the best of people.' She picked up his glass. 'Let me get you another one while you think about it.'

She returned to the bar and got him another drink.

'If I do it,' he said when she sat down again, 'you never come back to this club again.'

'What if I suddenly discover the joys of golf?'

'Not here. Ever.'

She nodded. 'OK. Deal.'

'No electronic transfer. Cash only. Nothing you can turn around and try to pin on me.'

'I can't just go to the bank and take out thirteen thousand in cash.'

'Find a way. And I don't want you bringing the money to my house.'

'You're quite paranoid, aren't you?'

'And I'm not coming to yours, either.'

Again, she nodded. 'You sure about this?'

'Not really. So where can we meet? Somewhere quiet where nobody's going to see me.'

She nodded. 'Agreed. Do you know a place called Boat Lane?' she asked. And she described the place in exact detail.

On her way out, she took a twenty-pound note and placed it in the yellow charity box on the table; the one that Ayman Younis must have put there. When she left the room she was sure she could hear him laughing, but didn't dare look back because she wouldn't know what she would do if she did.

— *You say you've changed in the last few weeks. In what way?*
— *I'm about to do something that would have been unthinkable to my old self.*
— *Is that good?*
— *You tell me. I've never felt less certain of something in my life. I'm letting someone who I believe has committed a terrible crime get away with it.*
— *How terrible? You know you probably shouldn't tell me. If you tell me about a crime, I'm not obliged to keep that confidential.*
— *Don't sound so nervous. I'll spare you the details. Remember I told you about that man I sent to prison?*
— *The one who likes birds?*

290

— *He's a good man. Best man I've ever known, really. He always looked out for Zoë, from the moment we knew each other. I let him down before by doing what I thought was right. I know he was very hurt by that. I want to do something good for him, but I don't think the old me would have ever done something like this.*

— *I can't pretend to understand what you're telling me, but I do know that at the heart of this is empathy. You care very much about what happens to this man. Empathy is good.*

— *Maybe you think so in your profession. In mine, I've never been convinced. If empathy means we only do good to the people we know, what good is that? Know what? I'm actually kind of sick of empathy. Empathy for one person means we value them over the people we can't see. We're just looking out for our friends and family. That's like the mafia. I don't want empathy. I want some rationality, for a change.*

— *Rationality isn't going to help you. If you're feeling that kind of empathy for this man, maybe it's like that part of you that you've kept under the skin for so long that's coming alive again.*

— *Maybe. I'm not so sure I like it, though. I miss my old, cold-hearted self who knew how she felt about everything and knew exactly what she was supposed to do. Why are you laughing?*

It was raining when Curly delivered the car to her door. 'It's a classic,' he said.

'I bet it absolutely soaks up petrol,' complained Zoë.

A twenty-seven-year-old gold Mercedes estate. 'I like it, though. I can see myself in a car like that.'

'I said we should get an electric car.'

'It's what we can afford. We're going to have to tighten our belts a little, one way or another. Is that rust?' Alex peered at the sills.

'It's a bargain, that's what it is,' said Curly.

'I don't see why we need a car at all, Mum.'

Curly handed her mother the heavy old key. 'Don't worry, Zoë. We're just taking it for a test drive, love. I somehow doubt your mother is going to like this one.'

'We'll be back in a couple of hours.'

'Don't I get a say on which car we buy?'

'No,' said Alex, getting into the leather driver's seat. She put the car into gear and moved away, turning the big wipers on to clear the rain from the windscreen. As she passed the new lighthouse, the wheel dipped into a pothole, and the sump cracked against the concrete track.

'Careful,' said Curly. 'I hate to see a car like this treated badly.'

After that, they drove, north, neither saying anything.

She dropped Curly at his house. It was already evening by the time she turned off a lane in woods just outside Ashford and drove cautiously down a hundred metres of uneven track beneath the trees, to a place where it was wide enough to turn the car around, then switched off the lights and waited.

The woods were thick and old. They smelt of decades of rot. Behind the silhouetted trees, small chinks of pinky blue sky broke into the blackness.

Terry Neill was late. She watched his headlights shining through the trees as they came towards her.

When he was alongside her, he rolled down the window. 'Why here, of all places?'

'Private,' she said. 'Out of public view. Like you wanted.'

'Bloody hell.'

She got out, and stepped into fresh mud, loosened by the day of rain.

'Jesus,' he said, looking down. He was wearing white trainers. 'Come on then. Get it over with.'

'Come and get it then.' She had the money waiting for him in a Sainsbury's shopping bag in the boot. He tiptoed towards the car. Before taking out the bag, he lifted a couple of the wrapped bundles and flicked through them. When he'd looked enough, he waddled through the wet soil with them and put them in the back of his own car.

'When will you do it?' she asked.

'Maybe at the weekend.'

'Sooner,' she said. 'He's about to sell his house. There's no time to be lost.'

'And then we never see each other again.'

'That's not soon enough.'

'Nice car, by the way,' he said as he opened his car door. 'It's a classic.'

She washed the mud off at the twenty-four-hour BP station in Ashford, and drove back towards the coast.

When she got home it was dark, and Zoë was sat on the couch on her own watching TV.

'Where's the car?'

'I decided it wasn't right for us,' she said. 'The petrol consumption was too high.'

'Told you,' said Zoë.

That night she slept for the first time in what felt like weeks. When she woke, thick-headed, as if she had a hangover, it was to a steady, welcome drizzle, blowing in from the sea in grey waves. 'Oh Christ,' she said out loud. 'What the hell have I done?' But Zoë was already up and out of the house.

FORTY-SIX

On the following Saturday she and Zoë walked down to Arum Cottage with a pot of coffee, half a dozen eggs, and a loaf of bread that Zoë had made. They walked with a big fishing umbrella covering both of them. Summer had turned into autumn. There was an *Under Offer* sign outside now. Rain was cascading out of the bird bath onto the stones around him.

'Did you hear anything from Mr Neill?' she asked when he let them inside.

'Guess what? Not a thing,' said Bill.

'What are you talking about?' Zoë dumped the bread onto his kitchen work surface.

Alex put her hand on Zoë's head and stroked her short hair. 'Just a man who owes Bill some money,' she said.

'That's so unfair. Is it a lot?'

'You could say so,' said Bill.

'That's horrible.'

'He's a very horrible man. Why don't you call him, Mum, and tell him to pay it?'

'Because I know exactly what he'll say. He'll say, "What money?" He must think very little of me.'

Bill put his arm around her shoulder. 'He thinks very little of everyone but himself.'

'I don't understand any of this,' said Zoë, looking from one to the other.

'That's good,' said her mother. 'It's much better if you don't.'

Bill changed the subject onto coal tits. It was September. The migrations were in full swing already. Zoë started arguing about the reasons why the continental variations of the species were turning up in larger numbers, which was, Alex guessed, exactly what Bill had intended. And then Zoë went on to say that Kenny Abel had seen a Eurasian treecreeper up at the wildlife sanctuary. 'That's, like, a mega-find,' she said.

'A what?' interrupted Alex. Zoë didn't bother explaining.

Alex and Bill ate scrambled eggs with mackerel that Curly had brought round. Zoë just nibbled her homemade bread.

'When are you going to exchange?' asked Alex eventually.

'Don't know. The client wants to do everything in a hurry.'

'Where will you go?' asked Zoë.

'I've lived round here almost all my life,' said Bill. 'I don't know, exactly.'

The conversation stopped. Alex pushed bread around her plate to soak up what was left there but no longer felt hungry enough to put it into her mouth. On the way back, clutching the half-eaten loaf, Zoë said, 'I didn't want to cry in front of him, so I didn't.'

★

When she got back home, she packed herself a lunch from the rest of the loaf and asked Zoë if she could borrow the binoculars she had given her for her seventeenth birthday.

'Why?'

'You don't need them today. You're going up to London to visit Gran.'

It was true. She was sending her daughter up to London for the day; she would spend the night and come back on the train in the morning. Jill had agreed to give her a ride to the station.

'And your poncho.' The camouflage one that Zoë had bought with her own money, which she used to improvise her own hide with.

'What?'

'I'm going looking for a Eurasian tree-sneaker. My own mega-find.'

Zoë didn't even bother to correct her.

At the Dungeness light railway station, Alex bought a return ticket and waited on the platform for the 12.40, which arrived, disgorging only a handful of tourists. The season had ended. Soon it would be quiet again here. Ducking down, she pulled herself into the small wooden compartment and thought about the day she had seen Stella and Tina arrive on the same train.

The little engine eventually tugged them around the big loop, across the stones, back towards the edge of the estate. In twenty minutes she was at New Romney station, next to the edge of the golf course. A family got off with her. She waited until they had disappeared into the station building before setting off in the opposite direction, walking along the narrow railway track.

Away from the road, the land opened out. It took her a little while to find the right spot, a rise of land to the east of the course, hidden by gorse bushes. Nobody had seen her. She watched Terry Neill arrive at around two o'clock, as he always did. He had made new friends now. Today he was wearing a yellow shirt that made it easy for her to keep an eye on him.

At the sixth hole, she opened her Tupperware and ate a cheese sandwich, drank a cup of coffee from her flask.

The eighth hole of the warren course was closest to where she was hiding. She watched them approach. Terry was playing with two men she didn't recognise, both older than him. She could hear them all laughing when Terry mis-hit a shot into the rough alongside the railway track.

The last of their group was teeing off again when she saw the first blue light. A police car moving at speed down the Dymchurch Road. Then a second.

She watched the two cars speed past the golfers towards the centre of New Romney, disappearing behind the houses.

It seemed to take an age before she saw the police officers emerge from behind the red brick clubhouse, almost half a kilometre away. They seemed in no particular hurry.

A couple of times they stopped to ask other golfers for directions. Watching them through Zoë's binoculars, Alex recognised Colin Gilchrist. He was talking to the women she had talked to the first time she had visited here. One of them was pointing straight towards the eighth hole. It was the former superintendent. Good for her, thought Alex.

She watched the officers walking towards Terry Neill; the group he was with stopped their golf and looked at each other.

Only Terry might have had an inkling of what was happening, but he didn't try to run.

The rest of the group watched, shocked, as the officers led Terry away, leaving his clubs unattended at the edge of the rough. They stood for a long while, as if dazed by what they had just seen happen, even after the cars had travelled back up the road past them with Terry inside.

Instead of completing the round, they put their clubs in their trolleys and wheeled them back towards the clubhouse, as if the whole day's sport had somehow been ruined.

When they had gone, Alex finished her flask of coffee, savouring every sip, then packed up and walked back to the train station in time for the 3.45 home.

FORTY-SEVEN

Jill arrived at around nine in the evening, in the red suit she sometimes wore for work. She was carrying a plastic bag from Tesco Metro as she made her way across the uneven ground in matching red heels. 'Something awful. I wanted you to know before you heard it on the news.'

At the back door, Alex tried to sound surprised. 'What?'

'They are investigating your boyfriend for the murder of Frank Hogben seven years ago.'

'Terry Neill?'

'Yeah. I know. Bizarre, isn't it?'

'Ex-boyfriend. Not even that. One-night stand.'

Jill was all sympathy. She put down her plastic bag, with a tell-tale clink of glass against the concrete door step, and flung her arms around Alex, squeezing her tight. 'You poor girl. Did you know that Terry Neill used to be a smack-head? Frank Hogben was his dealer.'

'Oh my God. No. Really?'

'They just dug up Frank Hogben's body. He never disappeared at sea at all. He was buried up in the woods off Boat Lane in Ashford.'

'Has he confessed?'

'We haven't charged him yet. They questioned him this afternoon. We're still making the case. God. To think of that. You must find this all so disturbing.'

'I do. How did all this happen?'

'Last night there was a call to Crimestoppers. It was a man's voice, but he didn't identify himself. He gave the location of Frank Hogben's body and the name of the person who murdered him, that's all.'

'Any idea who the man who called was?'

'No idea. Thing is, though, we found the body this morning up near Ashford in some woods, just where the guy had said it was buried. And they found, like, three grand in cash buried with him . . . Can I come in? I brought a bottle.'

She fished it out. Alex was touched. Normally Jill preferred pink wine; for Alex she had bought a nice red.

'Forensics say the grave had recently been disturbed. Like . . . dug up. The notes were mostly those old twenties. They're going out of circulation this year. We're working on the theory that whoever buried it realised they'd be worth nothing in a few months.'

'Wow,' said Alex.

Alex wondered where Neill had stashed the £13,000 she had given him. She doubted he would have banked it yet. They would search his house; soon, if they weren't already doing so. When they found the money, it would not take them long to

301

discover Curly's forged notes among them and to match some of the numbers on those twenty-pound notes to the ones they had dug up at Boat Lane woods.

'Can I stay the night? Can I? I miss us just talking like we used to? I really miss you at work and everything. It's not the same.'

Alex stepped forward and returned the hug. 'Soon,' she said. 'Not tonight. OK? I have things I need to do.'

Jill stood there, crestfallen. 'It's OK. I get it. You're still in a vulnerable place.'

'In a way you're right, yes. I am in a vulnerable place. Thanks for telling me in person. I love you, Jill, you know. You're such a pal.'

'Soon then? Promise?'

'Yes. Very soon.'

'Keep the wine. It's OK. You'll probably need it more than me.'

Alex watched her drive away, then took her bike out of the shed and locked the door behind her.

The advantage of not having a car was that her journeys were invisible. A car was traceable by the automatic cameras that stood along almost every road now. A bike was not.

In the darkness, she cycled out to Curly's house in Littlestone. Just to be cautious, she took the back roads.

When she knocked gently, Curly opened the door, peering behind her, checking she was alone. 'Everything go OK?' he asked, his voice anxious.

His living room was surprisingly neat. The furniture was brown, faded by sunlight. It looked like it had been untouched since the 1970s. There were two brass bedpans hanging on either side of the fireplace; above it was a black-and-white photo of a man standing on a trawler. 'You and Danny on the boat. That was like a big pantomime, then. You trying to scare me into realising how dangerous a trawler can be?'

'Sorry. Stupid idea. Didn't mean any harm.'

'Your father?' asked Alex, pointing at the photo.

'He was a good bloke, my dad. Before it all went to shit around here. Tea?'

'I thought you might need something stronger. I brought some wine,' said Alex, taking the bottle Jill had brought her from her backpack. 'You made the call, then.'

'Just like you said.'

'You said exactly what I told you to?'

'Yes. I told them where the body was, and gave them Terry Neill's name. Nothing else.'

'What did you do with the phone?'

'Smashed it up and threw it away. Just like you said.'

'And the Mercedes?'

'Took the plates off and towed it up to the scrapyard in Dartford yesterday. All gone.'

It was a shame. It had been a nice car. She would have liked one like that. A classic, as Terry Neill had said. There would be no record of Alex ever having owned or driven it. Nothing about his account of her giving him the money would tally with the apparent facts.

Alex cracked the metal cap of the bottle open. For Tina's sake, Curly had conspired to cover up a murder. For Bill's sake, she had just done the same. 'If people think Terry Neill killed Frank Hogben, they won't come looking for you and Tina.'

Curly relaxed a little, then went to the kitchen to fetch two glasses, while Alex studied the photo of his father taken before, as Curly said, 'it all went to shit around here'.

'I should say thank you, then. They charged him?'

'Not yet. But they will sometime over the next twenty-four hours, once they've found the money in his house and the mud from Boat Lane woods on his car, which they will do, even if it takes a few days.'

Curly nodded slowly. 'Reckon it'll stick?'

'Maybe. Maybe not. Too early to say.'

'But Tina is in the clear?'

Alex didn't answer. It was too early to tell that, either. They drank the wine for a minute in silence.

'Was it you who buried the body?' she asked eventually.

Curly nodded. 'It wasn't as hard as I thought it would be. I hated that man with every bone in my body, even before I found out what he'd been doing to Tina. When Bill South let out that he was abusing her, I almost killed him myself.'

He drained his glass. Alex poured him another.

'I stopped going out on *The Hopeful* after that. I couldn't bear to be around that man any longer. I'd have thrown him overboard, or vice versa. So when he was out at sea, I went to check up on Tina, told her I knew he was harming her. Course, she said everything was fine, he was just a bit moody sometimes. I could see the marks on her neck, though.' He held up the red wine. 'They were this colour. He used to choke her.' Curly put down the glass and held his hand out, thumb and finger parted; he looked at his hand for a while before he lowered it.

'How did you find out, then?'

304

'She told me it all, in the end, piece by piece. I took my time. Each time he was out on a run, I would know. I'd see the boat go out. So I'd go up and say "Hello, fancy a cup of tea?", just to make sure she was still OK. It took a long time for her to open up.'

'She described the abuse to you?'

'One time he choked her so long she was unconscious for, like, minutes. It was some stupid argument about her wearing a short dress in the chip shop. He didn't like it. When she came around he was on top of her, as if he was frightened he'd killed her that time. Which he almost had, I'd guess. He would have killed her in the end. I'm sure of it.'

'Maybe.'

'I was trying to get her to go to a refuge. I'd almost got her to agree to go. I was that close. Then that Saturday, she called up and said something terrible had happened. She was a mess. She told me she was going to kill herself.'

'The day she killed Frank?'

He scrunched up his mouth for a second, so it looked tiny, just a dark line across his face, then he spoke. 'I went straight up there with a tyre iron, all ready to have to fight Frank. Scared to hell. I'm not a fighter, Alex. Only, he was dead already, under the car. Frank had found out about how she was having this thing with Stella that morning,' Curly went on. 'His mother had seen the two of them together in town a few times when he'd been off at sea, and she'd put two and two together . . . That woman Mandy Hogben is a piece of work. When Mandy told him that, he went straight home and beat the crap out of Tina, and told her he was going to kill Stella. That day he beat Tina and locked her in their bedroom. And she believed that's what he was going to do: kill Stella. He went out, and then, maybe an hour later, he let her out – all smiles, you know? Asked her what was for dinner.'

The bungalow was on the main road. It had started to rain again. Alex could hear the sound of wet tyres on the tarmac.

'She said he had blood on his shirt. Tina thought he'd gone and done it to her, you know?'

'Murdered Stella?'

He nodded. 'Yep. He was all smug, you know. Wouldn't tell her nothing. The more she asked him, the smugger Frank looked. He wanted her to think that. I don't know . . . He'd probably just cut himself doing something stupid to his car. Maybe he put the blood there on purpose to make her more scared. But he was torturing her, mentally, you know? That's what he did to people. So Tina was convinced he'd done exactly what he'd said he was going to do. He'd killed her lover, the one part of her life that wasn't entirely shite. And then, after dinner, he goes back to work on his car. All part of the mental game. But then he's under it, and she, I guess . . . she comes and sees the two jacks, holding that bloody car above him . . .'

'She definitely killed him? Deliberately?'

'And then she called me, because she trusted me and, because as far as she knew, Stella was dead and she had nobody else to turn to. You should have seen her, Alex. He'd done a number on her. Her face was in pieces. Her lips were out here.'

'Did you take her to hospital?'

'Couldn't. Not the state she was in. The coppers might have come after whoever did it and found him there, dead. So I called up Bill and asked him what to do. He's a good man. And after

306

that I got rid of his body and I put every penny that cunt had ever given me in the grave with him.'

Alex nodded.

'You figure it out, Alex. Was Tina right, or not? She thought he'd killed her girlfriend. Far as I'm concerned, he would have killed Tina for real if she hadn't killed him first. It was just a matter of time, whatever you say.'

The point about being a police officer, thought Alex, was you never had to answer that question; you had the law to do it for you. She believed in that. She had relied on it all her life.

'Are we square, then?' asked Curly.

'Yes. We're square.'

The question he had really wanted to ask came just as she was at the door, putting on her hi-viz jacket for the cycle home. 'This man,' he said finally. 'You sure he deserves all this?'

She took her time cycling home.

Though the rain had stopped, the roads were still wet, and the water thrown up by her wheels soaked through her. Car lights blared off the wet road. She took the coast path, riding along concrete slabs that seemed to jolt every bone in her body, then rejoining the coast road, cycling cautiously on a surface where water-filled potholes looked like any other puddles.

The light was on in Arum Cottage when she passed, but she was exhausted and damp, so she continued up the hard track, dreaming of a shower, and was annoyed to find, when she reached the shed, that Zoë had left its door unlocked.

And by the time she had remembered that Zoë couldn't have done that, because she was in London, it was too late.

FORTY-EIGHT

Her helmet protected her from the first blow, but it knocked her sideways and she crashed against something hard and angular. Her balance gone, she fell hard onto to the concrete floor of the shed, and whatever she had banged into clattered down on top of her.

When she looked up he was there, then he was gone, then there, then gone, then there. The flashing lamp from her bicycle, propped in the doorway, illuminated him for fractions of a second in the darkness. She watched, fascinated, detached, as if she were viewing some grotesque animation rather than a man attacking her.

What had happened to that ability to predict the future? Her vigilance had deserted her, for better or worse. She had let her guard down carelessly.

Terry Neill was above her now, swinging fists. A second punch caught her on the cheek, but she was able to turn with it this time, absorbing the force of the blow. When she tried to raise her leg to kick him in the groin she realised what it was that had fallen on her; she had been knocked against Zoë's bicycle. It had tumbled and was now lying across her legs, trapping her. The man leaned down, grabbed her hi-viz jacket and tried to yank her upright, but her leg was caught under the bike and because he was standing on the frame he was forcing her lower half flat at the same time as trying to lift her. In panic, she screamed from the sudden pain in her legs.

He must have forced the lock. He had been just inside the door waiting for her all this time. 'Bitch,' he screamed.

He lunged at her a second time, trying again to pull her up. If he pulled any harder, she thought, curiously calm, he would break her trapped leg, the one he didn't realise he was forcing down with his weight. It was pure fury. In slow motion, she felt parts of her brain fizz; the amygdala sending messages to the frontal cortex. A new clarity emerged. Despite the pain, she arched her back, destabilising him, then at just the right moment kicked out hard under the frame, making him topple. In the flashing light, the moments of blackness were absolute. Disorientated, with nothing to brace his weight against, the bulk of his body sailed forward, over her. In the blinking light she shot an arm up and grabbed him by his shirt collar, tugging him down right on top of her. He landed with a thump, knocking the air out of her, but giving her a new advantage. This way she could hold him close where his arms could do no damage. He struggled to press himself away but in the next second she had an arm around his neck now, locking him down tightly to her.

He was a university professor, not a fighter, and now that he'd lost the element of surprise, she was the stronger. She was in charge.

She pulled her arm tighter, the back of his neck in the crook of her elbow, forcing his head into her armpit, and heard him rasp for breath.

'Let go,' he whined.

She started to laugh. Only days ago he had lain like this, on top of her. Tired, wet and wrung out from the last few weeks, she laughed like she hadn't done for a long time.

She held him a whole minute longer until he stopped struggling, then slowly loosened her grip.

'Bitch,' he gasped again, so she reasserted her grip a second time, this time a little tighter until she heard him start to choke.

'Don't ever call me that.'

When she guessed he had finally had enough, she released him again, pushed him off her, then sat up and pulled Zoë's bike off her legs and stood, leaving him lying on the floor. She would have impressive bruises in the morning. He too, she hoped.

She propped the bike back up where it had been, switched off the light, and then stood by the open door. 'Get out of here,' she said.

He sat up, rubbing his neck. 'You stitched me up. You gave the police some cock and bull story about me killing a man seven years ago.'

A light came on outside, shining on the ground behind her. She turned to see a man in grey tracksuit bottoms emerging from one of the back doors with a broom in his hand, held like a weapon.

'Who's there?'

Alex emerged from the darkness of the shed and did her best to smile reassuringly. In the light she could see he was wearing the same T-shirt he'd been wearing the last time she had seen him. 'Sorry. Me again. I fell over while putting the bike away.'

'Is that the woman from number seven?'

'Yes. Sorry to have disturbed you again.'

'Your face is bleeding. Are you OK?'

'Is it?' She held her hand up and touched the cheekbone where Terry Neill had hit her; when she lowered it, she saw blood on her fingers. 'Just a scratch. I'm fine. Go back to bed.'

She waited until the man had closed the door behind him, then returned to the shed. 'Go home, Terry.'

He was sitting cross-legged on the concrete floor. 'They took my bloody car away. They took the cash from my house.'

'Yes. If we're lucky, they'll start looking into your banking affairs too.'

'I told them you gave me the cash.'

'And if I deny it, as I will, and tell them I have no idea what you're talking about, who do you think they'll believe? A police officer who's always had a stick up her arse, or you?'

He grunted. 'You're trying to set me up for a murder I didn't commit. I did nothing but treat you well.'

She took the light off her handlebars and switched it on again, to full beam, pointing it right at his face.

He stood up, shielding his eyes from the light with his hand.

'You're framing me for murder,' he said.

'Because you are a murderer.'

He stared back at her, pupils shrinking from the glare.

'Let's get this absolutely straight, Terry. You are a murderer. You killed Bob Glass.' He blinked at her, scared now.

He shook his head vigorously.

'Bob Glass was squatting in the field when he heard you and Ayman Younis arguing. I guess that was you telling Ayman he wasn't ever getting his money back. He would have been pretty hurt, wouldn't he? When you heard about that, you figured that Bob Glass was the only person with real evidence to identify you as the one who had conned everyone out of their money, so you killed him. Given your past, I don't think you'd have found it hard buying some street methadone. Something way stronger than he'd have been used to. How did you make him drink it? Did he want to? Or did you force it down his throat? What? Is that "No comment" again?'

He found his voice again. 'That's crazy.'

'Isn't it though? I think it was you all along. I'm pretty sure of that.'

'I told them you gave me the money.'

'And I'll say you're lying. Know what? I've never put a foot wrong as a copper. I'm as straight as they come. Always have been. I even shopped one of my best friends. You, on the other hand, were a known associate of Frank Hogben, someone who bought drugs from him at the time, someone who lost their job because of their addiction and then lied about it. You're really asking the police to believe that someone like me would plant money on you?'

She switched off the torch, leaving them in absolute darkness.

'So which murder do you want to go down for, Terry? A seven-year-old murder of a drug dealer who nobody really missed very much, back when you were an addict and not in a good shape and not in sound mind? Or the premeditated murder of an ex-serviceman to cover up a financial fraud? It's your choice.

312

The more you tell them I gave you that money, or you don't know where that money came from, the more they'll dig into your finances. And I know you've covered your tracks, but what if they find something, and it all starts to unravel?'

Her eyes adjusted to the darkness. He was still standing at the back of the shed, his face a dim moon in the blackness.

'I'm going to bed now. Go home.'

She turned and walked back into the overcast night.

'I thought you were nice,' he called out from the shed, like a boy who had had his toy taken away.

'So did I,' she said. Heart still thumping, she made sure she was at the door of her house, and her key safely in it, before she let herself turn to see him slink out of the shed.

Letting herself in, she made her way through the dark house and upstairs to her bedroom. Through the window, she watched him walking away down the narrow track, bathed in orange light from the power station.

FORTY-NINE

— *Do you want to tell me about it?*

— *Not particularly. Best not, really.*

— *How have you been, then?*

— *Pretty good. Excellent, in fact. Last night I slept better than I have in months. I finally feel like I'm getting some control back over my life. Well. Maybe not over my own. I'm not sure I'll ever get there on that. Over other people's lives, at least. That's something, isn't it?*

The day after Terry Neill had attacked her, Zoë phoned to say when she would be back.

'I already called up Jill and asked if she'd pick me up from the station 'cause I know we've got no car.' Alex heard her mother's radio on in the background playing pop music so loud she could barely make out what Zoë was saying.

'I can't hear you,' complained Alex.

'I said, are you and Jill OK? Jill says she thinks you've been avoiding her. I told her that was nuts.'

314

The one thing she hated about all this was that she couldn't tell her friend the truth about what had happened.

When the mint-green car drew up outside, she stayed inside, but Jill came in anyway.

'Are you OK, Alex?'

'Yes. I'm fine. I just needed some time on my own,' she said.

'Mum! What's wrong with your face?'

'I fell off my bike.' Another lie. 'It was wet and I couldn't see the potholes.' Lie upon lie upon lie.

'When are you going to get a new bloody car?' demanded Jill. 'You can't live out here in the boondocks without one.'

'What's with the candles?' demanded Zoë.

'Something my therapist suggested. I thought you'd like them.'

'Scented candles give you cancer.'

Jill stood, waiting to be offered a drink or something. It broke Alex's heart, but Jill would be working on the Frank Hogben murder case, and having her around only meant she would have to lie to her more about what she knew.

Jill hovered uncomfortably by the door. 'I don't want to stress you out, Alex,' she said eventually, 'but you know they're going to question you about Terry Neill?'

'Really?'

'He's saying it was you that gave him the money. All sorts of stuff like that.'

'Why would he do that?'

Jill looked down at her feet. 'I didn't want to say it was too good to be true, you and him.'

Alex frowned. 'What are you saying?'

'Just . . . that he played you.'

Alex was suddenly offended at the suggestion, but unable to show it.

'Don't you see, Alex?' She shuffled her feet. 'I think maybe he was just using you. To me it looks like he was creating an alibi by going out for a copper. He probably never actually . . .'

'Never what? Never fancied me?'

Jill didn't answer. Zoë stood with her bag in her hand, looking embarrassed.

'That's absolutely ridiculous,' said Alex eventually.

'Yeah. Of course it is,' said Jill, backing out.

Later, at Zoë's insistence, she and Zoë walked down to Arum Cottage. 'We've got to tell him,' she said.

When they arrived there, they saw that the *Under Offer* sign had been modified. It now read *Sold*.

The bird bath looked splendid in the deep red of the evening, thought Alex, while her daughter knocked on the door.

'Are you going to tell him, or am I?' asked Zoë.

'Tread carefully,' Alex told her daughter. She was nervous now, in a way she hadn't been for weeks. A sense that everything could go very wrong. 'He's a very independent man. This might have been a mistake.'

'Weirdest thing,' said Bill, when he came to the door. 'Turns out I don't have to move out.'

'What do you mean, Bill?' Zoë pretended not to know what was going on.

He opened it to let them in. It was the first cool evening of the year. He had lit a fire in the stove and the red flame matched the colour of the sun on the stones outside.

'The woman who bought it is letting me live here on pretty much a peppercorn rent. She just bought it as an investment, apparently. I mean . . . I know they go for a fortune now round here, but it's, like, I've just been paid two hundred thousand pounds to live in my own house . . .'

'Well, there's a thing,' said Alex.

'What is it? Why are you grinning?'

Zoë was practically shaking with excitement. 'Is the woman who bought the house called Helen Breen?' asked Zoë.

'That's right. How did you . . . ?'

'You know . . . Helen. You know her, Bill. It's my gran.'

Bill's jaw dropped. As he stared at Alex, the smile left his face. 'Your mother Helen?'

'It was Gran's idea,' said Zoë, hesitant now. 'Not Mum's.'

Bill looked winded. 'I'm not sure how I feel about that at all,' he said.

Zoë looked from one to the other, worried now.

Eventually Alex spoke. 'I owed it to you. But it *was* my mum's idea, not mine. It's just a financial transaction, that's all. If you don't like it, that's fine. You sold the cottage and now you've got the money. But we'd like you to stay, obviously.'

'Right,' he said quietly.

Alex wondered if she had miscalculated this badly.

But Bill South was still living in Arum Cottage in mid-September when Alex's old colleagues from Serious Crime formally charged Terry Neill with the murder of Frank Hogben.

The headline in the Kent Messenger read: *Disgraced University Professor Charged with Drug Murder.*

317

Neill's protestations that the money police found at his house had not been his were contradicted by the fact that a forged note had been discovered in the till of the golf club where he regularly spent time in the bar; nobody noticed or remembered that it was Alex who had paid for the drinks on the evening she had spent with him there. The following day they found others had been passed in shops in the neighbourhood. There was even one in the yellow charity box on the table at the golf club. Members of the golf club who had previously vouched for his good character seemed to be falling away. It was easy for them to believe that a former drug addict had been up to something dark.

Checking in to see how she was recovering, DI McAdam visited after work.

Sitting in her kitchen, Toby McAdam let slip that they were working on the theory that Frank Hogben's murder had been a dispute over drug money; that Neill must have been involved with Hogben importing drugs. Neill denied it but was unable to explain the sums of money, not large, but very regular, that had appeared in his personal account over the last few years. There was something shady about his finances, for sure.

'I'm sorry. This must be painful for you,' Toby McAdam said.

'Yes,' Alex said.

'How's your daughter Zoë?'

Alex liked McAdam. He was the kind of boss who took care to know the names of his colleagues' children; though, she realised now, she had never once asked about his. 'Insane, as ever,' she answered. 'Though she looks after me well. Apparently I haven't woken up screaming in the night for at least a week now.'

'She must have been through a great deal.'

318

'I suppose she has,' said Alex, though she was a little offended by the suggestion.

'As you have, obviously. We'll see about bringing you back on light duties soon.'

And Alex's heart shrank again, but she tried to look grateful, for his sake.

FIFTY

'All you have to do is drop me at Tina and Stella's,' Zoë said. 'I don't see what the big deal is.'

Alex had finally bought herself an ancient green Saab off Curly, and so, in theory, she could have driven her daughter to Folkestone. Instead she said, 'I'm busy.'

'No you're not. You're hanging around the house all day. Is there a problem with me being friends with them?'

'No.'

'You sure? 'Cause you're acting like some kind of homophobe.'

'What do you see in them?'

'I don't know,' Zoë said spikily. 'Maybe I'm a lesbian, after all.'

'*Maybe I'm a lesbian*? Are you really saying that?'

'No. I don't have to decide, do I? It's just society that makes people have to decide. I just like hanging around with people who are a bit different. They have nice friends.'

'You don't have to decide. That's true.' Her daughter had always liked hanging around with people who were a bit different.

When they moved here, to Dungeness, Alex had thought it strange her teenage daughter had become so obsessed with nature that she hung around with adults like Bill all the time. Now she seemed more interested in hanging around with Tina and Stella, Alex found herself mourning the fact that she was spending less time with birders and naturalists, or out at the Marsh Visitor Centre.

That wasn't why she didn't want to drive her daughter to see them at their tiny house. Knowing what Tina had done, it was best not to spend time in their company. There were too many lies.

'I might stay over, Mum. Hang out with some people in Folkestone.'

'OK.'

Zoë softened. 'Don't sound so down about it, Mum. I'm seventeen. I mean, I can go out, now you've stopped having nightmares and stuff.'

'I never asked you to do that. I was OK. You never had to stay and look after me.'

'Didn't I?' said her daughter.

She no longer woke in the night to find her duvet twisted around her, and her daughter quietly sitting by her bed. She no longer smelt earth around her, weight on her chest, or the wetness of blood. She hadn't returned to work yet, but that would come soon. She wasn't frightened. Something had freed her, and now the ordinary dull patterns of the world had come back; tides came in and out, and they were just water. She felt in control again. She had done a bad thing, but she had made some sense of the world.

'Get in the car, then,' she said.

In a rare display of affection, her daughter kissed her.

'So,' Alex said, as lightly as she could as they drove past the bungalows that crowded the flat seafront. 'Do you really think you're gay then?'

'No. I don't think I'm anything.'

'Of course you're something . . . love,' she responded, too quickly.

'I don't mean it like that.'

'Sorry.' She loved her daughter more than she had loved anything; sometimes, though, she felt they were further apart than ever.

They pulled up at the small terraced house.

'Come in and say hello, Mum. They'd like that. Tina thinks you're ace.'

'Does she?' Alex smiled. 'That's nice. No. I'm OK.'

She waved at her daughter as she drove off.

In the hallway she noticed the umbrella. She had forgotten to return it. It would be nice, she thought, to sit in a pub on her own and read a book. Strapping it to her bicycle frame and putting a book in a backpack, she set off for the nearby town. The Dolphin was mostly empty. She handed over the umbrella to a barman, and then a couple of young American tourists approached her because she was on her own, and they chatted for a while, and when they learned she lived at Dungeness they told her how fantastic and spooky a place it was and how they had come here because they were on a kind of pilgrimage to see Derek Jarman's cottage, which was as close to a religious

322

shrine as you got on the Ness. They talked for a while, but then she pulled out her book and they got the hint, and she finally sat alone reading about neuroscience while eating haddock and chips and drinking Pinot Grigio. It felt utterly luxurious.

When Curly came in, she noticed him tense a little as he spotted her, but she nodded hello at him, and he nodded back. That's all. It was as if she had finally become a local; she was someone who held a shared secret.

'Sit with me,' she called to him. So when he had bought his pint of lager and a packet of sweet chilli crisps, he joined her at her table.

'Have you seen anything of Bill?' she asked. 'I think he's ignoring me.'

'He'll be fine,' he said holding out the crisp packet.

She shook her head.

'He's been alone his whole life. He doesn't know how to react when other people try to help him. Bird bath is one thing. But the whole bloody house is another.'

'So he told you, then? We had to do something.'

Curly nodded. He had grown up around here, but could no longer afford to live on Dungeness himself. 'Like I said. He'll be fine. He's a quiet man, best of times.'

'Tell me about it.'

Curly picked up another crisp and looked at it for longer than any bar snack deserved. 'He loves you, you know? Kind of this old-man crush. If it wasn't for that, he'd probably find it easier.'

'He tell you that?'

He popped it into his mouth and chewed. 'Doesn't really need to, does he? Want another wine? I'm getting another.'

When he returned with the wine he leaned in. 'I got you a large one as a thank you.'

'For what?'

He lowered his voice. 'I heard that professor guy is going to plead guilty. Tina is definitely off the bloody hook.'

Jill had told her that. Alex had been surprised, but his lawyer was probably advising him to. If he pleaded innocent, there was always the risk that the police would dig more deeply to make their case, and if they did, there was a risk, however small, they would find out the truth about Terry Neill and the bad things he had really done. However much money he had stashed away would be gone, and then they might start to connect him to the death of Ayman Younis and the death of Bob Glass. Pleading guilty to the murder of a drug dealer seven years ago was not the worst option. With good behaviour he would be out in five years and the money would still be waiting for him safely overseas or wherever it was.

'Going out tomorrow on the boat,' he said, as if he felt the need to change the subject. 'It'll be a bit of a blow out there. We'll have some bream, I dare say.'

It was a kind of pointless observation, and she was grateful for it.

Despite too much wine, she slept well, but was woken thick-headed by the noise of a car horn.

She blinked, went to the bathroom and looked down from the window.

Below, engine running, was a Ford Escort, sunburst red, with alloy wheels and a biplane spoiler. Her daughter, sitting in the passenger seat in a big, baggy pink hoodie Alex didn't recognise, waved.

Alex stared for a while, open-mouthed, then ran downstairs and opened the back door.

It was Stella behind the wheel. She got out and smiled. She was dressed in green dungarees and an orange sweater. Under her short, bleached hair, her face was still brown from the summer sun. 'Just wanted to say thanks,' she said, holding out her hand to shake. 'For everything you've done for Tina. And me.'

'I didn't do anything,' said Alex, leaving the hand where it was, in mid-air.

Stella tilted her head. 'Yeah you did. I know. I'm not stupid. But I am very, very grateful. You're a good woman.' She held out her hand a second longer, but still Alex didn't take it.

'You shouldn't be driving this car.'

The wind had come up, as Curly had predicted it would. Dry grey leaves from the sunken woods were flying up into the air around them. 'It's a real bit of history, this car. German-built. Bosch fuel injection. Get a hundred and ten m.p.h. out of it no problem. And Frank doesn't need it any more.'

'What's this about, Mum?' Zoë sounded uncertain.

'It's mine. I don't see why I shouldn't drive it.'

'Nothing, Zoë.' Alex turned to her daughter. 'Why don't you go inside?'

'I borrowed Stella's jumper, Mum. It got cold last night. I'm just going to change and give it her back. Want to come in, Stella?'

'I better not, Zo,' said Stella. 'I don't think I'm staying.'

Zoë ran inside the house.

'The old thing's been hidden away all this time. It deserves a good run.'

'I thought it was your brother who fixed it,' said Alex slowly, when her daughter had gone.

'What brother? Who told you I have a brother?'

Alex looked confused. 'Mandy Hogben said he was up there fixing the car at night.'

Stella laughed loudly. 'It was me fixed the bloody car. I don't know. Maybe she thinks a woman couldn't do something like that, poor cow.'

'Let me get this straight. It was you I saw up at the Air Force Memorial car park, wasn't it?'

Stella didn't answer directly but Alex knew she was right.

'You fixed my car, too, didn't you?'

Stella leaned across the roof of the red car. Alex could see her face reflected in the shiny paint. 'After a fashion. Yeah. Sorry about that. I was just trying to protect us, you understand? Me and Tina. That's all I've ever been doing.'

It was as if the temperature had dropped. 'You restored this?' Alex said again, looking at the car.

'Like I said. I'm good with machines,' she said quietly. 'Been working on it for years.'

Alex touched the scab on her face where Terry Neill had cut it. 'It was you, that day in the lock-up too. Not Tina. It was you who dropped this car on him.'

'What was it you said earlier?' Stella said. 'I didn't do anything.'

'Except you did.'

Stella got back inside the car. The Ford's steering wheel had a red leather cover on it, held on with a red lace. Stella put her hands on it and spoke to Alex through the open window. 'After he found out about me and Tina, it was a matter of time. You should have seen the state of Tina. It killed me. Curly just assumed it was her that killed him. So did your copper friend. And so did you.'

She started the engine. 'For a while I thought you were going to spoil everything. I tried to throw you off. But you're a good person, Alex. You did good. Back then, I stepped up and saved her,' Stella said. 'Just the same as you did now.'

'No,' Alex said. 'Not just the same. Not at all.'

'I know why you're angry.' Stella scrunched up her mouth. 'It just kind of worked out this way. If it's any consolation, I don't like what I did any more than you did. I'm not proud. It just needed to happen.'

Alex looked her in the eye. 'Just don't come back here, OK? Not ever.'

When Zoë arrived downstairs with Stella's bright-pink hoodie bundled up, the car had already gone.

Alex looked at her, standing there, disappointed that Stella hadn't waited to say goodbye, puzzled by her mother's hostility to her friend. Alex wasn't sure where to begin. Luckily, before she could say anything, Bill South rounded the corner of the end house dressed in a yellow sou'wester, a bunch of bright-red supermarket chrysanthemums in his hand.

An offering.

THANKS

It goes without saying that the trawlermen and their families portrayed in this book are totally imaginary. The Stade boasts a strong fishing community. I'm very grateful to Luke Noakes for taking me out on his trawler. If you're ever visiting Folkestone, you can sample his latest catch at The Fish Shop at 1 Fish Market on The Stade. At sixteen, Luke was the youngest ticketed trawler skipper in the UK. The man who certified him – and who introduced me to him – is the crime writer and translator Quentin Bates.

Thanks also to Jake Jones, Darren Cooke, Paddy Magrane, Liz Cowlett, Graham Bartlett, Jasmine Palmer, my editor Jon Riley and my agent Karolina Sutton and the team at Curtis Brown. Much gratitude to the old gang: Roz Brody, Mike Holmes, Janet King and Chris Sansom. And finally, thanks, yet again, to Jane.

Chapter one of this book was written almost entirely during a workshop I gave that was hosted by Dungeness Open Studios. Many thanks to the artist Paddy Hamilton and co-host Bridget Wilkins who have always welcomed me with tea and encouragement.

Discover William's latest thriller,

DEAD RICH

coming in 2022 . . .

PREFACE

They arrive in at luxury marinas, slipping up the Thames, shadowing the pink mansion houses that fringe the shores of Portofino, edging slowly into fat moorings off Brooklyn Marina. From the hills of Monaco, you see them crowding the harbour below.

Each one is different; each special. The cheapest cost mere millions. Sheikh Mohammed bin Rashid Al Maktoum, the ruler of Dubai, spent four hundred million on his. Roman Abramovich has a fleet of them, several costing as much as Sheikh Mohammed's. He paid over a billion for *Eclipse*.

Most of these floating palaces are gleaming white, though some are grey or even black. Their owners like what you can see of their exteriors to say something about them. There is one that you often spot cruising in the Mediterranean that has been painted in rich geometrical shapes of yellow, pink and blue by the artist Jeff Koons.

But more impressive is what you can't see. Yachts are secretive, like their owners. Their gleaming hulls conceal dance floors, fireplaces, spas, underwater observation windows and swimming pools with glass floors, under which you can see the fish swimming. Many have what their designers call toy garages, with doors in their hulls that open to launch other smaller versions of themselves, tenders and sailing boats, even mini-submarines.

The bigger, the richer. Compared, say, to the fragile carracks that took Columbus to the Americas, these are huge, fantastical monsters. Like castles, these vessels become a symbolic power, created to inspire awe; a physical projection of wealth and power and internationality. Like their owners' money, they can slide silently in and out of any port. Like castles, too, they are defended.

They are an entire world, separate from the rest of us. They are fabulous.

CHAPTER ONE

The house cleaner is Romanian. Her name is Mihaela and the first time she hears the phone ping in her handbag she does not look at it because she is under the bed in an apartment off the south end of Paris's Rue de Vaugirard trying to retrieve a pair of knickers that she has discovered there while vacuuming.

The second time it pings she doesn't pay it any attention either, because she is examining the knickers more closely; they are black, flimsy and not the kind that would belong to Mme Caron, who is a tall, broad-hipped woman. Mihaela is fond of Mme Caron; she tips Mihaela whenever they meet, much to M. Caron's annoyance. Mme Caron also remembers Mihaela's son's name, despite the fact that she has only met him once, when Mihaela had to bring him with her to work because he had an upset stomach.

'And how is poor little Florian?' she asks each time, as if she imagines her son to be perpetually ill.

Mihaela considers returning the knickers to the place under the bed where she discovered them; or innocently putting them into one of Mme Caron's own underwear drawers where she can find them and confront her husband about who they might belong to. Mihaela very much dislikes the idea of his infidelity. However, she is a cleaner and depends on M. Caron for her work.

Not just an ordinary cleaner, like so many others in this city. She cleans for a very exclusive class of client. The agency she works for boasts of their reputation for discretion, and lecture their workers on the importance of it. Confidentiality is of the utmost importance. So she puts the knickers in the pocket of her jeans and carries on with her work.

It isn't until after she leaves the apartment over an hour later, setting the alarm and locking the door, that she finally takes the phone out of her bag and looks at it. The message that arrived when she was under the Carons' bed is there on the lock screen.

Returning from Orly now will need to sleep today. No cleaning today. DB.

The colour vanishes from Mihaela's face. She clutches the dark wood banister of the staircase and sways.

It was Kiki's fault. Kiki works at a gay nightclub in the Quai d'Austerlitz and carries her sense of excess with her wherever she goes. It was Kiki who suggested they hold Daria's twenty-first birthday party in David Bullimore's apartment in the sixième arrondissement.

Though maybe it was Mihaela's fault as well, for boasting to Kiki about David Bullimore's hot tub. 'It has a built-in stereo and a TV.'

The neatest feature of the Englishman's apartment is a secluded roof garden from which you can see the Eiffel Tower, plus the six-person jacuzzi that he has installed up there. Sometimes, she cannot resist telling her friends the details of her clients' lives, just to remind them that though the hours are long and the pay could be better, her job is superior to theirs. She has told them about the woman who had a Swarovski-studded catflap; the couple with the vitamin-C infused shower; the chain-smoking academic who appears on TV and who has a genuine Mondrian in his toilet.

'David's jacuzzi has really cool lights,' Mihaela said, like she was a friend of his.

'I bet *David*,' Kiki mocked, 'would like to get you in there one day.'

Mihaela wouldn't mind if he did. She harbours what she knows are adolescent fantasies of a man like him taking her and Florian away from a life of short-term contracts. 'The water is always kept hot so he can use it whenever he wants.'

Kiki goes on Extinction Rebellion protests and thinks that kind of squandering of resources is unforgivable. 'Somebody should use it,' she declared. 'Otherwise it's a waste.'

Plus, Daria has been feeling miserable because she has no work and knows nobody in this foreign city. The Englishman David Bullimore was supposed to be away in Tel Aviv on business until next Tuesday.

There were a total of five of them up there last night dressed in their bikinis, drinking strawberry jalapeño mint juleps under the June stars, smoking weed, listening to hip hop and giggling, all except for Mihaela, who hated every minute of it. The breeze splashed candle wax all over the decking. She sat in the pink-lit bubbling water, fingering her crucifix, anxious about the babysitter she had hired to look after Florian, worrying that one of them would break something, or spill pink drinks on his white stair carpet, or that David's neighbour would spot them on his security cameras.

Unlike all her other clients, David Bullimore doesn't have a burglar alarm. He boasts that he doesn't need one because his neighbour, who owns the top three floors of the eighteenth-century building next door, is an ultra-paranoid Russian billionaire called Stepan Pirumov – *the* Stepan Pirumov – who has security cameras overlooking the front and back of his apartment. Having such a wealthy neighbour is good for the neighbourhood.

'Relax,' Kiki told her as she sat in the brightly illuminated tub. 'The Englishman isn't back for a week. I'll help you tidy up. It's not a problem.' For some reason, Kiki was wearing a black nylon wig like the one Uma Thurman wore in *Pulp Fiction*, and whenever Mihaela complained about the mess she said, in English, 'Don't be a . . .' and drew a square in the air.

But by the time Mihaela told them the party was over, Kiki was so drunk she had thrown up takeaway pizza into the frothing water. When they hauled her out, she could barely walk. She and Daria had to guide her cautiously down the back stairs to the servants' entrance in the narrow Rue de Nevers behind the house.

'What about my coat?' complained Kiki, loudly. 'I left my coat behind. It's Zadig and Voltaire and it cost me five hundred euros. Six hundred. I don't remember.'

'I'll get it tomorrow.'

'But I'm cold.'

The Uber driver refused to take her home unless they accompanied her, so Mihaela had no option but to leave the mess upstairs for another day.

She reads the message on her phone again, hoping she has made a mistake. She hasn't. It is an hour old. The Englishman will be on his way back from Orly now and the sixième arrondissement is at least twenty minutes away on the Metro. She fumbles with the key for her Piaggio scooter.

The Englishman is a neat freak. He has hundreds of vinyl records which he keeps in strictly alphabetical order. He sends her texts if the toilet roll has been installed the wrong way around, or if there are smears on the mirror above the fireplace, but as a cleaner she respects that. When she has her own apartment, she will be the same. She knows where she stands with him, and he with her; now she feels as if she has betrayed him. At Saint-Placide she cuts in between a cyclist and a braking car and the cyclist yells at her.

The Rue Guénégaud is close to the Île de la Cité. She dodges pedestrians on crossings on the Rue de Rennes. David Bullimore will already be there, she thinks. She will have to admit everything. He will tell the agency that she held a party in his flat and she will lose all her work. In this country good work is so hard to find. She has been an idiot.

The Rue Guénégaud is a one-way street. It's quicker to park at the south end and walk up. She has just made it to the junction on Rue Mazarine and is locking her bike when she looks up and she sees the black Mercedes rounding the corner at the top.

339

Somehow, she knows that will be Bullimore's car. She watches in horror as it pauses right outside number 15 and the door opens.

A uniformed driver in a peaked cap emerges. The passenger door opens.

It is him.

It is her fault for giving in to Kiki. She should have never listened to her. Now there is no way she can make it to the apartment before the Englishman to try and tidy the worst of it. To reach the servants' entrance from here – the only door she has the key for – she would have to walk all the way past the front of the house up to the Quai de Conti and then turn right into the narrow back street, and there is David Bullimore already ahead of her, taking his bag from the driver and reaching into his pocket for the front door key. Any second now he will be inside, calling the lift.

She picks her phone out of her bag. She will send him a note of apology right away before he sees the mess, and throw herself at his mercy, knowing that it will make no difference. Tell him she would work for nothing, perhaps. Of all her clients, he is the one who would be most outraged by the mess they had left. *I am most sorry, Mr David*, she begins to write in English.

As she hesitantly presses the keys, composing her message, she barely notices the noise, a dull *crump* coming from somewhere up the road.

She hears a man next to her gasp, but she doesn't look up. The screaming starts a second later. Finally she tears her eyes from the phone.

From where she is standing, she has a clear view up the pavement on the right side of the road. A man appears to be lying on

340

the ground barely a metre from where David Bullimore is standing. There is something strange about the shape of his body.

The woman who is screaming is on the far side of the man; she was pushing a child in a buggy. The man lies just in front of the little boy's dangling legs. Now David Bullimore's voice joins the woman's in an inchoate wailing, his voice deeper, but just as full of shock.

She watches, puzzled as her client staggers backwards now, tripping over his own suitcase, falling, then scrabbling up again, pushing himself away on his elbows.

A man has emerged from the gallery on the opposite side of the street talking on a mobile phone while pointing upwards.

It takes Mihaela another second to realise that the man is not just lying there; he must have fallen. There is blood, she sees now, on the grey of the pavement. He has landed between the woman and David Bullimore, missing both of them only by centimetres.

In no time the gendarmes seemed to have arrived too, blocking the street. Not just ordinary *flics* either, which is strange. They are RAID, a tactical unit, in full body armour, automatic weapons not just slung over their shoulders, but grasped in gloved hands. They hustle Bullimore and the others back from the prone body, away from the apartment's front door. A SAMU car arrives, blue light flashing, and two paramedics leap out. She watches them as they close off the whole street.

Looking up, she mentally traces the line between the pavement and the balcony he must have fallen from, and realises that it is the one next to Bullimore's – the Russian's. She glances again at the paramedics and the man they are busying themselves with and then turns away.

*

Through all of this Mihaela is strangely calm. She recognises the opportunity for what it is. God-given. Pushing past the shocked faces that have gathered around her, she walks the long way back until she reaches Rue Dauphine, turning left again into the back alleyway.

She guesses the front entrance will be blocked for at least half an hour, maybe more. That will be enough.

She is pulling out her key for the servants' door when she notices something strange, and her skin goes cold.

The black door is not properly locked. To any passer-by it would look closed, but she can see a couple of centimetres of white door frame. She was an idiot getting drunk with friends here last night. In her hurry to get Kiki out of the building she must have not even closed the door behind her properly.

If David discovered that she had left his back door unlocked, she would be sacked on the spot though. Another stroke of luck; another chance to set things straight.

Closing the door behind her, she climbs the stairs quickly. In the living room, Kiki's Zadig and Voltaire faux-fur jacket is lying abandoned across the back of a leather sofa, along with her Uma Thurman wig, lying like some creature on the floor.

Mihaela tuts; she doesn't even hear the footsteps behind her. Not until the hand is clamped firmly over her mouth.

In horror, she sees the other hand holds a kitchen knife.

She thinks of the body on the pavement below her; that this is all Kiki's fault. She thinks of her son Florian and how he will be alone here in a strange country without her.